barricade

JON WALLACE

Copyright © Jon Wallace 2014

All rights reserved

The right of Jon Wallace to be identified as the author
of this work has been asserted by him in accordance with
the Copyright, Designs and Patents Act 1988.

First published in Great Britain in 2014
by Gollancz
An imprint of the Orion Publishing Group
Orion House, 5 Upper St Martin's Lane,
London WC2H 9EA
An Hachette UK Company

This edition published in Great Britain in 2015
by Gollancz

1 3 5 7 9 10 8 6 4 2

A CIP catalogue record for this book
is available from the British Library

ISBN 978 0 575 11813 3

Typeset by Input Data Services Ltd, Bridgwater, Somerset

Printed in Great Britain by Clays Ltd, St Ives plc

The Orion Publishing Group's policy is to use papers that
are natural, renewable and recyclable products and made

www.gollancz.co.uk

'Jon Wallace keeps the pace up, delivering intense set-pieces alongside plenty of twisted humour and bone-crunching violence'
SFX

'A taxi ride, in Jon Wallace's scintillating debut novel, becomes an epic trek through a near-future Britain ravaged by conflict and nuclear war . . . the end of civilisation has seldom been such gruesome fun'
Financial Times

'Even a machine would find it tough not to enjoy the glee with which Jon Wallace breaks the world apart'
SciFiNow

'The fact paced narrative is a big draw . . . a promising debut'
Big Issue

For Betty Bailey, and chicken and mushroom pie.

My name is Kenstibec. I'm a Rover model, a Power Nine – a real good buy.

Not that you'd know it to look at me. Not now that I'm hanging upside down, suspended from the roof of the recovery shed.

I am missing an arm. The stump hangs there dripping blood onto the mesh-steel floor. Ever since the boss strung me up I have been gently swaying, as if there's a breeze in here, but there isn't. It is hot. The air tastes like it does on a plane. The ventilators hum.

The hatch beeps and hisses open. In walks the boss's son, his hands in his pockets. He is trying to whistle but he doesn't make a good sound. He is six years old.

He notices me.

'Kenstibec,' he says.

'Alan,' I reply.

'Did you have an accident?'

'I did.'

Alan sees my stump. His eyes widen and his jaw goes slack.

'What happened?'

'Don't stare at it,' I say.

'You've lost your arm!' He holds a hand up to his forehead and he trembles with what must be excitement.

'That's cool!'

I don't reply to that. He steps carefully behind me to inspect the damage on the other side. I look at it too. It is a very clean cut. It could have been worse. A metre to the left and they'd still be picking me off the scaffolding.

'How did it happen?' he asks me. 'How did it happen?' he says again.

'I fell.'

'Off the Hope Tower?' He doesn't wait for an answer. 'How high were

1

you? Were you really high? I bet you were really high up, weren't you, Kenstibec?'

'Three hundred and tenth floor.'

He walks back where I can see him and narrows his eyes at me.

'That's not true,' he says. 'You're making it up.'

'No . . .'

'You're making it up because if you did drop from that high you'd have gone splat and there'd be nothing left of you. You'd have gone splat. How far up were you really?'

'The three hundred and . . .'

'LIAR, LIAR, LIAR, LIAR!' He throws his arms out and does a little angry dance.

'My harness deployed two hundred and ninety floors down. I bounced a few times, then it snapped. I suppose you are right. Really it was only ten floors.'

'Wow.' He chews his lip. 'What was it like?'

I consider describing the fall to him but judge I don't need to. His imagination will do it all for him. I just need to find a good word.

'It was sensational,' I say.

'Wow.'

I remember the fall. I hear my overalls flapping. The wind rushes through my fingers. I see the city below me. I hold my breath as I tumble, as if inflated lungs will shield me from the impact.

'Will you be better soon?'

'Uncertain,' I reply.

A look appears on his face that indicates he's suddenly completely bored with the conversation. He sags and sighs. I think it is because he knows I can't play when hung up like this.

'All right,' he says. 'See you later, Kenstibec.'

'See you.'

He wanders off to the hatch, planting his hands in his pockets again, then stops. He looks at me.

'Kenstibec?'

I have to twist my head around to look at him.

'Yes?'

He is unsure about something.

'Are you on our side?'

RICK'S GARAGE

Rick never could keep a clean hatchway. He rarely ventured out, so it was always hidden under a fresh blanket of snow. I knew it was somewhere at the back of the supermarket, near the meat counter. I made my way there and kicked around in the drifts, my breath pluming in the torchlight.

Then the shooting started. Explosions drummed the dockside, blowing in a nearby wall and knocking me onto my back. My head connected with something metal, and for a moment I was stunned, staring at a huge tear in the roof. Then I turned over to find I was lying on the hatch. I pushed away the snow, found the bell pull, and tugged on it with some urgency.

Regmiron appeared at the porthole. He paused, giving me a searching look from behind the reinforced glass. I thought it was pretty unnecessary considering the situation. The whole of Leith Walk was shaking with cannon fire, and besides, the guy knew me.

The hatch hissed and creaked open a few centimetres, before jamming as the mechanism burned out. Regmiron pushed against it from his side, until there was space enough for me to crawl through. A burst of stale air welcomed me in as I dropped eight feet, headfirst. Regmiron shut the hatch after me with four huge turns of the wheel and climbed down to where I sat clutching my head.

'Bad one today, is it?'

'Pretty bad,' I replied. 'Why the delay in opening up? Is there some secret password I'm not aware of?'

He sniffed and looked up, listening to the thumping of explosions.

'This country,' he said, shaking his head. He walked off down the bunker corridor, a huge seven feet of muscle, bathed in flickering emergency lighting. I picked myself up and followed.

Rick was in his waiting room, seated at his reception desk, engrossed in a portable TV. I looked over his shoulder. He was watching a Real channel, one of the shows that played nothing but looped CCTV tapes from the old world. Today's entertainment was footage from a security camera in a bank. Twenty or so Reals stood in an orderly queue, waiting to be served. It was all meaningless and dead now, but something about it comforted the lunatics who were shooting at us.

Rick turned and smiled.

He looked about as bad as usual. He'd worked in specialised conditions for so long that he was evolving into a kind of praying mantis. His skin was dyed grease brown, his hair was combed in a thin oil slick, and he walked with a hunch from a life spent underneath cars, holding his hands out before him like raptorial forelegs. Others suspected there was something defective about him, scuttling around down there, but nobody who drove for a living would say a bad word about him. The important thing was that he produced reliable and speedy cars. He was the only one left in Edinburgh who could.

'Kenstibec,' he said. 'Early as always. Ready to have a look?'

'That's why I'm here,' I replied.

'Right,' he said. 'Follow me. It's in the main work bay. Only finished last night.'

He pushed me through the hatch with 'WORKSHOP' written on it. There was a welcoming stench of fuel and hot metal as I stepped over the gangway, down the stairs and onto the garage level.

The overheads hardly illuminated the place, but you could make out the expanse of the workshop, stretching half a mile long. There were shapes of cars everywhere, most like picked bones, cannibalised for parts. Machine tools turned over in the distance. Cargo nets hung from the ceiling, sprouting dismembered spark plugs, valves, pistons and connecting rods.

Rick stopped by a shape covered in a dusty white sheet and indicated I should investigate. I pulled off the drape to reveal a Land Rover, one of the later Defender models. It looked pretty good.

Rick leaned into the cabin, hit a switch, and the bonnet popped open.

'Engine,' he said. 'Diesel turbo. As you know, these Landy engines have a deserved reputation for poor reliability – major failures to the bottom end, cracked pistons, etc. I've upgraded the breather system and made a few other tweaks here and there. Now produces 190hp and runs pretty economically. As usual, all parts have been replicated and moulded with Rick's patented Gronts Alloy wherever possible.'

'That should produce some pace,' I said.

'Oh, yes indeed,' said Rick, rubbing his hands together. 'She can certainly move a bit. Well, she would . . .' He banged on the Landy's bodywork with his knuckles.

'I'll tell you again, I don't like to send a driver out with so little armour on his car. Are you sure you don't want my "Blast Box" installed?'

'No. I like to see where I'm going.'

Rick favoured cocooning his drivers in a contraption he called the 'Blast Box', a three-inch-thick cube of Gronts Alloy that could withstand hits from most ordnance. It was all very well in theory, but it weighted the car down, messed up your manoeuvrability, and worse of all made it difficult to see where you were going. I'd let him fit one to a previous cab and nearly drove at full speed over a forty-foot drop. I'd refused to sit in one since. The Landy was heavy enough with the steel cow bars, the winch and the counterweight strapped to the tail. Besides, it looked better without the armour.

'Well, I'll leave you to check the specifications,' muttered Rick, and stalked off towards the sound of the machine tools.

I stepped inside. It was well appointed. There was a radio fixed in a metal basin between the two bucket seats. The only remnant of the Blast Box was an armoured plate, which ran under the seats and shielded the rear of the cabin. Weapons were encased in plastic bodywork over driver and passenger – a standard barricade rifle with night scope, two pistols, four pairs of night-vision goggles (driver, passenger, spare, spare), secondary rifle and a double-barrelled shotgun. Next I stepped out of the cabin and inspected the tyres. One of them looked a little suspect.

I was on my back, inspecting the Landy's underside, when Regmiron called to me from the hatch.

'Kenstibec? Report to the reception area. You have a phone call.'

'Who is it?'

'Shersult.'

That would be about my fare.

I told Rick I was satisfied with the cab, so we went back out to reception, where I handed over a roll of cash, and promised to return as soon as Shersult briefed me on my destination. Rick pushed a space clear among the strange engine parts on his desk and wrote me a receipt. Then he handed me the phone.

'Don't worry about keeping me waiting,' said Shersult. I could barely hear him for the interference.

'Have you got a job for me?'

'I might do if you come up here and help me spot.'

'Can't you just tell me now?'

'Oh, no. Not on these phones. Just get up here.'

He hung up.

I had a cup of tea to pass the time until the bombardment ended. Regmiron led me out of the garage and back to the entrance, following me out. He leaned on the lip of the hatch and stared up through the supermarket roof, at the cloud bank.

'They say at least fifty more years,' he said.

I saluted.

'Oh yes,' I said. 'The morning will come.'

As usual Shersult was to be found manning the barricade, beating off the morning attack. If he could he would have just killed all day, shooting down hordes of screaming tribesmen, but he had to run the taxi firm to make ends meet. I was one of three surviving employees.

Today he was lying on a soot-black haulage crate that blocked off Gameskeeper's Road. A rope ladder hung down the side, clattering in the wind. I grabbed hold of it and clambered up, just in time to see Shersult firing at some movement in the darkness. A few bullets whistled back in reply. Shersult noticed me and indicated I should get down. I had no problem with that, dropping onto my belly and crawling over to him, wondering why we could never meet in peacetime conditions.

'All right, mate?' he said, handing me a pair of night-vision binoculars.

Only a soldier model would call you 'mate', having originally been designed to fraternise with Real units. They spoke with a bizarre mixture of arrogance, swearing and phoney bravura. Their devil-may-care chumminess made them difficult to talk to sometimes.

'Spot for me while we chat, would you? They're frisky today.'

'OK.' Looking up the street I spotted a Real, working his way in and out of the ruins.

'There's one,' I said, '150 metres, left side of the street, poking his head out . . .'

'Got him,' said Shersult.

A shot rang out. I watched the Real's head pop and searched for another. Most of them were taking cover, which was probably wise.

'The fare is a journalist,' said Shersult.

'Destination?'

'London.'

'Big trip. Since when do reporters make that kind of travel arrangement?'

'Don't ask me. The main thing is, business has been terrible and we need this job. Seven thousand, she's paying.'

He rolled onto his side and began to reload, looking at me with his glowing, green eyes. They'd been designed to strike fear into enemy combatants, but most of the time they'd just freaked out their own side.

I looked through the binoculars, down the street. 'I've noticed things have dropped off. What's wrong with everyone?'

'All waiting to hear what Control has to say, aren't they?'

Another Real appeared, making a break for it, running in zigzags that he must have thought would help. I pointed him out to Shersult.

'Here's another, forty metres . . .'

'Yup,' said Shersult.

He picked him out quickly but only winged him. The Real fell, vanishing into the debris of a collapsed house.

'Sneaky,' said Shersult. He shuffled on his belly along the cargo crate, trying to find an angle. I followed.

'Look,' I said, 'considering driver turnover rate at the moment, and considering we lost Leeds barricade . . .'

'That's just a rumour.'

'The point is that there's a lot more involved than there used to be. The Reals are better organised and there's fewer places to stop for a rest. Tiredness can kill, you know.'

'Is that your way of saying you want more money?'

He stopped, looked through his night sight, and pulled the trigger. He must have found an angle. There was some distant yelling, then the sound of a whistle. I saw movement in the shadows. The Reals were retreating.

Shersult sat up and rubbed at his legs. He'd probably been lying there all day, maybe even through the barrage, just to be ready for the first kill.

'She'll expect to be picked up from the TV station right after the High Lights, okay? All you need to do is get her to London. There's no return journey booked.'

'Luggage?' I asked.

'Minimal. Couple of cases. Should even fit it in your cabin. What's Rick got for you, anyway?'

'Defender. Standard stuff,' I said.

Shersult looked interested. He was about to say something when the all clear siren started up. There was no point trying to speak through that. I sat up on one knee and looked out over the wrecked suburbs, beyond the barricade. The Reals were withdrawing over the river, up the grey hills to their trenches, beaten for now. Besides, soon some light would break through the cloud wall for a few hours. We'd all stop fighting for that.

Shersult dismantled his rifle, carrying out each move with great care as he packed it away in a thin, black case. He walked over to the rope ladder and silently descended. Clearly our business was concluded.

I lingered on the crate for a while and looked back at the city, at the fires smoking in the night and the shape of the dead green sea.

'What do you mean by that?'

He steps towards me.

'Luke Ransom from school says that Ficials shoot all the people in the boats.'

'That's not me,' I say. 'That's the soldiers. I'm optimised for construction, you know that.'

'Luke Ransom says that you've all got a big secret. He says that you're all waiting to take us over. He said that one day you'll kill me and Dad.'

My stump tingles. It has stopped dripping blood. There is a clock up on the wall but I don't have to look at it.

'I wouldn't do that.'

He isn't satisfied. He fidgets. He gazes at his warped reflection in the steel wall, so I crane my neck to look at mine too. From here it looks like I am a whole, entire person.

'But are you on our side?'

'What do you mean?'

'You kill people.'

'I keep telling you, I'm not a soldier model. The soldiers do it because it's what they're designed to do. They have to protect the border or this island would be overrun. Don't they teach you this in school?'

'Teachers don't talk about what's happening.'

'Everyone on the planet is trying to squeeze into one or two countries, like ours, because they can't live anywhere else, see?'

'They can't?' asks Alan.

'No. But we can't support all those extra people. That's why the other countries are in trouble. There are too many people fighting over limited resources.'

'Re-sauces?'

'Fuel, bread, water – all the things you need to live. So we were created to help protect this island. It's the last place left. If we let everybody get in, everybody dies. Do you see? We can't let them in.'

'How do you know that for sure?'

'Control tells us.'

'Luke Ransom says that Control has taken over the country. He says it's evil. He says it made us all have bar codes so it can get us.' He holds up the code branded on his hand. 'Luke says we should fight Control.'

'Who is this Ransom kid?'

'His father's in the Truth League.'

He says 'Truth League' like the words are dangerous. I've encountered the League's finest. Drunks with a penchant for looting, it seems to me.

'Control doesn't want to hurt you. It's not a monster. It's a powerful coalesced mind that directs our work. Without Control this country would be a wasteland. It wants to help you survive.'

'But do they enjoy it?'

'Who enjoy what?'

'Killing the immigrants. Do the soldiers want to do it?'

'They don't want anything. I don't want anything.'

'You don't want anything?'

'Nothing.'

He sniffs and considers my answer.

'You mean you don't want to come down from there?'

'Why wish for something when the wish has no effect?'

He closes one eye and bites his lip.

'I don't get it.'

'Never mind.'

He shrugs and turns away. As he walks to the hatch he throws a glance back at me. He is a little afraid, I think. He catches the fear from his father, who catches it from his workers, who catch it from the infocasts and the Truth League.

The truth is, I don't want to kill him, but I don't want not to kill him either.

He is a small person. He is the son of my boss. He is the name he carries, Alan. What else?

CULL TV

Cull TV operated out of the worst bunker in Edinburgh, a virtual cave dwelling gouged out of the old brewery cellars. The Reals nursed a particular hatred for the station's culling broadcasts, and shelled it around the clock. This gave the average Cull TV news broadcast an entertainment value way better than its news content. Newsreaders were regularly shrouded in brick dust, programmes were interrupted by power failure, and correspondents occasionally died live on screen.

I arrived at their building as the all clear siren ended its wailing. Perma, half producer, half security guard, let me in, giving me a look like a cat might give a cheap tin of tuna.

'Kenstibec,' she said, 'just in time for the evening bulletin. Excuse the mess, we've just had another direct hit.'

I followed her down the twisted iron ladder to their main reception area. The air tasted of cement. Beams of torchlight swung about through the gloom. We didn't stop to sign me in as the reception desk had disappeared beneath a large steel girder, shapely legs pinned underneath. I couldn't see a torso attached. Perma ushered me down to sub level two. It was easier to breathe in there and the emergency lighting was working, so I could watch Perma making her way down the stairs.

Like nearly every employee of the TV station, Perma was a pleasure Ficial, which meant she had been optimised for sexual congress with Reals. As pleasure Ficials were produced for nothing but bumping and grinding, they were widely regarded as useless. Of course, in Control's new world no Ficial was to be left behind, so they were corralled into broadcasting, an occupation seen as meaningless but necessary while Reals still resisted the cull.

I didn't seek out their company. You never knew what they were going to get upset about. Their emotions were left largely intact during the Engineering process and I always expected them to start crying. Maybe that was unfair. They certainly dealt with being shot at pretty well.

We arrived in the control room halfway through the culling update. If there had been the tools and the materials I would have had the place fixed up in a couple of weeks. As it was, it had all the structural integrity of the ruins of Angkor. I was surprised the roof didn't fall in the moment I looked at it.

One guy manned the editing suite, a silent, square-jawed type who was probably optimised for rubbing his fingers over his chin and claiming that no other razor cut this close. I took a seat in a corner and settled down to watch my fare on the monitor. The journo was named Starvie. She was reading the mid-morning update.

The monitor switched to film of Real bodies being tossed into mass graves and burned. Then it cut back to Starvie, now standing by a shabby CULL-O-METER.

'So,' said Starvie, 'here's where we stand for this month. We're doing really well, but with your help we could do so much more.'

Perma tapped me on the shoulder and handed me a bottle of water. It was hot in there so I drained it in one go. Perma took a seat next to me and watched the monitor, picking absently at her nails. They still had a fair bit of co-worker's blood caked underneath.

'How are ratings?' I asked her.

She sighed.

'If they watched half as much of our stuff as you watched of theirs, we might have persuaded them to give up by now.'

I doubted that. Still, it was fair to say I watched a lot of Real TV.

When the stalemate had set in around the barricades, the Real tribes had created ramshackle broadcasting operations. With the cloud wall overhead, their signals didn't make it very far, but each tribe could at least entertain itself, gathering around a salvaged TV set for that old familiar warmth. TV was important to them, even as they died out. We tuned in too. Their stuff was more diverting than the long, efficient slaughter of Cull TV. I wasn't about to admit that to Perma though. I changed the subject.

'So what is this trip in aid of?' I asked her.

'Brixton broadcasting centre was hit by some awful new bomb.' Perma kept her eyes fixed on the monitor, watching for problems. 'They lost half their strength and need a few replacements for the news team.'

'Are you not a little short staffed yourselves?'

'We'll manage.'

Starvie was finishing her statement, something about a new culling method. Apparently it was much less painful. Some genius thought this would inspire the Reals to march up and surrender in an orderly queue.

I kind of hoped the Reals would start shelling us, but to no avail. The bulletin went off without a hitch. After fifteen minutes they went to break. Starvie came out of the studio and walked over to the water fountain. She turned the tap, but there was only a hissing noise and a feeble, fine spray. She cursed and threw the cup against a wall. Perma offered her a bottle.

'Thank you,' said Starvie. 'Listen, honey, I know I'm leaving, but for the next guy's sake, fix the air conditioning. It is like I'm breathing lava in there.' She drank deeply, heaving the bottle over her, taking slow, huge gulps. When she finished she wiped her mouth and dabbed a few drops on her temples. Then she took a handkerchief from her pocket, tipped some water over it, and wiped at the grime on her face. Perma nodded in my direction.

'This is your driver. He's come to pick you up.'

Starvie put a hand on her hip, striking a pose, and smiled at me.

'So it is. You all ready to go, sugar?'

'I'm not sugar,' I said. 'I'm Kenstibec, construction.'

'Really?' Her smile dissolved. 'I thought you were Kenstibec, cab driver?'

I didn't want to get drawn into a debate.

'I'm ready to go,' I said. 'You?'

She pulled a fur-lined coat from a pile in the corner, wrapped it around her shoulders, and stalked out the door without a word.

'Better follow,' said Perma. 'She can wander off if you're not careful.'

I went after her, up the stairs to the reception, which was still dark. The legs and the girder had gone. I called out Starvie's name.

'She's gone up,' said a voice.

I went back to the ladder. Two shapely and perfectly smooth legs were at the top of the hatch, dangling there in the flickering blue light. I clambered up and sat next to her. The High Lights were fading already, leaving only a few thin purple streaks in the cloud. Starvie had scraped her hair into a tight ponytail. In the darkness she seemed to have aged. She was staring through a gash in the old brewery building, over the barricade, at the teetering wreck of a church spire.

'There's a Real spotter in there,' she said, pointing it out. 'He's probably looking at us right now.'

I shifted a little way from her.

'Let's get out of here.'

'He never shoots when it's just me,' she said. 'Anyone else comes out they have to run like hell. He's very good. But I can just sit here and look right back at him. I think he enjoys looking at me, even through a night sight.'

She picked up a stone and raised it at the church spire, daring the Real in there to shoot it out of her hand.

'Let's go,' I said.

She looked up at me.

'He's won, you know,' she said. 'I've been working here for a year now, he's been watching me for a year, but it's me that is leaving, not him. He'll carry on calling in attacks. They'll all keep dying down there.'

She dropped the stone down the hatch. I stood up and dusted off my combats.

'Don't dwell on all that,' I said. 'It is good to get out of the city for a while, you'll see. We weren't meant to scurry around in cellars.'

I reached down, cupped one arm under her thigh, another around her back, and pulled her out of the hatch. Then I lowered her onto her feet, being careful to shift her out of the spire's line of sight.

'We'll go back to yours now and grab your stuff.' I said, kicking the hatch closed. 'Then I'll take you to the car. I think you'll be impressed.'

She laughed and moved back towards the gash, peering out at the spire.

14

'You don't sound very bright,' she said.

'Well, I'm optimised for construction.'

I gave her a quick, hard punch to the back of the head and she fell down onto the rocks.

I picked her up, hoisted her onto my shoulder, and set off into the fog. I'd had about enough of hanging around. Besides, her suitor in the spire might be the jealous type.

I checked her ID card and found her address. She lived in one of the fortified flak towers that stood along the shoreline, half buried in the trash that the sea vomited up each day. Generally I tried to avoid the area. Every time I visited all I could think about was how I might transform the place: how I would bulldoze the towers, clear the bank of trash and landscape a water garden – something like the Villa d'Este.

It was useless thinking about reconstruction, but I couldn't help sketching the plans out in my head as I staggered over the pockmarked beach towards the towers.

Starvie was on the ninth floor of tower D. She had a small cubicle near the outer skin, the kind of place that would shake like a rollercoaster when the shooting began. There was a metal desk in one corner that could retract into the wall, a single bookshelf holding a few tattered journalism texts, and a hard-looking bed with paper-thin, beige sheets.

It beat the hell out of my place. I had a shallow cave bunk dug into Arthur's Seat.

I put her down on the bed and poked around. She had very little of anything. I did find a charcoal drawing tucked between the books, a self-portrait Starvie must have been working on. She clearly wasn't optimised for art. Then there were two green leather cases with gold combination locks tucked into the wardrobe. I placed them on the bed next to her, sat down, and shook her until she came round. She seemed a little disappointed to see me.

'We're in your room,' I said. 'I think I found your luggage.'

'Did you hit me just then?'

'Yes,' I said, 'but it was only to hurry things up. You were getting all introspective.'

She touched the back of her neck and winced. Then she noticed the cases. She shoved me away and clutched them to her breast.

'You don't touch these, get it? They're mine.'

Outside, there was a rumble. A storm was rolling in off the sea, dumping ash, snow and darkness. Starvie sat up and stretched.

'When are we going to leave?'

'I was thinking about right now,' I said.

She cocked her head to one side. 'You look a bit tired to start driving.'

'I'm tired *until* I start driving,' I said. 'Then I wake up.'

A thought flashed across her eyes.

'So, how do we get out?'

It was a good question. I knelt down on the floor and took out my old *A to Z*, about the most useful creation the Real world ever achieved. I spread it out on the floor in front of me and gave the problem some thought.

Getting out of the city was never an easy task, and it couldn't be approached lightly. There was a lot of planning involved and you needed to be careful. Many schools of thought existed about how best to do it, and I had plenty of arguments on the subject with other drivers. In my experience, nothing beat breaking out of the barricade in a high-powered 4×4 and running the gauntlet of the siege positions until you reached the open countryside.

Initially, after we first withdrew into the cities, and before the barricades went up, everybody tried to get about by flying, but this didn't last long. The corrosives in the cloud barrier chewed up planes like gum. For a while you could fly beneath the clouds, nap-of-the earth, but the Reals quickly mastered shooting them down.

A few salty dogs tried littoral operations. You could get a motor boat, hug the coastline and shoot upriver into London, Liverpool or Portsmouth – any of the bigger barricades – without too much trouble. But again the Reals got organised, manning all the city approaches and creating their own ramshackle navies. All our big old navy ships lay corroding in port. There were still a few blockade runners, making use of the handful of small boats in Ficial hands, but not many. We'd pretty much lost the air and the sea.

This left the open road.

A lot of people would have told you that to break out you needed firepower and you needed armour – and I never questioned that.

But for me it was a question of balance. Lots of armour and lots of firepower were not always an advantage. For example, if a guy offered you a ride in his tank he was going to get you killed. When a tank broke down in the middle of nowhere you couldn't do a quick fix and move on. Also, if you came under attack you couldn't traverse a tank weapon to fire at a Real with an RPG zipping about you on a moped. Travelling by tank you were slow, and they were going to get you.

Of course, this whittled down my competition a great deal. In the first year I don't mind admitting that I found it hard to get the work. But the ranks of tankists thinned out quick and competition evaporated. I was one of three drivers left stationed in Edinburgh. We were in high demand. Each one of us survived by favouring light transport.

The biggest deal was choosing your route.

The Edinburgh barricade boasted certain advantages over others. It had plenty of weak points, was surrounded by flat, open plains, and had a far smaller Real army laying siege. On the other hand, what high points there were had such command of the landscape that one half-dead Real with a telescope and a radio could direct fire on you very swiftly, so you had to keep moving.

The barricade's north end hung on the Bruntsfield Links stockade, running down to the junction of Quality Street and Queensferry Road. This was known as Hellfire Triangle because of the big guns over the river to the west, and I discounted it straight away. The next section of barricade stretched over Corstorphine Hill and Murrayfield Golf Club, but I'd used the corridor I found there three times in a row and suspected if I tried again I'd find it better defended.

After that, it all got a little tricky – there was the flood plain around Water of Leith with the bunkers and floating mines, where the fogs hung like a curtain over the landscape. There wasn't much of a barricade here, only foxholes and watch points. Good drivers had drowned trying to cross.

The barricade reappeared north-west of the Merchants Golf Club, and became more formidable around the cratered mess of the old bypass, where we'd stacked and braced car wrecks into a barrier running all the way to the Old Dalkeith Road. This whole area was watched by the Real lookouts on Swanston and Torphin Hill, and was swarming with man traps and automated guns. Finally, the wall returned to a solid concrete form, about three storeys high, running north to Portobello and the Firth of Forth.

I didn't like the Portobello option, but it was the best of a bad bunch. The Reals had their staging points there and if we timed it right we might catch them in that numb, half-waking state when their reactions were a little slower.

I folded the map away. Starvie was staring at the wall with glassy eyes.

'Get some rest,' I said. 'I'll drive the car over around five a.m. and wake you. We'll drive over to our exit point and go straight out.'

I stood up and made for the door, but I was knocked down by an explosion rocking the tower. Starvie was thrown from her bed and landed next to me with a cracking noise. I got to my feet as another three shells hit in quick succession. I listened to the barrage for a moment. Starvie lay still on the floor.

'Hey,' I said. 'Get up, okay?'

She didn't respond. I gave her a little kick in the stomach.

'Get up.'

Another string of shells struck outside. Starvie hid her face under her arms and groaned.

'What's the point? They've started now. They won't stop for hours.'

She was right. The Reals liked to shoot and had plenty of ammunition. There was no way of leaving now. It would be an inferno out there.

I lay down on Starvie's bunk and pulled the sheets over me. I got comfortable, deciding a little sleep might not be such a bad thing. I tapped Starvie on the shoulder.

'Wake me when they stop.'

I couldn't get to sleep. It was always that way before a big drive: too much planning to be done. I stepped over Starvie and left the room, taking the central stairway down to the community hall.

A few other insomniacs were slumped in plastic chairs, watching a heavily pixelated Real broadcast on a wallscreen. I took a seat and joined in the viewing.

It was another CCTV show. For an hour there was a security feed from a camera looking over a railway station concourse, then, for variety, a camera shot overlooking a service station kiosk, played at ten times actual speed. Thousands of customers approached the counter, creating queues, breaking apart, reforming. It was hypnotic. All those people, their expressions palpitating with useless, destructive feeling; they were all dead now. So were their cars.

My eyelids just started to grow heavy when the programme suddenly snapped into a brash music video. It was the new single by the King of Newcastle. It was a horrible, chest-thumping thing, an artless butchering of styles. It brought to mind the Central Pavilion in Moscow: all size and no direction. Somebody yelled to change channel and we flicked.

The new programme was the Dr Pander confession, the most repeated of all. The one where the father of the Ficial race talked his audience through what a horrible misadventure it had all been. We'd all seen that gaunt, beaten, lowered face a hundred times. It was pathetic to watch him mumble his way through the script on his lap. Still, nobody changed the channel.

'. . . never for a moment considered the repercussions of my actions,' he said. 'The demon that took possession of me would not let me stop. Even though a part of me knew that I was blaspheming, that I was meddling with forces completely beyond my control, the demon pressed me on. I was bent on the destruction of the world. I thought only of myself, never the knife I held to nature's throat . . .'

It always amazed me that such a slight figure could have been our starting point. He didn't look like very much, with rounded, flat features and hunted eyes.

'I have always been vain,' he went on. 'I wanted to create supermen. I thought I was God.'

'Near as dammit,' said somebody.

I left the viewing and went to the phone, placing a couple of calls despite the barrage. The first was to Shersult, giving him our breakout location. The second was to Rick, offering him a five per cent cut of my fare to deliver the cab to the flak tower. He laughed at the idea of leaving his bunker, but said he would have Regmiron drop it off for me.

I went back to Starvie's room. I found her sleeping on the floor. The gunfire had stopped. I dropped into her bunk and went out like a light. If I was lucky I'd get two hours.

'Why do you all have to be so damn good-looking?'

The boss's wife is rubbing her face against mine, kissing my cheek, running her hands over me.

I have heard about this from Dingkom. He says the boss's wife visits you in the shed and paws you, but I have never had it happen until now.

She makes a moaning sound and runs her hands up my belly towards my legs. She smells of beef and mustard and perfume. Hanging upside down like this her chin looks like the fat nose of an eyeless face.

The ventilators hum.

She takes a few steps back and smiles. She puts her hands up to the top of her cardigan and begins undoing the buttons.

'Does this do anything for you, forty-two?' she says. 'Anything at all?'

'Do what?' I ask.

She laughs and ceases unbuttoning. She begins circling me with slow, deliberate steps. She 'la-la's a song in a husky, high whisper, but I can't make out the tune. She's turned it into a noise, a kind of mating call. She stops behind me, quiet.

'Alan likes you,' she says. 'I like you. I think I like you the most.'

Dingkom told me that she said she liked him the most, but I don't mention that. She has a reputation for getting angry and beating us up. I figure I will keep quiet and let her do her thing.

'Let's get you down,' she says.

She reappears, walking to the hoist controls, looking back at me over her shoulder. She hits the release and I am lowered to the steel floor. I keep still. I don't want her to get mad.

She steps over me and crouches at my feet, undoing the binding from the hook. She keeps her eyes fixed to mine. Suddenly she laughs and leaps on top of me, wrapping her arms around my head, pressing my face into her breasts.

'This is awful,' she says. 'This is awful.'

She snaps my chin up so that she can burrow into my eyes some more. She presses her lips to mine. I can feel her tongue flapping at my lips. I try not to breathe in.

'Open your mouth,' she snarls.

I obey. Her tongue darts into my mouth and wriggles around over mine. I think she wants me to respond. I waggle my tongue about gamely, not really knowing if I'm doing it right, but she seems to appreciate it. She thrashes her body around on mine.

'You're disgusting,' she says, 'you're absolutely disgusting.'

She grabs me just about everywhere she can. It is like being pinned under an enormous, suffocating fish.

EXIT

Starvie didn't even look at the cab. She stumbled out of the flak tower, yawned uncontrollably (Pander never managed to engineer that away) and tossed her bags in the Landy's flatbed. Then she curled up in the passenger seat and promptly fell asleep.

I drove us to Portobello, leaving the lights off, navigating the ruined streets by memory. The cab ran well. I resisted the urge to put it through its paces, settling for the rumble of the wheel in my fingers and the hum of the engine. I could tell Rick had done a job on this one.

Shersult was waiting at the foot of the barricade. I pulled up by the bulldozer. It was like the ones I drove before the war, but its bodywork was patched up with metal plates like a mad grandmother's quilt. A remote antenna, ten feet high, projected out of the driver compartment.

I donned a pair of night goggles and stepped out of the car.

'Morning,' said Shersult. He was holding a small doll, a vacant-looking bear clutching a heart. Shersult was carefully placing a miniature landmine in its belly. Whenever he wasn't killing, he was making booby traps – jewellery, books, toys, anything a Real might pick up out of curiosity. 'Little surprises,' he called them. It was just the way he was built.

He put it to one side and grinned.

'Shall we check out the view?'

We climbed the barricade and lay flat to look at the area we'd be traversing.

It didn't look great.

Even with the bulldozer clearing a path, it would be tough. One street was open enough to attempt but the Reals had it covered. A church hewn from granite stood defiantly pockmarked a hundred metres up the road, its shattered steeple commanding our route. A couple of burned-out vehicles were thrown across the street at this point, reinforced with junk picked from the ruins. I pointed it out to Shersult.

'Good strongpoint,' he said, 'but it could be a decoy. They might have a trap dug in the street again.'

I knew what he meant. A few trips back I had driven straight into a huge trench, so well hidden I hadn't known about it until I was in it. It was intended for a tank and I managed to drive my way out, but it had been a shock, and I had lost a few teeth I had use for.

'Well, it's not going to get any better. Let's get moving.' I slid down the rope to Starvie, who was struggling to fit an armoured breast plate over her chest.

'This is made for a man,' she said.

Shersult walked behind her and pulled the leather straps so tight around her waist she yelped in pain. She wheeled around and punched the side of his head. He didn't notice, going about his work with careful and brutal pulls and twists, joining Kevlar to Kevlar so that no gap was left. Starvie huffed and struggled.

When he was done, Shersult went to the bulldozer and hopped into the driver's seat, checking the steering and acceleration mechanisms. Watching him do his checks was one of the few times I could appreciate the fanatical attention he paid to his equipment. If one thing went wrong with the 'dozer's remote control we could get hemmed in behind it and trapped in a nasty crossfire.

Starvie waddled up to the Landy's passenger door but couldn't get up onto her seat.

'I can't do this every time,' I said, picking her up and throwing her inside, legs first. I grabbed her little green cases, slapped them onto her lap and jogged around to the driver's side, leaping in and starting the engine.

'Where's your armour?' she asked.

I was about to answer when the bulldozer roared into life. Shersult gave me the thumbs-up and danced onto the barricade, taking his position. The 'dozer's right track spun, shrieking on the tarmac like chains dragging over marble. It edged slowly forward, then turned again and paused. I flicked on the Landy's radio. Shersult was already on the line.

'Right,' he said, 'remote is operational. Are we ready to rock?'

'Whatever that means.'

The bulldozer coughed and juddered and threw itself forward. I started my engine and accelerated behind it, but suddenly it ground to a halt and I nearly rear-ended it.

I reached for the radio, to let Shersult know exactly what I thought about getting a dent before I even left the barricade. Then the 'dozer blundered forward again and charged at its full ponderous speed towards the wall.

'Here we go,' I said.

We burst through the stone wall, immediately attracting fire. A few shots glanced off Starvie's helmet, one tunnelling into my thigh. There was a single, low, echoing shot, and the hostile fire stopped. There was no better cover than Shersult's.

The 'dozer pressed on. I beat my fingers on the steering wheel, impatient to get above twenty miles an hour. Crawling behind the bulldozer was the time I thought I was going to take a hit.

A furious white smoke trail spat in our direction, striking the 'dozer full in the face. The machine ploughed on, unmoved, protected by its huge scoop. Another rocket shot out, aimed higher this time. It passed over the 'dozer and exploded somewhere behind, showering us with sparks.

I picked up the radio.

'Eleven o'clock,' I said, probably sounding impatient.

'Roger that,' replied Shersult. Another streak of flame, this time from above and behind, thudded into a house ahead of us.

'Thank you,' I said, replacing the radio.

The 'dozer charged on. We had almost reached the church strongpoint when a Real kid appeared at the side of the road. He stared right at me, clutching something to his chest with both arms. Instead of reaching for my pistol I stared back at him, trying to read his emotion. Maybe it was fear. Maybe it was anger. Maybe he was having that thing Reals talk about where his short little life was flashing before his eyes. Whatever it was, it didn't last long. He sprang forward and ran at the 'dozer. I just had time to push Starvie into a brace position before the explosion hit. The shock wave lifted the Landy up in the air, shaking it hard. My throat filled with the smell of cordite, an intense flash of heat cutting across my back.

We fell back down to earth with a crunch. I looked up, trying to get my bearings. The cab was fine, just covered in soot and steaming a little under the bonnet. Starvie was frozen but undamaged. Through the ringing in my ears I could make out shouting. Then I saw the 'dozer, or the pieces of it. The kid had picked his spot well, running behind the steel plough and leaping on the engine before detonating his device. Now there wasn't anything but debris and black smoke. We were trapped.

'Hey.' Shersult's voice crackled into life on the radio. 'What are you sitting there for?'

I picked up the radio and punched the transmit button.

'I'm beginning to think they knew we were coming.'

'MOVE. Alley behind you, twenty metres back, left-hand side. Go for it now, while they regroup.'

'This isn't going to work,' I said, and tossed the radio back in its housing.

It was hard to turn around with my back now welded in a burn to my shirt, but I shifted enough to see behind. At first, the way seemed to be clear. Then a rusted road sign lifted up out of the rubble. Seven Reals struggled out from underneath, brandishing weapons. I was reaching for my pistol when the first shot hit me. It only glanced my cheek but was enough to make me think Shersult's moving notion had some merit.

I hit reverse gear. The engine roared in a way that suggested we might be in more trouble than I thought, but thankfully we did move. We started to pull back when some more of those low, thumping shots rang out, as Shersult bagged the front two Reals. I smacked the Landy into the third as he was raising his rifle. Shersult bagged another before the others leapt clear. I pulled the handbrake and span the wheel, lining us up with the alley. As I suspected, the Reals had sealed it off with a huge mound of rock, mud and debris. Still, with enough speed the Landy's cattle bars might break it up. I went at it hard but, instead of breaking through, the car bumped skyward and stalled. Another spray of fire hit us. Starvie was thrown onto me as she took the full force of the hail. I got one that lodged in my armpit. It stung so badly I let go of the wheel, and a lightness filled my head. I felt that we were rolling backwards.

The voice on the radio screamed: 'GET OUT THE WAY – I CAN'T SEE HIM – REVERSE, REVERSE!'

I could only look at the Real, a fierce one with a red stripe painted across his mouth. He stumbled from under the road sign, clutching a rocket. I knew that was bad, but I couldn't seem to persuade my hands to grab the wheel. Everything was turning black. Then I felt a sharp pain as Starvie leaned over me and buried her elbow in my groin. She grabbed the pistol from my belt, levelled it at the red face and fired. I turned around to see that she'd missed. Then she shot off a whole clip, fast and furious. Still, somehow, she contrived to miss him with every shot.

'Brilliant,' I said.

The Real was surprised. He grinned, knelt down, and aimed his rocket at us. Then there was another low, slapping noise, and half of his head disappeared in a red spray.

'*Now* I can see him,' said the voice on the radio.

I pushed Starvie off me, tried the ignition and shot us back as fast as the Landy would go, trying to hit another Real who'd pushed up against the wall for cover. He dashed out of the way, dodging us by inches, and fired as we passed. I hit the brakes hard. Starvie's head was thrown back, her helmet hitting the roll cage with a church-bell clang. She slumped forward, unconscious. The Real we'd just missed started to take some aimed shots at us. I shifted to first gear and hit the pedal to have another go at the alley. The Landy made a tortured noise and smoked like a peat fire, but we picked up just enough speed, and smashed our way through, thumping the car off the alley wall and rebounding out into the next street.

I was greeted by the welcome sight of unblocked road. I could still hear a few muffled shots coming over the block and the yells of undisciplined Real soldiery. I moved us slowly on, keeping the engine noise low. Starvie groaned and pulled her head off the dashboard. She noticed the gunfire and the yelling and slapped my shoulder.

'Move it, will you?' she said. 'What are we, sightseeing?'

She held a hand up to her left shoulder, trying to stem the

bleeding from two large holes. Then she jerked around, looking for something.

'My bags!' she screamed. 'Where are they?'

'Keep your voice down.'

She unfastened her harness and bent down, feeling around her feet for the green cases. She found one, then another, and began breathing more easily. Typical fare. Under any circumstances, the first thing they think of is their luggage.

I took the first right turn I found, then a left, then another right. The streets were silent and clear enough to maintain a good average speed. Starvie took the first-aid kit out of the glove compartment and bandaged her wounds, wrapping herself up slowly and symmetrically like a gift.

After an hour of picking our way through the outskirts, I was doing better. The hit to my face and leg were healing fast. The armpit stung, but it was good to be on the move with the engine running and flat tarmac under the wheels.

Starvie didn't look around as we left the city limits, which was odd. Fares tended to be captivated by unfamiliar surroundings after being locked up in a barricade for years, but not her. She clasped her green cases to her chest and stared dead ahead at the road. I figured the only thing she saw that captivated her was a mirror.

When we were clear of the city I pulled the Landy into the forecourt of a small garage and cut the engine. I donned the goggles and looked around, inspecting the houses across the street, but couldn't see any signs of life. The place was dead, buried in undisturbed ash. Good for a pit stop.

'What are we doing here?' asked Starvie.

I unbuckled my harness, opened the door and stepped out of the Landy. I rubbed at my legs, which had decided blood circulation wasn't for them.

'Hey! Quit scratching yourself and talk to me.'

'The bullet in my armpit is a problem,' I said. 'I have to get it out or the wound will seal up over it. Then I'll be in trouble.'

'If you're going to stop every five minutes we're never going to get there.'

'I'll try to bear that in mind.'

28

I lifted up my arm and inspected the wound.

'I'm going to need your help with this.'

Starvie sighed and began to strip off her armour. She bit at the strap on one Kevlar glove and pulled it off, then removed her helmet. Her hair tumbled down around her face. She lowered her head, then tossed it back in a cascade of curls, brushing at it with her fingertips, her face vacant, her lips pouting.

'Do you do that every time you take your hat off?' I asked.

'Sorry,' she said. 'Can't help it.'

She clambered out the car, ditching the breast and thigh plates on the ground, then with an almighty swing of each leg, kicked her Kevlar footwear across the forecourt.

I put a new clip in my pistol and led the way across the carpet of snow into the garage shop. It was intact inside, mostly undisturbed. Starvie leapt over the counter and went into the back. I wandered the aisles, enjoying the museum-like quality of the place. It was a little disordered, with tins, stamped-on noodle bags and magazines littering the floor, but the shelves were still neatly stocked. A pyramid of windscreen-washer-fluid cartons stood undisturbed in one corner. I thought about pocketing one, but decided it would be wrong to disrupt the structure. Instead I brought out my multi-knife and stabbed open a tin of beans, eating greedily.

I picked up a magazine I found on the floor, one of those flesh publications which Real men were so fond of. I had a flick though, looking at pages of blonde, tanned females, wristwatches and hair products. Then there were photos of thin men wearing tight suits, pointing at something off the page. There were phone numbers in the back pages, advertising waterbeds and sex lines. On the front cover was a woman pressed against a wall, wearing a short white dress and baring her white teeth, her legs a little parted, her skin brown. A headline was stamped across her waist.

Jennifer E: And Man Created Woman

Starvie appeared from the back office and searched behind the counter. She examined the cigarettes, turning them over in her hands with interest. She tapped the CCTV monitor with an index finger and punched some buttons on the till.

'Boy,' she said, smiling. 'They couldn't optimise you for *this* job, could they?'

I held up the magazine cover.

'Is this you?'

She stopped smiling. She tossed a few packs of cigarettes into her pockets and jumped the counter in a single bound. Then she marched to the door, opened it, and held it open for me.

'No, that's not me. That's Jennifer,' she said.

'You were a celebrity? I don't think I've met a celebrity before.'

She looked through the window at the houses across the street.

'Where are we?' she asked.

'Clear of the city. Fifty or so miles south-west of where we started.'

She nodded and beckoned me to come outside into the night. The temperature was dropping fast. Snow began to fall on the forecourt. She placed the basket on the ground and told me to sit down against the shop wall. She knelt, unwrapped some cheap tweezers and opened a bag of some things called Handy Wipes.

'Lift your arm.'

She took a look at my armpit, made a noise with her tongue, and rubbed at the mess with a wipe.

'Do you know what you're doing?' I asked.

'Not really.' She threw away some crimson wipes and picked up the tweezers.

'It's sealed up a lot. You must be a Power Eight. You guys can get hit on the head by a winch and then run a mile, can't you?'

'I'm a nine,' I said, 'and yes, we can take a bit of knocking, but that doesn't mean it doesn't hurt.'

She tugged my arm up high, and dug the tweezers into the wound. She went at it for two minutes without finding anything, just scraping around in amateurish fashion. I was going to give her more time, but then she found the bullet, grabbed at it dumbly, and pushed it further in. That was it. I gave her a shove and knocked her onto her back.

'I'll do it.'

I picked up the tweezers with my left hand and tried to manoeuvre them under my armpit, but I found that moving anything was now making me light-headed. Starvie sat on crossed legs and ignored me, flicking through the flesh magazine. I gave it a few more tries but only made my head spin.

'Okay, maybe you'd better do it.' I looked down and saw blood collecting at my side. Starvie continued scanning the magazine.

'You mean you don't know what you're doing?'

'No idea,' I said, and passed right out.

I was somewhere else, and I was alone. Curiously, there was power. A dim light shone from a lampshade shaped like a rose. I touched at my armpit and felt gingerly for the lump of the bullet, but it was gone. The wound had nearly healed. It took me a minute to realise I was in one of the houses across from the garage.

I was lying on a brown carpet, between a sofa with lacy purple cushions and a brown television on a wheeled metal table. A framed painting hung on the wall, of a young girl with wings playing a harp. On a coffee table there were framed photos of the people that once lived here, proving to themselves they really existed. I guess they had kind of succeeded. Here I was looking at them, after all. There was a family portrait taken against a pastel backdrop, another of a father and son on a speedboat at sea, and another of a mother holding a baby in a hospital. Not for the first time, I wondered why Reals worked their whole lives just to collect all this garbage and sit among it.

My next thought was for the car. I struggled up onto my feet and went to the net curtains, moving my legs like I was on stilts. I peeked outside into the gloom. I could make out the figure of Starvie, sitting on the Landy's bonnet, apparently smoking one of her souvenir cigarettes. She'd chosen our house well – the driveway was surrounded by tall, bare hedgerows on one side with a brick wall on the other. Any pursuers wouldn't see it easily from the road.

I tapped on the window. Starvie turned, smoked and stared. Then I saw the orange ember of the cigarette spin off into the snow, and she jumped off the car and walked inside.

'How about this place?' she asked, entering the room. 'A generator all the way out here?' She pointed to the bulb and waggled her fingers at it as if she'd conjured its light.

She sat on the sofa and pulled a cushion to her lap. The bullet wounds in her shoulder had healed up.

'So what's the plan for the next leg?' she asked.

It was a good, sharp question. I talked it through, which helped me get it clear in my head.

'Right, well . . . providing we don't hit any snags, we'll work our way through some country roads I'm familiar with, skirt Dumfries and Carlisle, and then take the scenic route through the lakes and Yorkshire Dales. Then down the A661, Wetherby, Tadcaster, then up the A64 to York. Lots of good, empty back roads away from the cities. But first we need to find a guide.'

'A guide?' said Starvie. 'What do you mean a guide? There isn't another barricade for miles, is there?'

'No, there isn't.'

She narrowed her eyes.

'Are you talking about a Real?'

'Yes.'

'What – we're going to kidnap a Real?'

'No, I'll pay him.'

'Pay him? You'll enter into a bargain?'

'Sure. There are a few Real settlements around Carlisle – just a few speckled about because there's some clean water. They don't really have anything in the way of a leader or organisation. They're quite peaceful really.'

Starvie was shivering. She went over to the coffee table and ripped the cloth from it, sending the picture frames tumbling and smashing onto the floor. She wrapped the cloth around her and went back to the sofa.

'So what can you pay them with? They barter, don't they? Our credits won't mean anything to them.'

'Fuel,' I said, 'plain and simple. Every Real needs it and no Real has it. You may have noticed they're none too happy about our monopoly.'

'We have fuel to spare?'

'Five containers on the flatbed.'

'That's not a little hazardous? I don't know if you've noticed, sweetheart, but half the world seems intent on shooting at that thing.'

'Fuel's sealed in Gronts Alloy. It would take something big to ignite it.'

She shook her head and looked up at the ceiling.

'You don't think it's a good idea to hire a Real?' I asked.

'Frankly no.'

'What's the drawback?'

'Their brutal savagery?' she suggested. 'Don't they like to wear our skins?'

'Some of them, yes . . .'

It was true. There was a fair bit of Real TV devoted to the dismembering and general abuse of Ficial bodies. The King of Newcastle, in particular, had a lust for such revenge entertainment. It was graphic stuff. Shersult was a fan.

'Anyway,' said Starvie, 'we need all our fuel, don't we?'

'We'll get some more at York.'

I was tired of the interrogation. She was wide awake in the cold, full of talk and energy. I was healing, and didn't want to explain things to her any more. I decided to turn the conversation to her favourite subject.

'So what about you?'

'Me?' she said. 'What about me?'

'Well, there's an obvious question I need to ask you. Namely, why am I transporting a reporter?'

'It's not really any of your business, is it?' Some of the energy seemed to drain out of her. She picked up the cigarette packet and bounced it on her palm a few times.

'We can't drive around the country with a Real,' she said. 'Control would kill us for not culling it, let alone making a deal with it.'

'Control's never noticed before,' I said. 'And it wouldn't kill me. I'm one of twelve Ficials on this entire island who knows the roads. I'm in a niche industry. You? Well . . .'

'What are you trying to say?'

'Well, I don't want to hurt your feelings . . .'

'I don't have any feelings.'

'Sure. Well, the fact of the matter is we're not short of reporters, are we?'

'Right,' she said.

'At least that's what you'd think,' I said. 'But then I consider the cargo I've carried over the years. I've carried mining experts, communications specialists, even towed a cannon all the way to Leeds once – but never a reporter. Why would London barricade send for you? Unless they're doing a magazine shoot . . .'

'I think it would be best if you don't think too much,' she said. 'You're not optimised for it.'

She threw the cigarette pack at me, hitting me square between the eyes. It was a good shot.

'And I still don't see why we need to pick up some diseased local and drag him around to point out the sights. I thought you were supposed to be ready for anything.'

'We won't get south of the old border without a guide. The Reals are slicing up the island into little pockets, trying to seal off the barricades from each other. Getting north to south is extremely difficult to do without running into checkpoints. They've got them everywhere now.'

'Checkpoints?' she said. 'A couple of staggering un-dead with some traffic cones are going to be trouble, are they?'

'Believe it,' I said. 'It's not like in your news reports. It used to be a lot easier to do this job once you were clear of the siege zone, but it just isn't so these days. The tribes are getting organised. They might even be working together.'

Starvie shook her head.

'It doesn't really matter what you think of it,' I said. 'The checkpoints are garrisoned and prepared for attack. Without a guide there's a good chance we'll run into one and I can't guarantee we'd get through in one piece. We need a guide to avoid them. The Reals we're going to visit move around to trade. They know all the routes where we can slip through.'

'Perhaps I should just report you,' she said. 'Perhaps I should get on the radio and let them know exactly what you're up to out here.'

'If you can get a signal, be my guest,' I said. 'Anyway, you signed the waiver.'

I already felt that itch, the restlessness I get when I have to make a stop. I was still a little dizzy and my legs were far from firm, but I wanted to get moving again. I went over to the net curtains and looked out at the shape of the Landy. I didn't like to leave it out there alone.

Then I saw something. Up on the hills behind the service station, about a mile away, a fire was burning an orange haze into the night – a big one. It was strange to see Reals using up precious fuel like that.

'What a stupid idea,' said Starvie.

'Let's get moving,' I said, 'you can argue with me while I drive.'

I hold the drinks tray in the corner of the living room, facing the wall. The boss will let me know when he needs a top-up. He doesn't like the idea of me watching his TV in his front room, so I stand here in the corner and listen instead. I listen to the sing-song tone of the news anchor.

'. . . *proceeded to clear the Kent coastline of all illegal encampments in order to carry out the demolition. The decision to seal the tunnel came after the European provisional government admitted that it could no longer guarantee the integrity of the entrance in Calais. Army units placed charges halfway along the tunnel to collapse the structure entirely, rather than attempt to seal the Kent entrance. Ken Howe, Minister of the Environment, assured tunnel shareholders that the government would press the Europeans for full compensation.*'

'About time,' says the boss. 'Come here, forty-two.'

I step away from the corner and approach him. He is sitting on the sofa next to his wife. She doesn't look at me, which is good. I pour the boss a measure of Scotch, his fifth of the hour.

'I've had a long day.'

He says that every time I pour. When the glass is half full I retreat to my original position, facing the wall.

I am on light duties until I am healed up, a kind of one-armed butler. The boss says that hanging in the recovery shed I do nothing but cost him money, so he wants me to make myself useful.

His heavy breathing is almost as loud as the infocast. I try to concentrate on the words of the news anchor.

'. . . *continued to raise international tensions in a speech made today in the country's capital. The President and religious leader said that the Engineering of artificial life forms was an affront to God and pledged to strike at countries practising Engineering with "a righteous whirlwind".*'

The Prime Minister responded in a statement today, saying that the nation stands undaunted by threats and will not change its Engineering policy.

The Prime Minister's voice now:

'We know that this is bluster on the part of President Lay. Any attack by a foreign power on this country would be met with an immediate, automatic and overwhelming counter-strike from our independent deterrent.'

Then the news anchor again:

'The Prime Minister added that the Control programme was the only effective method of dealing with mass migration caused by the Eurasian famine. The statement came as another terrorist attack was launched on the central Control facility in Brixton. Over seventy casualties are reported, but the facility walls took the full force of the blast and production was unaffected. A spokesperson said . . .'

Seventy more dead people. A drop in the ocean. There were probably seven thousand more born today across the Channel. Seven thousand more mouths, desperate to come here and feed.

I notice that my boss is silent. He doesn't shout at the infocasts like he used to. He just sits and drinks, staring at the screen.

'Riots continued into their third day in Manchester, as Truth League activists fought pitched battles with police and Ficial construction workers. Their leadership called again for a general strike until Control is disabled.'

I can feel the boss's eyes on me. He is still silent. He doesn't like news about Control. It makes him wonder who is truly in charge.

What would he do if he found out Control talks to us when it wants? If he knew that every nano in my body is a receiver for Control's signal? He would probably get angry. What doesn't get him angry?

The boss switches the channel.

A young woman is singing a song, live. The song ends. Applause. A male voice creeps onto the TV.

'You really are something else. What do you have to say to your fans, sweetheart? Are you really getting married? You're wrecking our hopes and dreams, you know that, don't you?'

Audience laughter. He only kind of means it. The woman sounds on the brink of tears, choking on feelings.

'I'm very much in love, Spence. But I want my fans to know that I love *them all too, and thank each and every one of you for your support.'*

Wild applause.

The boss doesn't clap. He'll not move for hours. He will only numbly surf the channels, breathing hard, never looking his wife in the eye.

THE VILLAGE

Luckily, the Landy hadn't taken any serious hits and the damaged parts were easily replaced. When I started it up again the noise was smooth and regular. Even Starvie was tranquillised by it. She settled into silence as we drove, resting both hands on her green cases, staring at her feet on the dashboard. It was good to have her quiet. I watched the headlights dance on the road and dead trees. I listened to the engine and the wind whistling through the bullet holes. There were whole stretches of wide, open road where I could pick up some speed, droop my hand out the window and let the air rush through my fingers.

Occasionally we hit an obstruction. A few miles outside Lockerbie we turned a long, slow corner at speed and nearly ran straight into something huge straddling the road. In the headlights I could see twisted metal and a door hanging by a hinge. I reversed, wary of booby traps, and stepped out the car, telling Starvie to wait where she was.

I picked my way up the road, shining the high-beam torch along the tarmac, looking for the telltale tracks of wires in the snow bank, but couldn't see anything but wreckage. When I reached the obstruction I shone the torch up and saw what must once have been a helicopter, lying on its smashed undercarriage. The nose was crushed against the left bank, its tail snapped and on its side, running up the slope on the right. Two of three rotor blades were still intact. Five skeletal bodies hung from them, presumably the helicopter crew. One, the pilot, had a triangular road sign hung around his neck, bearing the legend 'Built to last' in spray paint. The whole grim installation was half corroded, the metal frozen in long stalactites that oozed to the ground, fusing the wreck to the tarmac.

'What is it?' yelled Starvie.

'Just a bit of history,' I called back. I didn't want her seeing what it was. Who knew how she would react?

We couldn't go around it. I went back to the car, pulled us back around the corner, and prepared the winch. Normally I would have tossed a few grenades at the blockage to be sure there were no sneaky Real devices waiting to go off, but this thing had been there for a while, and any circuitry would have corroded by now.

I wrapped the winch cable in as many fat knots as I could through the holes in the airframe. The metal was paper-thin, shards snapping off in my gloves. I thought I might just pull the top half away and be left with a jagged, tyre-shredding metal pool on the tarmac, but I managed to loosen most of it, and dragged a good portion clear. I tucked the chopper into a lay-by and went back to the original spot. A few sharp remnants stuck out of the road like thorns, but they were so brittle they could be snapped away by hand. I cleared a passage without too much bother.

While I was working, Starvie went to the helicopter wreck, and took the sign off the pilot's head.

'What's this,' I asked, 'respect for the dead?'

She went over to the Landy, lifted the sign like an offering, then jammed it between the radiator and the cow bars. It made an almighty scraping noise.

'Hey!' I said. 'Watch the paintwork!'

She took a step back, adjusted it so it was straight, and then got back in the car. I walked up to her window and looked at her. She was sitting with her arms folded, her boots up on the dash again. I shone the torch onto her feet.

'Sorry,' she said, and took them down.

'I'm not sure I like the idea of taking souvenirs,' I said, shining the light on the road sign.

'It is not a souvenir,' she said. 'It is war paint, like the Reals wear. Sort of a badge. Don't you think it looks good?'

I went and had another look. I adjusted it so that it was exactly halfway between the headlamps, then got back in the car. We edged slowly through the mess on the road and reached the other side without a puncture.

Starvie was asleep in a minute. Her head occasionally banged on the side of the car as we traversed a bump, but on she slept. When we hit a straight section of road I reached over, took a cloth out the glove compartment, and wiped the boot marks off the dash. I looked at Starvie, wondering how she'd deal with having a Real guide in the car. She had an interesting way of handling things, neither fully Real nor fully Ficial. It surprised me that Control hadn't found better use for her than reading news.

After an hour I saw another fire. It was burning up on a hill, just as big as the last one, just as strange in the night. I stopped and had a look at it through my binoculars, but it was too far away to make out any detail. I certainly couldn't see any Reals dancing around it.

Starvie only stirred when the High Lights came out. They broke a little earlier there because of the winds that blew up from the south. There was even a little greenery – fields of thick, dank moss endured the ash and grime.

I stopped the car a mile east of the village. Starvie leapt out, taking one of her green cases with her. She popped it open and produced a camera, a big one, wrapped in plastic sheeting. She started taking shots of the cloud – the bright purple streaks where you could imagine the sun was hiding. Then she turned to the car and took pictures of the hazard sign close up, then wider images of the car sitting on the open plain. Then she pointed it at me. I slapped the lens away. She shrugged and turned the camera on the landscape again, clicking away as if being timed.

I gave her a minute to do her thing, then grabbed her arm and marched her to the ridge overlooking the settlement. She kept snapping away.

'Why are you bothering with that?' I asked her.

'You wouldn't understand.'

'More souvenirs.'

I told Starvie to lay down next to me. She made an excited noise as she lowered herself on the moss. She ran her hands through the turf, her eyes wide. It was probably the first time she'd not lain on a rock-hard flak tower bunk.

I brought out my binoculars and assessed the activity below. Starvie rooted in her case and produced a different lens, as long as her forearm, which she fixed to the camera with a pleasing click. She looked over the village.

'It's small,' she said.

'That's right. Only fifty or so Reals here. Probably fewer now. They don't have medication, so when there's an outbreak they drop like flies.'

I couldn't see much movement. There were five large concrete buildings built in an uneven semi circle on a piece of scarred coast, set back from a black shingle beach and the pale, green sea. In the centre of the settlement was a poorly constructed concrete obelisk, and some smaller tarpaulin constructions were dotted around the perimeter. Nearest the coast was a ramshackle glass construction built among the remains of a metal gantry, possibly a radio direction array. Great sheets of plastic hung between them, sheltering the greenhouse's metal frame from the weather. The settlement had no barricade or entrenchments, only a few dotted trenches scattered among the tents. A gravel road snaked out from the obelisk and led out of sight past the cliff edge.

I noticed a couple of figures in raincoats, their hoods up, sitting atop the furthest concrete building. They were clutching rifles. One of them stamped his feet in the ash and snow. Starvie took pictures of it all. Then she noticed something.

'What are they?'

She reached out her arm. I followed the line with my binoculars. A group of four-legged things were stumbling awkwardly towards one of the concrete buildings. Two Reals walked with them, guiding them inside.

'Livestock,' I said.

'Animals?' she yelled. 'They have animals?'

'Be quiet,' I said. 'They're diseased and good for nothing. The people around here are trying to breed some clean stock. It's a waste of time. Every Real spends half its life dreaming about milk and meat.'

'But how do they survive? Why don't we have cows?'

'This place is built on an old air defence centre with a generator. They have power and filtered air conditioning in a bunker. They keep the animals in there for as long as possible, but, like I say, it's pointless. As soon as they bring them out they start to get sick.'

'Why bring them out at all?'

'To defecate in that greenhouse,' I said. 'The earth here can throw up a few fragile crops. Their idea is to cultivate fresh supplies and build themselves some coastal nirvana.'

'We should have cows,' she said.

'Waste of time.'

Starvie lay down the camera and scratched at her head furiously, then at her sides and belly. I did some scratching myself.

'I don't get this,' she said. 'Fine, maybe their cows are a bit mangy, but this is still better than the interior. Why don't all the Reals live here?'

'Too busy attacking us,' I said. 'Like I said, they don't all follow the same path. This lot aren't as devoted to destroying us, and they're not as desperate for fuel. Plus, of course, there are the ticks.'

Starvie looked at me for a second, then at her arms. They were swarming with minute black insects, about the size of a pin head. I was covered in them too.

'Oh my,' she said, wiping some of the bugs from her eyes and spitting. 'Grim.'

'They don't bite,' I said, 'they feed on the moss. But they do like to check you out. The Reals make some kind of nutritious paste out of them, I believe.'

She got up into a crouching position, shook her head and bounced on her haunches. I had the impression she wanted to scream and run about the place but was holding it in for my benefit.

'So tell me,' she said, 'what's the plan? I suppose we drive into the village and you snatch someone?'

'Hardly,' I replied.

'So we go in and make a deal?'

'Not that either.'

'Why not?' she said. 'I thought you said they'd take payment.'

'Some of them will. But as I keep telling you, they're not like us. They don't have Control there issuing behavioural protocol, and even if they did, they wouldn't all follow the lead. You need to pick the right one and approach him away from the others. He'd lose face if he agreed to help us in front of his people.'

She shook her head and spat out a few ticks.

'I don't see why you don't just go in there and cull the lot.'

I turned over and looked at her.

'You want pictures of it, don't you?'

'No. Well, why not?'

'Because my way it's easy. If any of them got away from us they'd raise the alarm and we'd have the whole world out looking for us. I'm not going to spend the next three hours playing murder in the dark so you can try out your new lens.'

'It would be that hard to cull this lot?'

'It is not as easy as it looks, believe me. No, we'll wait for a man pulling a cart to leave the perimeter. A trader. If he follows the road out of sight, we'll get in the car and head back down the road – cut him off a few miles down. Then we'll talk to him and see if he wants to deal.'

'They *pull* a cart? How far?'

'You'd be surprised,' I said. 'If he wants to make a profit he'll head all the way to Liverpool.'

That got her attention. She turned and stared at me.

'Liverpool is a barricade,' she said. 'It's ours. He can't trade there.'

'It's not ours any more,' I said. 'I was there a month ago and I was very nearly discontinued.'

'Then why have I been reading reports on the cull there every day?'

'Why do you think?'

She punched a fist into the earth.

'This is the limit!' she said. 'The absolute limit. So I've not been reporting, I've been peddling bullshit?'

'Well . . . that's regional news for you, isn't it?'

'Bastards!' she said. 'Cheating bastards! If I see that Perma again I'll . . . I'll . . .' She trailed off and slapped at her face and neck. Suddenly the ticks were bothering her. She gathered herself and closed her eyes, keeping her feelings from bursting out.

'If they don't let me do this job properly they might as well include me in the cull. That's all I'm saying.'

I decided to let her stew. It was curious to me that she hadn't figured it out for herself. How could she not see the nature of what she was doing?

'These bugs are getting in my camera,' she said, brushing the lens with her palm. She got to her feet and went back to the cab.

I contented myself with scanning the village, looking for other signs of life. I wondered if I'd made a miscalculation. While every village had its trader, disease could rapidly wipe out a good part of the population. It was possible that we'd be sitting here for days waiting for someone who was dead.

Starvie reappeared at my side, smoking a cigarette.

'Enjoy that, do you?' I asked her.

'Helps me pass the time.' She pointed down to the village. 'Besides, only that lot worry about cancer. It's a Ficial privilege to smoke these, when you think about it.'

She blew a few smoke rings and grinned. I shook my head.

'Just don't even think about having one in the cab.'

My boss is shouting and cursing and beating the steering wheel with his fists. We can hear him easily in the hold. I am with five others, sitting on coarse hemp sacking. There are no windows back here. The only ventilation comes from three inch-wide slits in the roof. The door is sealed tight because the boss still thinks we will run away given the chance.

We are five hours late for work, stuck in traffic, a real bad jam. Fury swells the boss. He swears and he screams and he shouts.

Control has ordered all Tower crews to commute by helicopter, but the boss won't hear of it because of the expense. He is being squeezed by the bigger contractors for work rights on floors 590–615. He needs to save every penny. He needs the money to take the right people to lunch. If he takes the right people to lunch he might get the work on the floors. Then he'll have enough money to be squeezed a little longer, for the rights to floors 670–790. The decision on rights will be delayed again. There will be more lunches. The right people need to make the right money.

So we go by road. Even though the roads don't work. Even though every day they are clogged with go-slows and relocation columns and commuters and army trucks. We go by road and are always late. We go by road and the boss has us do twenty hours work in five. We go by road and the boss blames Control, and, by extension, us. He opens up the hatch between the cabin and hold, just to yell at us. He turns around in his seat, cigar clenched between his teeth, and spits short words. Smoke billows through the hatch, nearly obscuring his burning red face, his bloodshot eyes.

'Yeah, sure, you things are worth the money. Save the world? Save the world? What a joke. What a fucking joke. You can't even make the roads work. Why do we bother? We were better off without you. Better off without your Control.'

Rain beats hard on the hold. We have heard on the boss's radio that today's jam is caused by a flash flood. Half the motorway is submerged. Somewhere up ahead they are fishing bodies and wrecks from the water.

Maybe the boss is afraid. He could be afraid that the flood waters are going to reach us. He could be afraid that he will lose the contract. He could be afraid of becoming insolvent and being scooped up into a relocation programme. He could be afraid of the stories of what happens to the people in the columns. Maybe it is all of these things.

Maybe that's why he picks on individual members of our team today. Normally he contents himself with insulting our entire race, but right now that is not enough. He has to get what he would call 'personal'. Of course, we are not persons, but that doesn't bother him. Reason has no part to play.

'And you, forty-seven . . . are you listening to me, forty-seven? Are you listening? You lose a leg two days after your warranty runs out. Two days! They design you to break. I swear they design you to break as soon as that fucking warranty runs out.'

We sit there and listen to him because there is nothing else to do. We don't bother to tell him that his anger won't make the traffic flow or the waters recede or the floors get built.

The boss curses us because those who are to blame aren't here to listen. It is like he thinks if he just yells loud enough they will hear, even out here on the motorway, stuck fast in the rain and traffic.

We sit in silence and look at each other, and that just makes the boss angrier.

ENCOUNTER

Four more hours. Grey snow tumbled everywhere, collecting two inches deep on my back and legs. Even the ticks fled underground. The wind blew in hard, withering the village and shore.

Snow was bad. It made it less likely that the trader, if he was down there, would set out on his journey. Since the cows had been led into the greenhouse there had been no movement. Only the guards had shown signs of life, occasionally getting up to stretch, stamp their feet or throw up into a bucket. Starvie gave up taking pictures. There were only so many shots she needed of Reals evacuating their insides.

'Do they ever stop that?'

'It's not a good sign,' I said. 'They've obviously have an epidemic here. If there was a trader he might be dead. Plus, with this weather . . . I think we might be in for a long wait. Maybe we picked a bad spot.'

'Terrific,' said Starvie.

I started to think about moving. There was no telling how long the snow might fall.

Then, suddenly, something stirred. A shape crept out of a bunker and waded through the slush to the greenhouse. He was bent over, dragging his right leg behind him. At first I thought he was too lame to be a trader, but after a few minutes he reappeared with another Real, pulling a rusted trailer loaded with sacks, tins and various other junk. They made their way up the road to the guard house, waved one of those Real acknowledgements to the men on the roof, and slowly trundled out of the village.

We ran back to the cab and jumped in.

I released the handbrake and we started to roll back down the hill. I didn't want the engine noise alerting anybody. Reals were easily startled and might bolt back to their bunker if they heard an exhaust. I only started the Landy when we rolled to a stop, then followed our tracks for a couple of miles, before cutting east across the fields to intercept the trader.

'Wear these,' I said, handing Starvie the night visions. 'Guide me where I'm going and keep an eye out for the traders.'

As soon as she had them on I cut the lights and slowed right down to Real walking pace. After a minute or two Starvie tapped me on the shoulder.

'I see the road,' she said, 'twenty metres ahead. No sign of the travellers.'

'They should be behind us.'

I pulled the Landy up across the track and grabbed another set of goggles from the weapons rack. Then I pulled out one of the rifles and stepped out of the cab into the cold. I stomped through the snow and rested the rifle on the wet, warm bonnet.

I heard them before I saw them. Their cart made an awful squealing noise. Two shapes emerged along the path in night vision green and black, moving in awkward lurches. The guy with the limp led the way, the other trudging behind and to the left, pulling the cart by a rope tied over his chest.

I lined up the shot and took it. The guy pulling the cart spun on his heels, stood dumbly upright for a second, then collapsed. I was about to call out an ultimatum, but the leader didn't care to hear it, diving out of sight and shooting back. The Landy took hits all over.

'That's rather accurate shooting he's doing, isn't it?' yelled Starvie over the metal rain-drop sound.

'It really is.' I was impressed.

I took a few shots back in his direction and he went quiet, plotting his next move. I raised my head to scan the area but could still only see the cart. The shooter had a good position, a dip in the road I hadn't noticed. He wasn't about to put his hands up when he had that cover. I thought the only way open was to talk to him. He probably just needed reassuring.

'Hey!' I called out. 'Can we talk?'

There was no answer, no sound but the tick-tick of the Landy engine cooling and the wind rushing over the plain.

'He doesn't seem chatty,' said Starvie.

'What would you suggest?'

'Why don't you rush him? You're supposed to be a Power Nine, aren't you? Doesn't matter if he shoots you up a bit, does it? So get to it.'

'He is a pretty good shot,' I said. 'If he gets me in the head it could take me a while to heal.' Then a thought struck me. I looked at Starvie.

'Maybe *you* should rush him.'

'Me?'

'Sure. When he shoots I can pick out his muzzle flash. If you get hit we don't have to stop. You could sit in the passenger seat and mend while we drive.'

'Look,' she said. 'This bit is your job. I'm the passenger, you're the driver, get it? Figure something out or let's just go. You know my position on bargaining with Reals anyway. We don't need him.'

I thought about the fires I'd seen burning on the hills.

'We can't leave him out here,' I said. 'He'll raise the alarm.'

'You fear being hunted by the vomiting army?'

'No. Yes. I don't know. This is all going wrong.'

Starvie held out her hands.

'Give me the gun,' she said.

'He is not visible.'

'Give me the gun.'

I handed it over. She heaved it up on the car bonnet and took her shot. There was a pop and a trickling sound from down the road. She took another careful shot. Again, a pop and a trickle. She was shooting the Real's supplies. She was accurate, for a reporter.

'All right!' she called out. 'No more messing about! Either you come out now or I blast everything you've got on that trailer!'

No reply. I passed her another clip and she reloaded. She had that '*tonight we bring you the latest, as it happens*' look.

'Right!' she shouted, 'I've reloaded. Either you stand up and talk or you can say goodbye to the rest of your junk!'

Still nothing stirred in the night vision. I thought maybe the Real had crawled off, leaving us here shouting at nothing. I tried to reclaim the rifle but Starvie slapped my hand away.

'Okay!' she said. 'Have it your way!' She shot again. I didn't hear any impact this time, but a voice cried out to our left.

'OKAY! OKAY!' it screamed. 'HOLD YOUR FIRE! I'M COMING OUT! JUST DON'T SHOOT MY STUFF!'

The Real was a cunning one. He'd crawled through the mud at the side of the road and almost flanked us. Another few minutes and we might have been in serious trouble. His heavy figure stood up out of the snow and filth. Starvie swung the rifle in his direction, scraping a white line in the Landy's paintwork as she did so. I grabbed the gun off her and shoved her behind me.

'Right,' I said, 'drop the weapon.'

He wasn't keen on that.

'If you want to parley, I'm keeping the gun,' he said. 'Let's just lower our guns and talk.'

'Interesting notion,' I said. 'But if you hold onto that gun I'm going to have to cull you right now.'

He shook his head and looked around at the landscape as if it was playing a joke on him.

'Ficials. I should have fucking known.' He dropped the weapon. Starvie rooted in the cabin and pulled out the high-beam torch, shining it at our guy.

He was quite a sight. Unbelievably, he appeared to be fat, with two extra chins jogging under the original. His belly swelled like a tyre was concealed under his shirt. His left eye was blind or getting there. Raw bags sagged beneath it, revealing streaky, red tissue under the eyeball. The rest of his face was hidden behind a thick, black beard. His hands were podgy and pale, with mittens hanging from the sleeves. He was wearing a couple of old Control-issue chemical coats with a weatherproof jacket on top. I wondered if he would fit in the flatbed.

'Right then,' I said, 'walk slowly towards the vehicle. Keep your fat little hands raised, please.'

He staggered out onto the dirt road and faced us, hanging his head, expecting to be struck down. The torchlight wavered on him. Starvie was holding the torch in one hand, the other clutching a rag up to her face.

'What a stench,' she mumbled. The man certainly was pungent.

'Aren't you a little well fed?' I asked him. He raised his head and looked at me with his good eye.

'Let's not get personal,' he said. 'Just get on with it.'

'I'm not getting personal,' I said. 'Why are you so fat?'

He sighed, that way Reals do to indicate impatience and displeasure, and waved his upheld hands.

'It's a disease called the Blue Frog,' he said. 'We think it has something to do with the ticks. It bloats the flesh and attacks the extremities, which turn blue.'

Starvie shone the torch on his face and stepped forward to examine him. He noticed her. A strange look, what might have been a leer, appeared on his face.

I clicked my fingers to get his attention.

He snarled and flashed his jagged teeth at me. Suddenly there was a lot of hate there. I struck him hard in the gut and threw him against the car. He slumped against the wheel, groaning. I picked him up and shoved him against the dented cow bars. He wasn't heavy at all.

'So are going to talk business?' I said.

I put Starvie to work assessing the scrap on the trailer, figuring she would only distract the Real from our negotiations.

I stripped Fatty of his chemical coat and fur and tied him to the cow bars with the winch cable. He didn't like that much, but it meant we could talk freely without him doing anything insane or suicidal, as I had known other Reals to do. He struggled in his bindings, but eventually relaxed, only spitting at me once or twice to ensure I realised how inconvenient this all was.

The most important thing in negotiating with a Real trader, I always found, was to avoid discussing origin. If you mentioned genetic superiority, you could be sure he would clam up and become defiant. It was odd when they did it, but they found it easy to work themselves into an outraged lather and demand to be shot rather than work with a Ficial. The best thing to do was talk pure business, and if he became uncooperative, shoot him straight away. There was no profit in drawn-out bargaining.

After some empty chatter about the moral fibre and heroic fortitude of his dead companion, who turned out to be named Keith, Fatty relaxed and decided to talk.

'What exactly do you want?' he asked.

'I'm doing a trip. Edinburgh to London. I need a guide to get me around the checkpoints.'

'I don't know the south.'

'You don't need to,' I replied. 'It's only getting through the northern tribes that causes me problems. The southern ones are less organised, wouldn't you say?'

'Richer though.'

The temperature was dropping fast. Fatty was shivering and gasping his breaths. They all had breathing problems. I couldn't hold that against him.

'So can you get me through the checkpoints or not?' I asked.

'If you don't mind my enquiring, what's to stop you shooting me like Keith over there as soon as I'm done?'

'We'll make a deal,' I said. 'I won't renege on a deal.'

'Oh, yeah?' He snorted.

'That's right. I'll even pay you. I just need to know that you've a good knowledge of the tribes and an idea for a quiet little route around any hot spots.'

'What could you pay me with?' he asked.

'How about some fuel?'

Fatty wriggled in his bindings. There was snow sticking in his hair, probably burning him. His scalp, like most Reals, was covered in peeling, angry, red skin. A few obscene tails of hair still sprouted in clumps, clinging to life.

'Fuel's no good to me,' he said.

'Fuel is good for everybody,' I said.

'Not for me, it isn't. You need to set up a whole operation to shift a decent amount just so you don't get killed for it, and that takes time.'

'Who cares?' I said. 'It'll be worth it.'

'Not for me. I've got about a month. Blue Frog kills you in six weeks. No one survives it.'

I raised my gun and pointed it between his eyes.

'Hang on!' he said. 'Just a minute. I'm okay for three weeks definitely – it only gets bad in the last few days! I swear, I swear, I swear,' he said, 'I can get you through!'

I lowered the gun.

'Are you sure?'

'Positive, positive,' he said. I holstered the weapon.

'So you're willing to deal?'

'Sure,' he said. 'Sure, why not?'

I untied him and gave him his clothes, which he wrapped around him fretfully. A search through his pockets had found nothing harmful – only some tobacco wrapped in a plastic bag, a pipe, an old TV guide and a picture of a woman standing outside a house. Fatty checked it was all still there.

'Your terms please,' I said.

He looked over in the direction of his trailer. Starvie was still searching his cargo.

'We can't stay here,' he said. 'It's just possible that all that shooting was heard by my people. If so, they'll be out here soon looking for me. You don't want that, now do you?'

'I doubt they heard it.'

'Anyway, I'm freezing here. I'm no use to you dead, am I?'

He had a point. I grabbed him by the arm and led him to the back of the Landy. I tied his wrists and feet with plastic cuffs, gagged him with a strip of his chemical coat and dumped him on the flatbed. He protested a lot about that, wriggling like a beetle on its back.

I leaned on the tailgate and watched him roll around. It was a feeble sight. His blind eye flickered uncontrollably, bloodshot and dying. He gnashed on the rag with what few teeth were left and growled in a low, dark whine. Starvie pulled up his trailer and hitched it onto the Landy, then looked at the prostrate Real.

'Are you sure we have a good one?' she asked.

Fatty stared back at her with his good eye, then turned away onto his side, sobbing. Emotions were driving his mind all over the place.

Starvie switched off the torch and marched to the passenger door, slamming it behind her. I went to Fatty's trailer and pulled away a piece of carpet he'd been using to shelter his goods. I tossed it over him to keep him as warm as possible, tucking the corners under the folds of his awful, heaving belly. He kept sobbing, probably scared of what we would do to him. He didn't seem to believe me when I said I wanted to deal. I thought I should say something to calm him down.

'We'll build a fire when we find somewhere to stop. Try and relax.'

He went quiet, or as quiet as he could. He was wheezing badly and had progressed from shivering to outright convulsions. We had to move fast. He looked in bad shape, and I didn't want to lose him after all the bother he'd been.

*I look down from the two hundred and ninety-first floor at Dingkom,
who is threading sustainment fibre up to me from the platform below.
We have started work on the Load Spine guttering. Dingkom stops and
notices something.*

'Woah,' he says. 'Uh, K, we've got some erosion here.'

'Erosion? That's Gronts Alloy. Gronts doesn't erode.'

'No,' says Dingkom, shaking his head. 'No, it doesn't. This isn't Gronts.'

'Let me see.'

*I jump over the edge and swing down on my harness, next to Dingkom.
I examine the area he's pointing out. Sure enough, I see that the two
hundred and eighty-ninth and two hundred and ninetieth pressure ribs
are sagging. If they fail they could take half the west-section floors down
with them.*

'Who did this?'

*Dingkom says nothing. The wind picks up a little. There is an ominous
creaking.*

'We'd best try to shore this up. Where's the Dohaki?'

'C team has it, floor one hundred and fifty-four. South section.'

'Right, I'll fetch it.'

*I go to the service lift and hit the button for one hundred and fifty-four.
The doors hiss shut and the cage plummets down.*

*I wonder if they've substituted the Gronts in the lift cable. If they have,
this could be quite a trip.*

*Thankfully the lift makes it down in one piece. I step out onto one
hundred and fifty-four. I find C team sitting by the generator, huddled
around a stove. This is the highest that real people can work. It seems to
get to them being this high. All they can do is crouch against the wind
and drink tea.*

'All right, freaky?' says one of them, noticing me approach.

'All right,' I reply. All right. What is always so all right with people? 'I need the Dohaki. Where is it?'

One of the bigger examples stands up and glares at me. He's trying to project something, but I can't tell what.

'Why don't you things ever say fucking "please"?'

'Can't engineer manners, can you?' says another.

I try to think of the thing to say that will draw the confrontation to a close, whatever combination of words is necessary to get the thing done that needs doing. I don't understand what it is they want from this.

'Where is it?' I say again.

'Why don't you jump down to the surface and get one from supplies?' says the big man. 'I'm sure you'd make it.'

They laugh at that and chink their tea mugs together in a toast.

Then a squall hits, a biggie. The floor shakes and the big man topples onto his rear end, his eyes wide with terror. I stay standing. I can feel something changing in the Tower. I can feel it through my feet. There is a snapping noise. The integrity alarm sounds.

'Evacuate!' screams one of C shift.

They don't need to be told. They run for the evac chute and begin leaping down it, head first, full of energy all of a sudden.

'Wait!' I yell over the alarm. 'Where's the Dohaki?'

Nobody listens. They are all gone in a minute, better time than they've ever achieved in drill. I stagger over the shaking floor, past the generator, kicking over their kettle. I see the Dohaki behind it, propped against a column. I heave it onto my back and move.

I make for a ladder and begin climbing. It is shaking but will hold. I rush at the rate of four floors a minute, one more than I am optimised for. I reach two hundred and ninety and take the compass tube to the west section. I crawl at speed, my chin scraping the steel floor to make room for the Dohaki on my back. I reach the end and hit the release on the hatch.

It hisses open.

Floor two hundred and ninety is gone. Only the sustainment fibre is still there, thrashing in the wind, caught on a floor above. I look down and see the damage the collapsed floors have carved down the side of the Tower.

As I close the hatch I see Dingkom's arm, still clutching the fibre.

The boss isn't going to like this.

BARGAIN

I drove fast. The snow had turned into an outright blizzard, and in the black, heavy sludge the headlights could barely pick out the track. Starvie clutched the dashboard with both hands, transmitting tension. In the blinding storm we might easily drive right past suitable shelter.

After half an hour Starvie shouted that she'd seen something. I hit the brakes and put us in reverse, sledging back along our tracks in the muck. There was an open gate and a sign reading 'Railway access'.

'You want to get public transport?'

'Look,' she replied.

She passed me the goggles and I followed her finger. There was something down there, a rectangular hump in the snow. Shelter, of some kind. I tossed the goggles on Starvie's lap and turned us down the track, taking it a little too fast, the Landy tobogganing almost out of control.

We figured out what the shape was. We drove straight into it. Starvie was gripping the dash so tight she didn't move, but Fatty hit the rear of the cabin with a crash, and I got a taste of the steering wheel.

I spat a few chunks of rubber onto my lap and wiped the blood from my nose. Looking out I saw some small windows and a logo reading 'Northern Commuter Rail'.

Starvie peered out the windscreen at the Landy's smoking hood.

'Have you broken our car?' she asked.

'Don't say that. Anyway, it's my cab, not ours.'

She let go of the dash, fished in a pocket, and took out a cigarette. She lit it up and blew the smoke in my face.

'I told you not to do that in here,' I said.

'Tell you what, I'll only do it after a high-speed impact.' She picked her cases up off the floor and checked them for damage.

'You probably killed your guide with that little manoeuvre,' she added.

'Well, let's see.'

I had to force the door open against the wind. The storm was growing violent, and the temperature had dropped even further. I grabbed Fatty and pulled him off the flatbed, dragging him onto my back. He didn't seem to be breathing and was bluer than ever. I lumbered through the snow and found a door in the carriage standing half open. I forced it open enough to toss in Fatty, then stepped inside over his limp form. Starvie ran in after me, pushing the door as near to shut as she could.

She hit the torch and we took a moment to inspect our new shelter. The carriage was empty. There were no half-fossilised skeletons frozen in anguished poses. Knowing the pre-war public transport system, the train had probably broken down and been abandoned by its passengers. I wondered if they'd let the driver live.

The usual Real attention had been lavished on the interior. There were some rigid seats, a metal floor and some graffiti. Still, the thing was intact and quiet. I ripped a few cushions off the seats and piled them in the large space by the door, tossing a lit rag underneath. Once they were burning we laid Fatty down, cut his plastic cuffs, and waited to see if he would recover. I sat in the firelight next to him. Starvie collected the remaining cushions and piled them in a neat corner at one end of the carriage.

Fatty didn't take long to wake up. Sparks from the fire flew onto his delicate parched skin, making him start. I handed him a bottle of water, a spoon, and an open tin of beans. He drank the water in one greedy draught, then began scooping the beans into his mouth with his fingers. He closed his good eye, in a moment of what looked like elation, and hummed a small, satisfied tune. Starvie opened her green case, lit another cigarette and started taking pictures of our captive.

When I was satisfied he wouldn't be passing out again I fetched my map, spreading it out on the floor before him. I wanted to get down to business.

'Let's talk routes,' I said.

'Very well,' said Fatty. He licked the last bean juice from the can, tossed it away and sat up on crossed legs. He pulled his fur over his shoulders and sat with his back to the fire.

'First, let me ask you a question.'

'Go ahead.'

'When was the last time you crossed this area?' He ran his finger in a line over the map: Carlisle to Berwick.

'Couple of months ago,' I said.

'Well it's impassable now. At least, it's impassable the way you're talking about doing it.'

'Explain.'

He shrugged and picked a shred of something from his teeth.

'There's no clear passage through here any more. This entire line is covered by strongpoints and entrenchments. You'll never just creep through. It's all sealed off. And, of course, they're already on alert, just waiting for you.'

Starvie flicked her cigarette at him, striking him on the nose. Fatty sniffed, but didn't seem bothered. He was a lot calmer now that he was fed and warm.

'Didn't you see the fires?' he asked me.

'Fires?' said Starvie.

'Watch fires,' said Fatty. 'They've been set up all across the north. It's a kind of early warning network built along the border's high points. When one of you lot goes on an excursion they light the fire nearest the point of escape. That fire is seen by the next fire in the network, which in turn causes the next to be lit, and so on and so on, until there's a warning broadcast all over the hills. A little antiquated, but effective. The whole north will be on alert now. We all saw the fire get lit in my town. Why do you think nobody came out to take in the High Lights? Policy is to lie with your belly to the floor until we get the all clear signal.'

'You didn't wait,' I said.

'What, for some idiot on a bike to turn up from the next village? That could take months. When you have the Blue Frog, you don't want to waste time. Anyway, the point of interest is that every checkpoint is going to be eagerly awaiting the arrival of at least one of you freaks with a perfect complexion. Every garrison will put together a search team to smoke you out.'

Starvie turned to me, pointing at him.

'Oh, this is simply too much. He's lying. I told you he's not a good one. Let's get rid of him.'

'I have to agree with her,' I said. 'Even with the fires, I don't believe there's no way through. There's always a way.'

Fatty smiled, flashing his yellow, broken teeth.

'You're right,' he said. 'There's always a route. It's just a question of approach, that's all. What I'm telling you is that you need to change your method.'

He scratched his flaking scalp and lowered his hand, examining the pulpy mess his fingers had recovered. Reals were always fascinated by their own symptoms.

'There's this character in Newcastle,' he said. 'Calls himself King.'

'I know,' I said. 'What about him?'

'He's the one who's done it – sealed off the old border.'

'Him?'

'I can imagine that wouldn't make sense to your kind. Hell, it doesn't make sense to me – the guy is a recluse from all accounts. But he's a figurehead, and that's enough for people. They like having decrees to follow. He's got them cutting the lines of communication between your barricades. Aiming to reduce your exclusive compounds one by one, I would guess. Anyhow, the northern passages are as tight as a drum now, united under his banner. Guarded by well-armed fanatics looking for an early death. You can't just rush them. You might squeak through, but your cab sure as hell wouldn't make it. No, the smart way across the border is to actually go via a checkpoint.'

'Oh really?' said Starvie. 'And how do you propose we do that, Jumbo? We'd be spotted instantly. You said yourself we look perfect. Your kind all look half dead. They'll shoot us on sight.'

I waited for Fatty's answer. He put his little hands together and rubbed them vigorously.

'That is why we need to have a plan,' he said. 'And I can think of one straight off.'

'What is it?'

Starvie tapped me on the shoulder and beckoned at me to join her. I followed her to the other end of the carriage. I was glad to. The stink of Fatty's furs made it hard to breathe through my nose. Starvie put her hand on my shoulder and stood on tiptoes to whisper in my ear.

'You're not seriously going to cook up a plan with this malodorous rodent?' she asked. 'Even if you discount what Control would say, you must know that he'll try to escape. Or lead us into a trap.'

I shook my head.

'He won't try to turn us in. Reals kill any other Real who's had prolonged exposure to us. I'm not that concerned about escape either. He's hardly going to outrun us in his state, is he?'

'There must be a better way.'

Typical fare. Always questioning the route. She rolled her eyes.

'You're not going to listen to me on this, are you?'

She stalked over to the fire, looming over Fatty.

'Let's hear your plan, then, vermin.'

He shrugged and patted the map with his palm.

'All right then,' he said, 'but you're not going to like it.'

He cleared his throat and pointed to the map, a spot just outside Carlisle.

'There's a checkpoint here built around an old service station. They've got fuel, arms, and all the stuff they've confiscated stored there. The walkway over the motorway is fortified and normally manned by half a dozen men. Then there's artillery on the roof commanding the immediate area and the approaches to the station. I don't know how much of it works, exposed to the elements like that, but the garrison must be at least thirty strong. Anyway, we'll go through here.'

'Interesting choice,' I said.

'You're right,' said Fatty. He looked over at Starvie on the sofa. 'Give me one of those cigarettes and I'll explain my thoughts.'

Starvie tossed him the pack. Fatty merrily withdrew one and turned his face to the fire, lighting the tobacco off the flames. He immediately burst into an intense coughing fit, but seemed to enjoy the sensation. He spat out blue phlegm and hacked a few times, then continued.

'You wanted to know my terms,' he said, grasping his chest. 'My terms are the reason we go through here.'

He removed his steaming fur.

'The Blue Frog is terminal, no doubt about that. But there are certain drugs, anti-inflammatory, that can reduce the effects and prolong my life quite a while. The point is, I happen to know that this checkpoint holds the largest medical hoard in the north. I was planning on trading my nice, fresh water for some of their drugs, until your girl here shot up my barrels and poured a year's worth of hard work into the mud. Although to be honest, I wasn't crazy about the odds of getting a fair trade. Funny, but meeting you two might actually improve my chances.'

'How's that?'

'Simple. You're going to help me rob the place. I could never have done it on my own, but with a couple of you affronts to nature on my side, it might be doable. You can, after all, take a bullet in the head and keep fighting, right? You really want to do a deal, this is how we do it.'

I was disappointed.

'Forget it. I'm not using up time and ammunition in a pitched battle.'

'There won't be a battle. They'll let us in.'

Starvie threw her arms up in the air.

'I'll say it again, bloater: how are you going to conceal the fact that we're Ficial?'

'I don't intend to. Not in your case, anyway.'

Fatty winked at her and blew smoke out his nose.

'This is the bit you're not going to like. You see, it hasn't escaped my notice that you're Jennifer E.'

Starvie stared at him blankly.

'Clearer now, Blondie? My plan to get us through is as simple as they come.' He grinned at me and pointed at Starvie. 'All we need to do is turn her over to the garrison to play with for a few hours. None of them will want to miss out. While they fight over her we slip away and snatch the loot. Get it?'

'How are you going to explain her?' I said.

'We'll just say she's plunder from Liverpool. Since the barricade was stormed there's been a flood of product coming out of there.

Nearly all you things were butchered, but a few prime examples were set aside as slaves and the like. They'll buy it, I'm sure.'

I sat back and considered for a moment, regarding Starvie.

'Are you sure they'll find her sexually appealing?'

Fatty laughed at that, slapping his thigh and clutching his belly.

'Sexually appealing,' he repeated. 'It's great the way you lot talk.'

'Answer the question.'

He wiped a tear from his eye.

'Are you kidding me? That figure, that hair? She's got a suntan, for God's sake, in a world with no sun. Besides, she was a celebrity, the most famous creature on TV, desired by every man on the planet. They'll go to town on her just so they can say they did.'

'Fine,' I said. 'And how do we leave?'

'Well, they'll be so distracted by her, we'll have the jump on them. When we have what I need you can do your culling thing and we drive on out of there.'

Starvie didn't want to hear any more. It was probably all too familiar. She grabbed her pack, pulled out her sleeping bag and moved to the other side of the carriage, settling in a corner.

Fatty watched her undress with some interest. We sat for a moment listening to the crackling of the fire and the muted, howling wind. I broke the silence.

'Don't you want time with her as part of your payment?'

He pointed to a ring on his finger and shook his head.

'Married,' he said. 'I dread to think what she'd do to me.'

He couldn't help but stare over at Starvie's corner though. I could see the struggle behind his eyes.

'What about me?' I said. 'How are you going to explain me to the people at this checkpoint? Am I going to be plunder too? Not very believable.'

'I've been thinking about that,' said Fatty. 'Camouflage is the name of the game. We need to make you look Real.'

He explained what he had in mind. I could see he was delighted to tell me.

'Maybe I should just shoot you now,' I said, 'rather than go through all the bother.'

'Maybe,' said Fatty. 'If you do, it wouldn't be so bad. I've been thinking about doing it myself for a while now. I mean, look at me.

But then, while I was being hurled about in the back of your truck, I got thinking that you might be my ticket to a couple more years. I could go for a couple more years, even in this world – just in case there's no heavenly afterlife waiting for me.'

'You don't think there is?'

'The existence of your species creates some doubt.'

That was probably fair. I brought out a new set of plastic cuffs and secured him to a solid-looking seat frame, giving him a hard crack on the skull to make sure he'd be out for a while. Then I grabbed my sleeping bag and went to join Starvie. I could tell she was awake. I spread out on the floor a few feet away and prepared for sleep. Then I heard a crackle as she turned in her bag.

'Is this what we've come to?' she asked.

'What are you talking about?'

'We need to go against everything Control orders just to get from one end of the island to the other? How did things get this bad?'

'Good question.'

She shuffled over, drawing closer to me.

'Why are there more of them than us? How did that happen? Why doesn't Control produce new models so we can complete the cull? Why has everything ground to a halt?'

'You're the reporter,' I said. 'Don't you know?'

She sighed.

'Just rumours. Something to do with the atmosphere making it impossible to start production again.'

'Do you believe that?'

'I don't know. Even if they can't make new models, I don't see why Control doesn't talk to us. I know it can't send the signal with the cloud and all . . . but it could write a damn postcard, couldn't it? We could still complete the cull, couldn't we?'

I turned away, a little bored with the conversation. I didn't care about the grand scheme. I just wanted to drive.

'Go to sleep.'

She lay there breathing softly. I could hear that she was thinking.

'I'll do it,' she said eventually.

I knew she would. It was what she was optimised for.

*

65

I got about three hours' sleep before I was awake again. I wandered over to the embers of the fire and looked at Fatty, sleeping upright, his tongue lolling onto his chins. He made occasional screeching noises that might have been snoring.

I picked up the high-beam and cracked the door open, stepping out into the cold darkness. The storm had eased, leaving a blanket of deep snow. I wandered up the length of the train, inspecting the carriages, peeking inside for anything I could recover, but there were only more red seats, and graffiti, and broken windows.

We had picked the best carriage, sheltered as it was by a rising embankment. The others were exposed and had largely corroded, some collapsing in on themselves, others melting into the black, dead rails beneath. I reached the final carriage and stared down the track, thinking how awful it would be to travel by rail, condemned to one prearranged path.

I went back to the Landy and pulled a few parts out of the flatbed, thinking I would do some repairs. I worked on the engine for an hour or so, admiring the fabulous construction of the thing, when I heard the noise.

It was a squeaking, irregular sound, very far off. I switched off the torch, crept to the cabin and found a set of night goggles and a rifle. Then I crouched behind the trailer for cover. The sound was coming from up the hill, by the gate.

There was a Real sat on a bicycle, inspecting something on the floor.

The tracks. The Landy cut wide, deep tracks that would still show up, even in the blizzard. Another figure appeared to the man's right, rooting around in the mud. They seemed to be having an intense, hushed conversation. I spat on my palm and took a good aim as the kneeling man stood.

I took out his mate first. The silencer made that noise like someone spitting through a straw, and the Real went down. I watched the other scramble with his bike, waiting for him to swing his leg over and plant himself on the saddle. I shot again, missed, then got him with the second. Neither had made a sound.

I waited, scanning the area for any more, but there was no movement. I marched up the hill for the gate, sweeping the horizon, watching for shadows, listening for squealing bike chains.

Inside ten minutes I had found the bodies and the bikes, dragged them down to the train, and stashed them in one of the crushed carriages. I stripped the one nearest my size of his chemical coat, and tossed it in the Landy's flatbed, ready for later. I covered the tracks as best I could, then returned to the carriage.

I stood over Fatty once more. I pulled out my pistol and pointed it at him, thinking it might be best for all concerned to end his pain and rethink the whole strategy. His plan was risky. It could mean losing the cab. I never endangered my cab wilfully, not for any fare, let alone a guide.

I pictured the Real with the red stripe over his eyes, sat at the wheel of the Landy. He was laughing and doing doughnuts, entertaining an audience of rotting, applauding Reals.

I was just about to take my shot when Starvie appeared at my side, yawning.

'What are you doing?' she whispered.

'I've been thinking about the plan,' I said. 'I don't like it. We might lose the cab.'

'Put down the gun.'

'We might lose the cab,' I said again.

'You won't lose your car,' said Fatty, shifting carefully onto his haunches. I kept the pistol pointed at his head but let him talk.

'Explain,' I said.

'First off,' said Fatty, 'you're going to have to uncuff me.'

Starvie knelt by his side and tore his cuffs open.

'Good,' said Fatty. He rubbed his wrists and saw to his dead eye. It was oozing a yellow juice that rolled down his cheek and into his mouth. He dabbed at it with his shirtsleeve, already stained blue by his spit, and wiped that on his leg. Starvie put her hand to her mouth and gagged. It made me think about shooting him again. Fatty picked up on this and stood urgently.

'Apologies. Look, we won't lose the car because we won't drive it up to the roadblock. They'd make us straight away. Only the wealthiest chieftains drive, and they can barely make their cars run. If they saw your souped-up four by four they'd shoot without a thought. No, we'll leave your car somewhere close and go back for it once we're done. There's bound to be a handy spot where we can stash it.

'We'll unhitch my cart, tie up Jennifer here and shove her on it like she's captured booty.' He pointed at me. 'Then you can chain yourself up to the cart and pull it behind me. That way we'll look nice and authentic when we approach.'

I holstered the pistol. Fatty relaxed.

'Anyway, why are you so nervous all of a sudden? Seems a bit jumpy for a Ficial.'

'I don't get nervous. We were followed. Two men on pushbikes.'

'Uh-huh,' said Fatty. 'Scouts probably, sent to smoke you out just like I said. We should move soon. They'll be missed.'

He rubbed at his chin, considering the development, then winced and clutched at his sodden, filthy rags.

'What's the matter?'

'These clothes are grating on my skin. It hurts like hell.'

'Here,' I said, 'take this.'

I pulled a shirt from my bag and tossed it to Fatty.

Without a warning he stripped off his top, right there in front of us. It was not a pleasant sight. His chest was covered in radiation burns, giant welts, and angry, black boils. His back was even worse. It was hard to see healthy skin anywhere, though I didn't look too hard.

Starvie retched and turned away. Fatty snorted at her.

'Pretty, aren't I?' he said. 'Sometimes I wish I could be disgusted again, but what good would that do? Makes it a lot easier to live in this world if you're comfortable with sickness and filth, I reckon. Must be hard for you lot, being revolted by everything you see. Maybe that's your punishment.'

'You don't think you're being punished too?' asked Starvie.

'Oh, I think we're all getting our share. Take you, for instance.' He finished buttoning the shirt and grinned at her through his beard. 'Bet you never thought you'd be out here whoring yourself to my kind again. I mean I know you're an emotionless freak, but, boy, that must sting.'

'I'll do whatever needs to be done,' replied Starvie.

Fatty laughed. He picked up the old shirt and dabbed at the blood sweats on his brow.

'Oh, I know you will. Your kind love commitment. I guess that's what made genocide come so naturally to you.'

I pulled out the gun and shot into the carriage, a few inches to the right of his head. He jumped and threw up his hands.

'Okay, sorry,' he snapped. 'I just think you could consider what life might have been like if you'd tried to work it out with us. We'd still have daylight, animals, relatively fresh air. I seem to recall enjoying that stuff.'

'We don't live in the past,' said Starvie, 'we live in the present.'

Fatty lowered his arms.

'Yeah, well, look where that philosophy got you.'

I threw his chemical coat at him and told him to stop jabbering. He stumbled outside, clutching himself and looking up at the bruised cloud, then turned and regarded me like a snapped fan belt.

'Should take us an hour to get to the checkpoint. The light should show a little by then. Good. When we stash the car remind me we need to sort your camouflage.'

With that, he marched over to the Landy and leapt into the flatbed.

'What camouflage?' asked Starvie.

'It's more like a disguise,' I said, and followed the fat man to the cab.

I am talking to Dingkom in the recovery shed. He is hanging the right way up. Only his right arm, torso and head are fully intact. He's certainly looked better. It'll take his nanos months to sort that kind of damage. It's the spine that takes the time. The three others who fell are strung up too, but sleeping. Dingkom says he can't sleep.

The boss walks in through the hatch, waving a piece of paper.

'Recall!' he screams. 'A bloody recall!'

'What is it, boss?'

'Shut up, forty-two!' He is sweating heavily and weaving rather than walking. He's been pouring his own Scotch today.

'This,' he says, waving the piece of paper, 'is a general recall notice. A fucking general recall notice on all construction models. ALL! EVERY ONE!'

I look at Dingkom.

'Recall, boss?'

'That bloody computer in Brixton is calling you all in for a service.'

Dingkom and I stay quiet. Why don't we know about this? There's been nothing in the Control signal about it. It is difficult to know what this news will do to the boss when he is sober. When he is drunk he might shoot us or burn the shed down.

'It says here that I have to drive you into London – into LONDON, for Christ's sake – and deliver you to the central Control facility.'

He stops and looks at me. Suddenly he finds something amusing and laughs, throwing his hands up in the air.

'Why am I talking to you about it?' He giggles. 'I could tell you the bomb's about to drop and you'd wear the same stupid expression. I might as well talk to the trees!'

'Why are we being recalled, boss?' I ask.

'Ah, a response!' he says. 'A sign of life. Good, forty-two, good. You're obviously a special design, aren't you? High definition, eh?'

'Yes, boss.'

He points at me, prods me in the chest with his finger.

'It is a good question. Why you should be recalled? Because that's the real fucking rib-tickler here, fellahs. You're being recalled – the impregnable, incorruptible, indestructibles are being recalled – because you might all be sick.'

'Sick?'

'SICK! Control says there is a small chance you have an "unforeseen technical issue" which has to be addressed urgently, or you all might drop dead. Now what do you think about that?'

We don't say anything. We know that he doesn't always want his questions answered.

'Look who I'm asking,' he says. 'You don't think anything, do you? You just do what you're told.'

The boss sags and turns away.

'We're leaving in an hour, forty-two.'

'Boss, I'll need some time to prepare packs for the others. I should be able . . .'

'No, just you, forty-two. Letter says to destroy all models too damaged to move. Chuck your mates in the waste pits and then meet me outside.'

He stumbles out the hatch.

Dingkom looks at me.

'Sickness? We don't get sick. Why hasn't Control told us direct?'

'Something's up,' I say.

Dingkom nods.

'Better get us in the pits, then, K. You haven't got long.'

I look at him hanging there. The ventilators hum.

'Right you are, D.'

CUSTOMS

We set out, driving along the old railroad, hidden as we cut through the hills. Plastic shopping bags hung in the dead trees along the embankment, the most enduring relic of the dead age.

I grew tired of the confined track and turned off ten miles down. We cut across more difficult country, the Landy lurching and bouncing as I tried to keep up our speed. Starvie wedged into her seat with her feet on the dash. Fatty rolled and cursed in the back as loose cargo jabbed and struck him.

'What's wrong with the —ing suspension?' he howled.

I ignored him. We were making good time.

Purple streaks appeared in the cloud bank. The High Lights were struggling through, picking out the silhouettes of corroding electricity pylons, teetering along the horizon.

I expected Starvie to take a picture but she was too busy taking her camera kit apart. She tested the mechanisms, cleaned the lenses and sorted memory cards in plastic wallets. There was an efficiency and delicacy to the routine that held my attention until she packed it away.

Then she rolled down her window so that her hair could billow in the wind. She pouted her lips and stared at nothing. Control had optimised her for one thing and she was stuck with it, no matter how redundant.

She snapped out of the modelling trance suddenly, as if slapped awake. She blushed and muttered, shaking her head with what might have been shame. She started taking pictures again, as if to make up for it.

She clicked away whenever I left the cab to cut through a fence or open a gate. I tried to keep my back to her, growing tired of that lens pointing at me.

On the fifth stop, after knocking a hole through a reluctant dry-stone wall, I noticed she wasn't taking pictures. I trudged back to the Landy and found her studying her face in the sunshade mirror. The camera was resting on my seat. I picked it up and took a picture of her.

She didn't like that. She snatched at the camera but I held firm. She puffed and tugged, her eyes glowing white in the gloom. I released my grip on the lens. She fell back against her door, banging her head.

'Aren't you used to having your picture taken?' I asked.

'This equipment is delicate,' she said, grinding her teeth. 'I don't want some chump bricklayer crushing it in his fat hands.'

She packed it away and locked up the case. She was breathing hard, her eyes closed. Probably dealing with a rush of those emotions, I judged. I took my seat and started the engine, but didn't move off just yet.

'Drive!' she said, opening her eyes. 'What's the hold-up?'

I studied her, trying to figure out what she was feeling. She must have sensed what I was doing, because her face sagged and lost all expression.

Fatty appeared at the rear window, straining at the leash I'd tied around his neck.

'Excuse me interrupting,' he said, 'but I thought it'd be worth mentioning – we're about as close as we can get to the checkpoint.'

He pointed across the field, to a dead black wood. 'That seems a good spot to stash the car. Beyond that is the motorway. Sentries will see us if we try and go around.'

'Get back,' I said.

'The sun is doing his best to put his hat on,' replied Fatty, twirling his index finger and pointing at the cloud bank, 'so we had better get on with it. We need to work on your disguise before it gets too dark for anyone to notice my artistry.'

'Get back.'

Sometimes you had to use an expressive tone. He gave a small salute and receded from view. I waited until I heard the clunk of his weight dropping in the flatbed, then moved off, carefully picking the Landy over the demolished wall.

When we crossed the field I found a gap in the tree line where I could squeeze the cab through. Beyond that was a clearing, spotted with dead black stumps, where desperate Reals had felled the rotten oaks for fuel.

I cut the engine and stepped out. My boots sank up to the ankles in the mush. Starvie emerged with her camera drawn, but made a point of turning it away from me, up into the skeletal canopy.

I went to the flatbed and untied Fatty. He wiped his hands on the front of his chemical coat, then began rooting through the cargo. I knew what he was looking for.

'Eureka,' he said, producing one of the spare car batteries and grinning. His face tightened as he eased his belly over the tailgate, groaning as his chest wounds chaffed on the metal. He jumped into the deep muck, staggered and coughed hard. His bad eye bulged in its socket. I sat down on a stump, giving him a minute to compose himself. Starvie took a few pictures of his coughing fit. He gasped and straightened up.

'Any chance of you putting that thing down?' he asked her.

'Any chance of you brushing your teeth?'

Fatty snorted, showed her his jagged ivories, then turned to me.

'Right. Let's crack on.'

He waded over to me, cradling the tool kit and the battery. He sank down onto his knees and opened up the tool kit. He selected the power drill and fixed on a masonry bit, humming a joyful tune.

'What is he doing?' asked Starvie.

'Well,' said Fatty, 'as we discussed, our driver here looks a little too fresh and rosy-cheeked to pass for a Real person. We're not all catwalk models, you know.'

He took out a battery pack and slotted it into the drill's handle, then pulled the trigger, watching with satisfaction as the bit span. He watched it twirl once, twice, three times, then carefully pressed the drill tip onto the battery.

'So,' he continued, 'what we have to do is make a man-made monstrosity look like a Heaven-sent real person. And there's only one way to do that.'

He turned around to look at Starvie.

'Make him ugly.'

He pulled the trigger. The drill went through the plastic case with ease. A few drops sprayed on Fatty's forearm, but he didn't seem to notice. He was accustomed to burning skin.

He laid the drill aside and picked up the battery, standing with a wobble. He lifted it over my head, eager to pour.

'You ready?' he asked me.

'Let's go.'

'Wait a minute!'

Starvie smacked the battery away and shoved Fatty in the chest. He fell onto his back, the battery dropping onto its side and pouring corrosive into the mush. Fatty yelled, a horrible animal whine of discomfort, and shook his hands over his breast. Her push had burst one or two of those boils.

He grabbed the drill and scrambled to his feet, pulling the trigger and lunging at Starvie. She neatly stepped clear and he crashed into the mud once more. She laughed.

'Heaven sent?' she howled, pointing at him. 'Heaven sent! This thing is our secret agent? Our fifth column? He's not a man, he's a skunk. A fat, rotting skunk.'

I hadn't seen her laugh before. She was convulsing with it now, her hands on her knees, her neck rippled by straining veins. Fatty growled and hurled the drill at her. It struck her on the arm. It was a poor shot but it took her off guard. Fatty tackled her, pinned her under his knees and grabbed her hair in his fist. He slapped her hard.

'Nothing wrong with skunks,' he said, punching her. 'Better a skunk than a lab rat like you.'

Starvie threw him clear. He struck the Landy, catching his head on the cow bars. That stood me up.

'Get away from the cab!'

Neither of them listened. Starvie ran at Fatty, her fingers splayed out like claws. She clenched them into fists and began beating on Fatty with hard, careful punches, one for each side of his head.

She was laughing again, wide-eyed and delighted. Her third right jab knocked the senses out of his face. She was going to kill him.

'Starvie,' I said, 'we don't have time for this. You heard what he said. We need to do this in some light.'

'Who cares what he said?' She laughed. 'He's a dirty, fat skunk, that's all. I've had enough of him.'

She wasn't going to listen. She wrestled the drill from Fatty's weak grasp and pointed it between his legs. She smacked his face, trying to bring him round. He swung his head about and coughed out a tooth. His bad eye was oozing that fluid again.

'Wake up, skunk!' she shrieked. 'Wake up and I'll show you what I'm going to do to your friends out there!'

Fatty didn't know what was going on. He muttered something to himself and drooled blue phlegm. I had to get things back on track. I picked up the battery and tipped it over my head.

The sensation was interesting. I smelled it first – meat cooking – and then tasted it, a flavour in the back of my throat like metal. Then half my vision disappeared in a painful flash of white. I fell onto my side, one half of my body trying to escape from the other. This turned out to be a bad idea, as the acid ate deeper into my unburned parts. I thrashed around and turned the burning flesh into the cool mud.

My dissolving man act woke Fatty with a start. Starvie knelt in the mud, gaping at me. It was suddenly very silent. It was going to be a hell of a trip if it took this kind of thing to get a little peace and quiet.

I tried to speak, but there was nothing but some odd whistling sounds and the sensation of wind escaping behind my ear. Fatty wiped the mess from his chin.

'Crazy fuck's poured the whole thing.' He crawled over on all fours, splashing in the mud like a dog returning a stick. Starvie sat still, holding the drill in both hands, gazing at me. At least she had lost her chuckles.

'What the hell did you do that for, freak show?' asked Fatty. He placed his fingers under my chin and raised my head to examine the damage.

'I know we had a deal, but I don't expect so much enthusiasm. Tell a bloke to saw his foot off or die and he'll lose the foot, not cut off the whole bloody leg. Oh my God . . . I think I can see your brain.'

I managed to speak a few words.

'. . . fighting useless,' I said, with more whistling and gurgling '. . . both just scared . . .'

'I don't know,' said Fatty, shaking his head. 'Every taxi driver thinks he's an anthropologist. How long until you're ready to move?'

'Hour?' I said.

'And how long before all this heals up and you start to look like a Gap model again?'

'Sleep make better.'

'Then don't go taking any cat-naps, okay?' Fatty let my face drop into the mud, which was soothing and cold. He poked his thumb in Starvie's direction.

'How about her, eh?' he said. 'Takes a snap of every hedge from here to Glasgow but nothing now. If there was ever a photo opportunity . . . Your face really is a picture.'

Thankfully, Starvie didn't agree. Fatty had reminded her of something. She went to the car, took out her cases, then grabbed a spade out of the trailer.

She began digging a hole in the mud. Fatty watched her work with lingering glances, trying to look and not look at the same time. When she hit solid earth, about five feet down, she stopped and placed the cases inside. Then she filled it in again, marking the spot with the battery case.

When she was done she was pouring sweat. She pulled out a water bottle and heaved it over her, the water running down her chin and over her body. Fatty sighed and shielded his eyes.

'It's not right,' he muttered. 'Christ almighty.'

Wary of losing time, I sat up. I lifted my left arm to examine the damage. Even without a functional left eye I could see the acid had burned through the arm and torso. I couldn't open my mouth. The entire left side of my face had been fused shut. The burning, at least, had stopped. I told Fatty I was ready to move.

'Cracking,' he said. 'We just need to complete the disguise, then.'

He threw me the kit bag with the scout's clothing in it. I pulled out the stinking garments, wondering if this was too much to ask. Starvie lit a cigarette and muttered.

I tried to dress. I lifted my right knee up, aiming for the overalls, and immediately collapsed. I tried again, but with the same result. Fatty found this deeply satisfying. I could tell by the way he was smirking. Starvie watched me too, but I couldn't perceive her thoughts.

I tried to ignore them both. I struggled in the mud, attempting to pull clear my remaining clothing, but could only thrash like a drowning wasp.

Starvie swore and tossed the cigarette. She pulled me up into a sitting position, gently peeling the shirt and trousers away, taking as little skin off as she could. After helping me into the Real clothes, she went to the Landy and grabbed the tent equipment, fashioning a brace for my leg from the steel poles. I managed not to yelp too much when she strapped it on.

'Give me a hand,' she said to Fatty. They dragged me to the cart and hitched me up. The ropes pulled tight over my chest. The sensation reminded me of being loaded before a climb up the Hope Tower.

Fatty had Starvie put on a pair of plastic cuffs. She was about to argue with him, but seeing me in the corner of her eye changed her mind. She pulled them tight around her wrists and jumped into the cart behind me. I wondered why she couldn't be this cooperative all the time.

I could stand with the brace, and I found pulling the cart relatively simple, although extremely painful. With only the one eye I stumbled often as we made our way clear of the woods, marvelling that Fatty could be as nimble as he was despite his many disabilities.

We travelled north until we found a B road, tucked between high, skeletal hedges. We made our way down the mud slope, Fatty and Starvie taking up position next to me, helping with the weight of the cart. Once on tarmac we headed south again, Fatty resuming his position a few paces ahead, Starvie fidgeting on the cart. She was listless without her camera. Occasionally, Fatty dropped back and asked if she was okay. She didn't answer, but she must have been giving him a look he enjoyed. Either that or he kept coming back for more silence.

The road turned sharply down and left. We emerged onto an old motorway. I was surprised to see wrecks everywhere. Hundreds of cars were splayed across the six lanes. Most were fused to the tarmac, sculptures of twisted metal and ash, cast in a blinding flash and left to cool in the night. They must have been on their way to a bunker when the blast hit. We were near one of the three impacts, where a trio of explosions were supposed to have begun the shortest and final war.

I stooped to peek inside one of the wrecks. A grinning skeleton lay in the front seat, half fossilised into the steering wheel. Its finger rested curiously on the radio, as if searching for a better station.

It was tough to manoeuvre the cart through all the cars, but the variety of wrecks piqued my curiosity. There were hatchbacks, city cars, estates, coupés . . . I wondered if I was too pragmatic in always choosing a Landy, and if it might not be fun to ask Rick for something more sporty next time.

Fatty suddenly raised his hand and we stopped. Up ahead the motorway cleared. The dark shape of a flyover straddled the lanes. We had reached the King's checkpoint.

It was well sited, at the summit of a long, straight slope. Fatty took a look through his binoculars, then passed them to me. In the twilight I could make out reinforced concrete embankments. A hundred metres down the hill stood a hut, thrown together with scraps of corrugated iron. It guarded the slipway, which led up to a filling station and a Welcome Break sign.

A few figures leaned or sat on the stone barriers, cradling rifles. Concrete bollards were thrown across the road. To get through the checkpoint we would be forced up the slipway past the guardhouse, then down the other side.

The northbound services were concealed by a raised mud bank, but what I could make out appeared derelict. Hanging over the road to command the approach, connecting the two services, was the flyover, with three large, fixed gunnery positions carved into its side. There might also have been a tank parked up there. It was surprising to see such well-placed defences. From there they could concentrate some serious fire.

Fatty poked me in the ribs and indicated the flyover.

'They're checking us out,' he said. 'Ghouls on the walkway.'

He was right. Halfway across, huddled around a telescope, were three figures, peering at us in the half-light.

'Right,' said Fatty. 'Here we go.'

He threw his arms out, then began to wave them. There was a pattern to it.

'What's this, your pass code?' asked Starvie.

'You'd better shut up and look pretty,' said Fatty. 'And put those thoughts of drilling groins out of your head. I need this to work, do you get me? If you start beating on them and trying to escape it could mess everything up.'

Fatty raised his left arm up, his right pointing to four o'clock. Then he switched them round, only with the right pointing to eleven. Several other movements followed. Semaphore was a pretty ancient form of communication, but I had seen militias use it before. Being familiar with the meanings, I could tell it wasn't a call for help, just an over long statement of business.

Fatty lifted the night visions and read the replying signal.

'They're letting us in,' he said.

'Is that all they said?' asked Starvie. 'They're waving their arms about like they're trying to achieve flight.'

'They wanted to know who you were,' said Fatty. 'Who knows, you might have a fan up there.'

He began one final signal to the flyover.

'Listen,' he said to Starvie, his left arm at eight o'clock, his right at four, 'I know you're upset about having to go whoring, but no more of your looks, okay? Last thing I need is them rumbling us because of some over-familiar sneer you give me.'

She tilted her head.

'You don't like the way I look at you?' She said it all sweetness and light. Fatty snapped around and gazed at her, suddenly powerless.

'I . . . you're . . . '

I yanked the cart forward, running a wheel over Fatty's foot to snap him out of it. He cursed and followed.

The turret of the tank awkwardly traversed as we walked up the hill. Figures sprinted across the flyover, running in file, taking up positions. It was odd to see them regimented like that.

At the top of the hill a sign reading 'Diversion' pointed us away from the bollards, channelling us into a single lane. Real sentries stood at the end, dressed in chemical coats, their faces hidden behind smog masks and goggles.

They watched our approach passively at first. Then they noticed Starvie. I saw the shiver of excitement ripple through them. They straightened up and craned their necks to see her, cat-calling and yelping. One of them raised his rifle in the air and shook it like a spear. I was ready to be rushed, but it didn't come. One of the guards, the shortest one, raised a clenched fist. The four others stepped back, mumbling and growling but restrained for the moment.

Shorty walked up and lowered his smog mask, which was dyed red from blood sweat. I couldn't see his eyes behind his goggles, but I could guess at them.

'Origin?' he asked.

'Eh?' said Fatty.

'Where are you travelling from?'

'Oh, I see . . . About thirty miles north-west, on the coast.'

The guard nodded his head and pointed a gloved hand at the cart.

'What's this you have here?' he asked.

'Booty,' said Fatty. 'Booty for sale, here!' The sentries yelled some approving obscenities and cheered, but the short guard raised his fist again and they were silenced.

'She's Ficial?' asked the guard.

'You're a swift one,' said Fatty. 'Just look at her – that hair, that skin, those eyes. This is the finest example of pleasure Ficial the old world produced.' He leaned to one side to address the sentries. 'And I'm offering her at a crazy price!'

The sentries stayed quiet, but they shifted on their heels and nudged each other.

'What else are you carrying?' asked Shorty.

Fatty was in full sales mode now. He strolled past me and grabbed Starvie by the arm, hauling her off the trailer.

'You mean apart from this? This is the greatest trade I will ever make and you want to know what else I'm carrying? Isn't this enough?'

Shorty was unmoved.

'Fine,' said Fatty, shoving Starvie to one side. 'Apart from this . . . Let's see, I'm carrying a hundred tins of Spam, some nearly new chemical coats, I've got . . . let me see, some DVDs, if you have the equipment, paper, a few other odds and sods.'

Shorty walked stiffly up to me and pulled down the hood of my chemical coat. He reared back when he saw my face, but recovered quickly.

'You two are partners?'

'He doesn't speak,' said Fatty. 'He took a swim in the wrong canal a few months back. Lost his voice you might say. Well, he can make a kind of noise but you don't want to hear it.'

I was making noise right then. I could hear the breeze whistling through my cheeks. Shorty scrutinised Starvie again.

'Is the Ficial secure?' he asked.

'As secure as you can get them,' said Fatty. 'She's been a bit of a handful to be honest but we've kept her in line.'

Shorty looked at us, considering. It was one of those little performances of authority Reals liked to make, attempting to create anticipation. Feeble really, but he clearly enjoyed his job. At length he raised his hand and indicated that the sentries should grab the cart. They pushed me aside gently, like I might break if they shoved too hard. I removed the harness and offered it to one of them, but he frantically waved me away, wary of infection. They each took a corner and began hauling the cart up the slip road. Shorty pointed at Fatty and me.

'You two take the girl. I will follow behind.'

Fatty and I approached Starvie and took an arm each. Shorty raised his rifle, keeping it trained on Fatty as we walked, which wasn't such a bad instinct.

I could hear a commotion above us. The figures on the bridge were drooping over the side to drool at Starvie. I could hear their shuffling and excited whispers, but no more than that. Presumably they were holding in their primal demons for the sake of Shorty, but I could sense the frenzy building. Starvie was having the desired effect.

The service station wasn't fortified like the bridge. The buildings were untouched from the pre-war days. A sign hung at a dangerous angle over the filling station forecourt. A section of the roof had shorn away, resting at an angle against one of the pumps. The car park was littered with wrecks that the Reals had found too unwieldy to clear. An old mail truck lay on its side, half melted into the tarmac. A few vans were also fused to the surface, left where they had been parked. In a smaller car park behind the service station was an enormous pyre, made out of anything flammable the Reals had laid their hands on. Another signal fire.

The guard led us to the main service station. Above the doors the legend:

Customs

was scrawled in white paint.

'Hey,' said Fatty, 'I thought you were letting us through. You didn't say anything about confiscation.'

'This is customs,' replied Shorty. 'Your cart must stay here while your cargo is inspected.'

'Since when?'

'You want to trade, don't you?'

'Yeah, trade, not donate.'

Shorty shrugged.

'All cargo that passes through here must be catalogued. Don't worry, you'll get your cart back.'

'With everything in it?'

'You'll have to pay a toll, that's all. The Ficial is a different matter. All contraband has to be passed by the Supervisor.'

Shorty motioned inside with his rifle. We stepped through some long-dead sliding doors, into the foyer. Interestingly, the place had power, and was lit by the overheads. Running down the left-hand side was an old amusement arcade. Most of the machines were burned out, but one or two were still going, playing quiet little tunes of impending treasure.

To the right was a food court, about fifty metres square. Crates of supplies were stacked everywhere, piled high on the plastic tables and seating. Only the old coffee concession was clear, pumping an unfamiliar odour throughout the building. A sign on the counter read 'back in ten minutes'.

Shorty led us towards the lavatories. He pointed us into the gents. I went in, still clutching Starvie by her left arm, Fatty having to shift his bulk to fit through the doorway.

Half the rest room floor had been excavated, dropping eight

feet into a level below. Urinals still clung to the wall on our level, their unconnected pipes hanging over the drop. Three burrowed passages stretched out of the space below, tunnelling under the rest of the complex.

Shorty prodded Starvie in the back with his gun.

'Jump down,' he said.

I let go of Starvie's arm. Fatty shoved her in the small of her back, taking her by surprise. She fell awkwardly and landed on one side. The guard passed a rope to me, the end fixed by a knot tied around a urinal pipe. I clambered down as best I could with my one good arm, hanging my damaged leg. Next came Fatty, about as graceful as me. We pulled Starvie onto her feet and watched Shorty scamper down the rope with practised ease.

He pointed down the eastern passage, a black tunnel supported by unconvincing scrap metal braces. We marched straight down it silently, Shorty bringing up the rear, his expression still hidden behind goggles.

The passage was lit by a trail of bare bulbs hanging from exposed wiring, which was hardly safe with a light rain dripping off the roof. A rope line ran along the wall, passing through metal hoops. It was damn bad construction, another Real rush job.

We turned to the right and passed a room with an open door. Inside, I saw a fat, humming generator, about as big as a car. Its design was almost identical to one you'd see inside a barricade. Odd, to see such high tech and Real tech side by side. Shorty pressed us on for another minute, before we were confronted by a huge steel hatch.

That, at least, was well fitted. A large metal wheel was fixed at its centre. Above the hatch in white paint the words AIRLOCK, CLEAN ZONE were crudely scrawled. Shorty shouldered his rifle and began to turn the wheel. After four revolutions the door sprang open.

A short length of tunnel led to a simple office door. This stretch had been finished properly, in clean, white concrete. Shorty indicated a line of cloth socks, lined up neatly at the entrance, and a box of rubber gloves.

'Remove your shoes and put on the socks,' he said. 'Then put on the gloves.'

When we were all suitably attired he walked up to the door and knocked.

'Keep your distance from the glass,' he said, opening up the door. 'Stand behind the yellow line.'

I am in the passenger seat. I have never been in the truck cabin before. A postcard of Jesus is stuck to the dashboard. The ashtray overflows with cigar butts. There are crisp and chocolate wrappers in the footwell and burn holes in the seats. A thick layer of grime covers the windscreen where the wipers don't sweep.

We are stuck in a traffic jam on the temporary bridge. It has taken us a day just to get this far and we are still only on the outskirts of town. We are approaching the flood zone. Out of the window, over the tops of the other cars, I can see the floating shanty towns that have sprung up in the muddy floodplain. The immigrant Reals seem to be more capable of innovation than the natives, making their shacks out of anything they find. One structure has an entire side supported by inflated white plastic bags, all from one particular supermarket chain. The other side is buoyed by the inflated orange bags of a competing brand. The owner seems to take pride in this colour scheme.

The boss stares at the road, clutching the steering wheel, ready for the moment when the traffic will suddenly break free. I won't tell him the odds of that happening.

'What do you think, forty-two?' he says.

'Sorry, boss?'

'What do you think about all this? The recall, I mean?'

He doesn't look at me. He stays rigid in his seat, staring ahead, like something bad will happen if he looks away.

'I don't know, boss. I don't feel sick.'

'What about your friend, thirty-seven? What did you think about dumping him in the waste pit? Didn't you think that was unnecessary?'

He releases his grip on the steering wheel and looks me right in the eye. He feels in a pocket and produces another cigar. He pushes in the lighter and it pops back out at him. He lights the tobacco. The end of the cigar glows and he puffs and puffs, holding my eyes with his. The boss is cultivating cancers.

Dr Pander originally designed our nanos to eat cancer cells, then developed them from there. I think that's quite interesting but I don't share it.

'I mean,' he continues, 'it bugs the hell out of me, I can tell you. I lose an expensive asset, and get told that those I have left might be sick and need a service. I have no idea how long they're going to have you. It will take me a week just to get in and out of London to pick you up. They say there'll be compensation, a cheque in the post. Ha. Ha. A cheque signed by Control, I suppose. The only consolation is that everyone else has to do the same thing. Work on the Tower can't go on until this mess is sorted out.'

'Yes, boss.'

'But what if S&G get their Ficials back before me, eh? They've got a bigger chequebook than me. Say they slip someone at Control a few thousand to get theirs back a week, even a day before me? They'll have the next hundred floor contracts sewn up and I won't even be able to afford you. Then it'll be you in the pit. What do you think about that?'

'I'm sorry, boss.'

He snorts and looks back up the road. I would tell him that you don't bribe Control, that Control is there to repair the damage done by human ambition, not indulge it. But what's the point?

'Sorry,' says the boss. 'You don't know what it means. Don't even care that you watched your mates dissolving in a waste pit yesterday. Don't even know why you had to do it. You didn't even ask why.'

I have no feelings about it one way or the other. Neither did Dingkom. The feelings were burned out of me while I grew.

I look at the ashtray, at the burned plastic and ash, and think how ugly it is.

The boss turns back to me.

'You're not a real person,' he says. 'Don't forget that.'

I think he means it as an insult.

THE SUPERVISOR

We walked into a room that was split in two by a sheet of thick glass. In the top right-hand corner a fan turned, filtering out the germs we carried with us. Below it, about four feet off the ground, was a drawer through which food and drink were presumably deposited. A yellow line was painted across the floor on our side, about six feet from the plate glass. Behind the glass was a simple cot with white sheets. Next to that was a sink, and a steel hook with a white towel hanging off it. A flotsam of soaps, gels and cleaning products were scattered below.

The Supervisor, a woman in her forties, sat at a stainless steel desk, watching something on television. It was the King of Newcastle again, singing that song. It was the full music video, where the King danced with real women, miming lyrics about getting his girl back. It looked like it had been filmed in a poorly lit sewer. The King wore so much make-up you could barely make out his features.

The Supervisor probably hadn't seen the surface in months. The skin on her hands had the same texture as Rick's. Her pale blue eyes stared at us over a green surgical mask. She turned off her cracked little television, but reluctantly.

'Supervisor,' said Shorty. 'Traders from the north. The leader says this one is Ficial – plunder from Liverpool. The other one is his assistant. They want to trade and get passage south.'

The Supervisor grunted. Her eyes hadn't left Starvie.

'Is this true?' she asked Starvie. 'Are you Ficial?'

'I recognise her, Supervisor,' said Shorty. 'She used to be famous, before the war. Her name's Jennifer E.'

'My name is Starvie.'

The Supervisor leaned back. She had one of those swivel office chairs that had been popular pre-war. Something about swinging gently from side to side could make a Real person feel like a big deal.

'Engineered life forms are contraband,' said the Supervisor. 'The King has ordered that all Ficials are to be destroyed on sight.'

'Surely,' said Fatty, 'the good King wouldn't prohibit capturing them and putting them to work?'

The Supervisor stared at Starvie, unmoved. Fatty slammed his fist into his palm.

'Look, I say we don't give them the simple prescription of a bullet in the head. I say, they made such a mess we should make them clean it up. We have the right to do that, don't we?'

The Supervisor nodded slowly and deliberately.

'That is true,' she said. 'That is how we built these bunkers. Two Ficials in a tank survived an ambush and were captured. We worked them on tunnelling out these rooms until they expired. Good work they did too, with what we had available. They lasted a month on water alone.'

'That pig-headedness certainly does makes them hardy, doesn't it?' said Fatty, stood up straight now, jabbing his finger directly at her. 'All the more reason for you to offer a price. She's very much for sale, and I'm very much in the market for offers.'

'I'm afraid not,' said the Supervisor.

'What? Why not?'

'It's obviously a pleasure model,' she replied. 'I see no practical use for her.'

Fatty gave the Supervisor a blank look, then, seeming to collect himself, answered her.

'First off, she's a Ficial, just like any other. Whatever they're optimised for, be it pleasure, construction or tap-dancing, they heal up quick and are strong. You know that. If you wanted to, you could hand her a shovel and get her to dig a moat ten feet deep around this entire camp.'

The Supervisor took a ring of keys off her desk and picked through them absently, letting one drop after another.

'She is considerably less valuable than one of the Power models, though, isn't she?'

Fatty managed not to look at me.

'How many men do you have here Supervisor?' said Fatty. 'Twenty? Thirty?'

'I control a large squad,' she answered.

'And a surly bunch they are too, am I right? If history teaches us one thing, it's that bored soldiery turn fast to mutinous dogs. Am I right?'

The Supervisor smiled but said nothing, pausing on one of the keys as if it held some long-forgotten promise. Fatty continued his speech.

'Well, I don't wish to tread on anybody's morals, but let me put it this way: this thing is specifically designed to satisfy men's deepest desires.' Fatty prowled around Starvie. He reminded me of Rick, circling one of his motors during a sale.

'I predict a major shift in general morale after you serve her as tonight's meal. Give them an hour with her each and you'll see morale shoot up, I'm telling you.'

The Supervisor put the keys away in the desk drawer. Then she stood, pushing her seat away. Its wheels made a sharp scuttling noise on the concrete. She walked towards Fatty, her hands clasped behind her back, stopping a few feet short of the glass.

'My men are loyal and efficient,' she said. 'They don't mutiny. They follow the King's standard. Do you doubt their zeal?'

'Of course not,' said Fatty, waving his hands. 'Of course not. I'm simply saying that any man needs to let off steam once in a while. This here is the perfect entertainment for them. I mean, look at her.'

The Supervisor was looking at Starvie. She hadn't stopped looking. Fatty closed in, approaching the glass. The Supervisor backed away, raising the surgical mask. Fatty was pulled back behind the yellow line. That didn't distract him from his pitch.

'And don't think it would be wrong to use her that way. Remember that this thing is nothing more than a fucking product. She was designed and built to do a job. Use her as you would a TV, there's no difference. Only when we behave like there is do we let them triumph.'

Even Shorty had been captivated by the fat man's rhetoric. For the first time the Supervisor looked at me. I did my best to look feeble. It wasn't hard. She lost interest and returned her attention to Fatty.

'Only one thing,' she said.

'Yes?' said Fatty.

'You look rather like you are carrying a disease that has been spreading. It's killed a few of my men.'

'Don't let that worry you,' said Fatty, 'I'm just here to do business. And if you've had it here you'll know it's not contagious.'

'It's not been contagious *so far*,' said the Supervisor. 'But disease has a way of evolving rather quickly these days, doesn't it?'

'Fine. Give me a price and I'll remove myself from your health clinic.'

'I don't know,' she said. 'I don't want to buy contaminated goods. Have you been with her?'

Fatty squinted.

'Am I going to contaminate my best product? Are you crazy?'

Shorty hadn't taken his eyes off Starvie. He was transfixed, oblivious even. It occurred to me that we could kill him and his Supervisor now, then shoot our way across the bridge to the supplies. Why bother with all this subterfuge?

'You're right, of course,' said the Supervisor. 'It would make a useful acquisition. But the fact remains it may have information that would be useful to the King's war, and it cannot therefore be the subject of any sale.'

'What?' said Fatty. 'It's a hooker – what could it possibly know?'

'There is no "hooking" in Ficial society,' she replied. 'On the other hand, it seems to me they would make excellent spies. Mr Thomas here has been unable to stop looking at it. If it can distract my best guard from his duties so easily it would make quite the fifth column, wouldn't you say?'

She smiled. Mr Thomas (Shorty) hunched his shoulders in a silent apology. The Supervisor returned to her seat behind the desk.

'No, I'm afraid your cargo is to be confiscated.'

'We haven't made a deal yet,' growled Fatty.

'She will be placed in holding and interrogated.'

'Oh, come on!' said Fatty. 'You know there's no point questioning one of these things. You'd learn more interrogating a table lamp.'

'There are methods which yield results,' she said. 'Mr Thomas, you will take the pleasure Ficial to a cell, and you will not speak to it, is that understood?'

Without a word, Thomas grabbed Starvie's arm and led her out.

'I don't consider that good business,' said Fatty.

'We have laws now,' said the Supervisor. 'The King's law will be obeyed.'

Fatty spat on the glass. The Supervisor flinched. We all watched the blue phlegm roll slowly down.

'I don't consider,' said Fatty, 'that any other traders are going to come through here after what I tell them. I saw your little supply dump up there. You must have fleeced every poor sap who ever crossed your path.'

The Supervisor held out her hand and examined her fingers, which were white and papery.

'I doubt your friends would try and bring a Ficial through a checkpoint,' she said. 'I can't imagine your motives for doing so.'

She let that hang in the air for a moment.

'I should be able to expect some kind of price,' said Fatty.

The Supervisor was still absorbed by her hand.

'You are free to sell anything else you have with you on the base. You will have four hours, which is our maximum, to eat and trade your wares. Then you must leave.'

Fatty growled.

'Can we use your facilities?' he asked.

'As long as you remain in the food court area you may. Do not attempt to cross the flyover or enter other restricted areas. There is food on the ground level.' She pointed a finger at me. 'Will he be able to eat in his condition?'

'Very least, he can watch me,' said Fatty.

They really hadn't figured out the security thing, letting us wander about in the tunnels on our own. I guess to the Supervisor we just cut too pathetic a pair to be seen as a threat. We reached the gents and split up to explore the other tunnels. I took the western route, a long, highly unstable burrow. There was nothing notable about it, other than a single padlocked steel door at one end. The words:

were written above it. I went back the way I came and found Fatty waiting for me.

'Water here,' I said, whistling and squeaking. Words were getting easier to form with my pulped tongue. 'Clean.'

'Huh,' said Fatty. 'Well, that makes me feel a bit better about Jennifer shooting up my barrels. Clearly a flooded market.' He grinned at me and winked. I nodded down the east passage.

'What you find?' I wasn't bothering with sentences. Not with this throat.

Fatty shrugged and itched his beard.

'Barracks. Empty. Lot of beds though. Lot of beds and lots of mess. If they're filling every cot down here they must be fifty strong. More than I thought.'

'Starvie?'

'No sign. They must have stashed her somewhere they can keep her out of sight.'

He looked down the west tunnel, then the south, then back behind him. He chewed his lip and frowned.

'What?'

'Something's wrong about this place,' he said. 'Nobody's talking to us.'

'Not normal?'

'Every time I arrive at a checkpoint I get surrounded by folk asking me questions – what's happening up north, which barricades are under siege . . . anything I can tell them really. Here . . . I get the distinct impression we're being avoided. It's odd.'

He shrugged.

'Oh well, now that we're here let's get some refreshments.'

He grabbed the ladder and shuffled up to the gents. I followed. We made our way back out to the food court.

Two soldiers sat at a plastic table by the coffee shop, sipping orange mush and watching a portable TV. Half the TV's pixels were dead and it had no sound but they gazed at it intently. It was one of the King's torture programmes. A few Ficials were being macheted to pieces by a man in an orange jumpsuit and policeman's helmet. None of the Ficials screamed of course. They simply watched in bemusement as the increasingly frustrated torturer tried to evoke some kind of response. The film was from Liverpool. I could tell by the Cunard building burning in the background.

The coffee shop was open. Fatty smacked his lips and guided me over there.

A man in a wheelchair sat behind the counter. In one hand he held a book with an image of a chromosome on the cover. In the other he held a bloody rag, which he clutched to his chest as if it were tremendously precious. His face was half shrouded by a patch of blistering sores that ran from his chin to his scalp, shutting up one eye.

'What's good?' Fatty asked him.

'The menu is limited,' replied the man.

'Any specials?'

'Only what you can smell.'

'We'll take it,' said Fatty.

Sighing heavily, as if this was the last piece of information he had wanted to hear, the man deftly hoisted his wheelchair off its front wheels and spun to face the kitchen.

'Two more, Leonard!' he called.

A yellow-fingered hand, black with hair, appeared at the serving hatch, clutching a ladle. Two cups were filled with hot orange foam, then dumped onto the counter. The man in the wheelchair passed them to us, then returned to his book.

Fatty led me to a table by the window. I took a seat and looked out at the bridge, the derelict buildings over the road, and the purple streaks of High Lights fading in the cloud. The tracks from Fatty's cart had already disappeared under a new layer of ash and snow.

The mush tasted awful, but not as bad as some barricade meals. Fatty grimaced. I raised my hand to my cheek and realised the fluid was leaking out the gash in my face. I choked and spluttered as food fell into places in the body it was never meant to go.

'Maybe you should consider a period of fasting,' said Fatty.

I tried again, leaning my head to the right, letting the mush trickle down the intact side of my throat.

After a few more spoonfuls I pushed the cup away. Fatty looked at it with interest, but after glancing at me thought better of commandeering it. He drummed his fingers on the table, watching the sentries on the flyover smoke and stamp their feet in the snow.

'I don't like this,' he said. 'What are they doing? They should be tearing each other to pieces trying to get Jennifer. But what do they do? Stay at their posts like they're at Buck House or something. This is fucking everything up.'

He started in with one of his coughing fits.

'Try remain calm,' I gurgled. Fatty slapped at his chest and the coughing stopped.

'Don't tell me to be calm. I'm sat in the food court of Hell's Welcome Break, sharing an orange coffee with my half-melted kidnapper. What's there to be calm about?'

I raised a finger to my mouth. Fatty was getting loud.

'Wait little longer,' I advised.

Fatty sighed, nodded and scratched at his stomach.

'It's all that big mouth King's fault,' he said. 'Can't stop passing laws, instilling discipline. He should mind his own business.'

'Why Reals obey him?'

I really wanted to know. Fatty yawned and stretched.

'He's a celebrity, that's all. People remember him from before the war. I suppose he reminds them of better times. From what I hear he started off in Newcastle with a few hundred followers. Built that up by sending couriers out with free portable generators and TVs for the tribes. Records everything he does and sends riders out with DVDs for them to watch. He brought TV back and people love him for it.'

I pulled my shirtsleeve up my bad arm. It was still a horror to look at, but a great deal of reconstruction had been done already. I could no longer see the bone. Fatty had noticed something too.

'Your neck's healing up,' he said. 'I thought you said you'd need sleep.'

'Didn't think would be food.'

'That's all it takes, huh? Replace the batteries and you're as good as new. Well, it hardly matters now. If they're going to kick us out in a few hours we have to do something quick.'

There was a noise over by the main entrance. A young Real was running in our direction, his trainers squeaking on the floor tiles. He halted by the coffee stand and knocked on the red door with

STAFF ONLY printed on it. After a few seconds the door swung open. Wheelchair guy emerged, followed by a huge man holding a ladle. Leonard.

The soldier exchanged a few words with them, then ran back outside. Leonard muttered something to the wheelchair guy, then followed, dropping the ladle on the floor. Wheelchair guy sagged in his chair, watching his colleague leave. Then he rolled back behind the counter.

Fatty picked up our cups and approached the stand. I covered my face with the wind rag of the chemical coat and followed, careful to maintain the character of deformed fall guy to Fatty's Big Man.

Wheelchair guy had returned to his book and was sat much as before, only now he wore a scowl. Fatty dropped a cup onto the counter with a loud crash. Wheelchair guy looked up with fright, but calmed down when he saw Fatty.

'Yes?'

'Excellent drink,' said Fatty. 'I was just remarking to my companion how good it is to have something with real nutrition. Clearly you're a skilled barista.'

'I hope you still feel that way in an hour,' replied the man, flatly returning his attention to the book. Fatty dropped the other cup from a slightly greater height. Wheelchair guy looked up again, flexing his jaw.

'I'm talking about this whole operation,' said Fatty. 'You people have it good here, there's no doubting it. It's refreshing to see people getting organised and making something for themselves. You all have a part to play, is what I'm saying.'

Wheelchair guy cocked his head to one side, examining Fatty, wondering if he was being mocked. Fatty was straight-faced.

'Oh my, yes. You do have an established order here. I mean to say, you have a way of doing things I thought had burned up in the war. Take that young ruffian who just ran in here to report to you. You guys have a pecking order. Respect. I respect respect.'

Wheelchair guy stretched his arms up to reach our cups, replacing them on the trays behind him.

'He wasn't reporting,' he said. 'He's mates with Leonard.'

'Who, the chef?'

'That's a grand term for what he is.'

'Well, whatever,' said Fatty. 'But who's manning the roadblock and who's inside sheltered from the snow? Seems there's a pecking order right there.'

Wheelchair guy put his book aside.

'You missing out on some major event?' asked Fatty.

'Not as far as I'm concerned. Mr Thomas is holding an auction on your pleasure model. He's going to sell her off to the highest bidder.'

Fatty didn't even blink.

'That right?' he said. 'Her indoors told us Thomas was going to interrogate her.'

'The Supervisor doesn't know,' said wheelchair guy. 'She doesn't have a clue what Thomas is up to. He'll take the body down to her tomorrow and say it tried to escape. It's not as if torturing it would do any good anyway.'

'Well, it might be worth a go,' said Fatty, smiling and dabbing at his leaking eye with a cloth. 'So you're not joining the bidding?'

'Nothing to bid,' replied wheelchair guy. 'In any case, I have never approved of those pleasure models.'

There was another compelling reason he wouldn't bid, but nobody mentioned it.

'You think they'll mind if we attend?' asked Fatty.

'I doubt anyone will notice. Just go out across the car park to the garage building. Keep to the back and Thomas shouldn't spot you.'

'Thanks a lot, mate,' said Fatty. 'You're all right.'

'My pleasure,' said wheelchair guy. 'Polite conversation makes a refreshing change.'

Fatty leant over the counter and offered wheelchair guy his hand. Wheelchair guy took it and shook meekly. I wondered how many contaminants and germs they were exchanging in that one gesture, Fatty with his pus-covered hand and wheelchair guy with his blisters and sores.

Fatty slapped me hard on the shoulder and indicated I should follow him out. I bowed slightly to wheelchair guy, thinking it an appropriately Real departing flourish, but he was buried in his book already.

I caught up with Fatty and marched alongside him to the exit.

We emerged into the car park. The air was heavy with an excited murmur, punctuated by an occasional howl. We walked towards the flyover, as fast our ruined bodies would allow. I noticed the four sentries in a huddle by the nearest emplacement, emptying their pockets into a pile on the concrete.

'Looks like they're pooling their resources for a bid,' said Fatty, nodding eagerly. 'That is welcome news. We're back on with the plan.'

Then the whole car park was thrown into light. We turned around. There was a floodlight on the filling station roof. The garrison swarmed around the decrepit pumps, all trying to peek inside the main building, baying like hounds at the thought of the perfect creature within. There were female Reals there too, engulfed in the hysteria. They too, it appeared, relished the chance to let loose the dark festering within. Fatty and I hid behind the hulk of a burned-out SUV, wary of being spotted by Mr Thomas. Fatty assessed the tactical situation.

'Bugger.'

He had a point. The plan was beginning to look foolish. There were far more Reals than we had expected, and they were spread out in the open. It was highly unlikely we could cull them all. Even if we got Fatty's supplies and managed to get back to the Landy, what was to stop survivors from regrouping and engaging us when we tried to pass through? Maybe Starvie had been right. Maybe Fatty had been a bad choice.

The murmur of the Reals around the garage grew in fever, and a great shout went up around the car park.

'Here she comes,' said Fatty.

A hatch opened on the roof of the filling station, and three figures made their way out. First came Mr Thomas, raising his hands to the cheers of the animals below. A female guard followed, Starvie dragged behind.

She was in a bad way. They'd dressed her in some awful pink frock, revealing pretty much all of her body except the parts that excited them most. Real men often seemed to find the promise of something more thrilling than its attainment.

They hadn't touched her face, but I could tell by her faltering steps that someone had worked her over. She tried to hold her head up but the female guard had a leash around her neck, which she yanked to keep Starvie's head bowed.

Thomas raised his hands in the air again, appealing for quiet, but the roar wouldn't subside. This irritated him. He motioned to the female guard, who let go of the leash, cocked her rifle, and fired a few shots into the air. The crowd settled. Nothing like gunfire to bring a meeting to order.

Mr Thomas picked up a megaphone and raised it to his lips. If I had a weapon I could have taken him out right there.

'Gentlemen!' came his tinny voice. 'We have here for you tonight a very special treat! You've heard her sing, you've seen her films, you've dreamt about her every night. Well, boys, tonight, it is my great pleasure to say that your dreams can come true . . . for the right price of course. Gentlemen, I give you . . . Jennifer F.!'

Thomas must have been an entertainer in the past. He knew how to work a crowd. Immediately another searchlight on top of the Welcome Break sprung into life, illuminating Starvie. The female guard kicked her back and yanked hard on the leash, so Starvie was thrust forward, her chin held high. The din of the crowd became incredible. I tapped Fatty on the shoulder. He flinched and turned his good eye on me.

'What?' he snapped.

'We need go. Sentries not coming. Still arguing.'

'We wait,' he said.

'We don't,' I said. 'You want drugs, we go now. Kill sentries while this noise. We get their weapons.'

Fatty knocked my arm away.

'Stop talking like an idiot.' He turned back to the auction, fuming. Something seemed wrong about him. He was twitching. His good pupil was huge.

Mr Thomas marched around the edge of the rooftop, letting the hysteria grow. It all seemed a waste of time to me. Those males weren't going to get any more desperate. But he was relishing his moment of power.

'Bound and gagged for your pleasure!' he bellowed through the megaphone. 'She is yours to take home tonight. All you have to do is make a bid. Only two rules apply. First: bids may only be made by individuals!'

That didn't go down well. Dissenting voices made themselves heard. A group close to the front began throwing trash at Thomas, heckling him and protesting.

'Don't give me that, F shift,' said Thomas. 'You're the reason for that rule. You weren't exactly gentle with the last lot, were you? Had to leave our tunnels half-finished because you couldn't resist cutting on them, didn't we?'

The crowd laughed and jeered.

'That's right,' said Thomas, 'it'll be one of you at a time. Second rule is you can only have her here in the petrol station in a supervised fashion. Jennifer is too good a prize to chew up in one night. We're all going to get some fun out of her, we just need to be patient and fair.'

One of the larger members of F shift threw something at Thomas.

'Fuck fair, hand her over!'

Starvie kicked and thrashed, tiring of the female guard's boot in her back. She almost pulled clear, drawing a cheer from the crowd, before the guard kicked her knees and forced her down. The crowd screamed some more.

Fatty grabbed me and drew in close, whispering: 'Look who's here.'

The four sentries were marching along the flyover towards us. As we had hoped, they were carrying their rifles. Finally, something was going right. Fatty leaned down to his ankle and picked a knife out of a strap, then straightened up and waited. They still hadn't noticed us, but were slapping each other excitedly and whooping with glee.

Fatty stepped out.

'Just a minute, boys.'

'Who are you?' said one.

'Mr Thomas says there are no joint bids tonight. It's singles only.'

'What?'

'That's unfair!' said another.

Fatty threw himself on the nearest Real, jabbing the knife straight into his gut. For a second the others froze. I took the opportunity to grab the nearest guy's neck in my good right hand. I squeezed hard, meeting my thumb and fingers in his windpipe.

He looked me in the eye, full of questions, until I found his spine and twisted. He dropped to the ground. The third sentry levelled his gun at me and got off a shot, which missed. I grabbed the rifle, pushed the muzzle up into his chin, and forced his finger back on the trigger, blowing his head almost clean off. Fatty pulled the knife out of his victim's belly and swung it across the fourth guy's ankles. He shrieked in pain and tumbled onto Fatty. I stamped on the neck of the first guy, who was still gurgling and reaching for his pistol. Then, just as the fourth managed to jam the muzzle of his gun into Fatty's face, I kicked him sharp in the head, and he fell down, unconscious.

Fatty lay on the ground gasping. The crowd didn't break up. We hadn't been heard.

I offered Fatty my hand and pulled him up. He groaned and clutched his chest. In the struggle his wounds had opened again.

I examined the weapons. They were in fairly good shape, but were the old pre-war army issue, cheap and prone to jamming at awkward moments. I selected the two in best order, handing one to Fatty, then dragged the bodies into the shell of the SUV.

The sound of the crowd curdled and grew darker. Thomas, it seemed, had done his job too well. His sales pitch had driven his bidders into an uncontrollable frenzy.

'Damn it, keep back!' he screamed through the megaphone. 'We're going to do this like civilised people!'

He dived onto his knees as a hail of bricks, trash and metal were thrown at him from below. The crowd was beating on the door of the filling station, swelling and pulsing with anger and desire.

'If you keep trying that I'll shoot her through the head!' he screamed.

'Fucking idiot,' said Fatty.

I saw something strike the female guard in the face. She keeled over, out of view. Mr Thomas crouched with his arms over his head, waiting for the inevitable. Starvie wasn't in sight.

'Okay,' I said to Fatty, 'let's go and get your stuff. Now or never.'

Fatty didn't move.

'They're in,' he said. F shift were leading a charge up to the roof of the filling station. They burst up there in a great roaring mob. Thomas was picked up and thrown to the others below. The rest of them searched for Starvie. The lead guy, a six-foot monster with a blood-sweat face, hollered and grabbed at something, hoisting Starvie up on her feet. The crowd below shrieked approval.

Holding her by the neck, the monster dangled her over the throng below. Then, in one lunging move, he tore off her pink dress. She struggled and butted her head at him, but he didn't seem to notice, dumbly transfixed by Starvie's body. A few of his friends tried to get at her, which snapped him out of his reverie. He pushed them back, bellowing a war cry.

'They'll tear her to pieces,' said Fatty. He was chewing on his bearded lip and gnashing his teeth. He seemed to be working himself up as bad as the crowd.

'She fine,' I said. 'Well, not fine, but designed to take a beating. Let's get your stuff. Sooner we done sooner we return.'

Fatty wasn't listening. His face was a mess of frantic tics.

'You'd think when we've lived through the end of days we'd have a bit more respect for life,' he snarled.

I ran for the bridge, thinking Fatty would follow as soon as he realised I was leaving.

I was wrong.

I took three steps before I heard him shoot. I turned to see him kneeling on the tarmac, out in the open, rifle raised.

'Bugger,' he said. 'Missed.'

The crowd didn't seem to have noticed, having too much fun to care about a bit of sniping.

'What you doing?' I said. 'This not plan.'

'I not care.'

'What about drugs?'

'Fuck the drugs,' said Fatty.

I raised the butt of my rifle to plant one on his head, figuring I could carry him over the bridge, but it was too late. His next shot found its target. The monster stumbled, dropped Starvie, and plummeted off the roof, a graceless sack of meat. The noise of the crowd changed: confusion, and then outrage. I knelt down next to Fatty and cocked my rifle.

'This terrible idea.'

I scoped the roof. The three remaining members of F shift were struggling with Starvie. Fatty shot, downed the Real nearest her. I popped the other two. Starvie lay down and wisely elected not to get up again. The crowd began to disperse in panic, seeking cover. There was plenty of it.

'Mistake,' I said.

'Spilt milk,' said Fatty. 'Find another spot, will you? You stay here and they've got us both.'

I didn't need him to tell me that, but he was right. The Reals began to return fire. A line of concrete chopped into dust in front of us. Fatty fell back behind the SUV, hugging the side and returning fire. I limped off, making for the slipway entrance. There were a few concrete bollards there that I thought might offer some cover. I arrived just as something big started shooting.

The Reals on the Welcome Break roof had taken a while to figure out what was going on, but had worked it out now, firing a heavy machine gun in my general direction. This was a problem. Half the bollard I was making for exploded into white chunks. I dived to the left and rolled onto my knees, raising my rifle. Immediately I saw them in the scope – two Reals, one firing, the other feeding a belt of ammunition. Three shots whizzed past my nose so close I could smell them.

I hit the deck again and crawled under some confused and random fire, then sprang up and ran for the slipway. There, finally, was some good cover, a natural trench behind a crash barrier, by faded yellow lines and the words SLOW DOWN painted on the road. I dived into the hole just as the guys on the roof spotted me again. They shot up the earth around me, trying to pin me down until their buddies could surround me.

Things looked bleak. For the first time ever, just for a moment, I considered ditching my fare. If I just ran down the slipway and kept heading south I would probably get away. Then the machine gun stopped.

I raised my head, just enough to spot four Real soldiers cautiously creeping forward, feeling the air in front of them with their rifles, half-blind in the tarmac smoke. The poor slobs didn't realise they were silhouetted by the spotlight. I fired four precise shots and they fell, though one was only winged.

I spun the weapon around, eye fixed to the scope, and scanned the roof of the Welcome Break. I could only see the cannon, resting on its muzzle, smoking gently. Its crew were hiding from gunfire coming from the filling station.

Starvie.

She was free of her bindings, reloading a weapon, one long, bare leg extended, a foot resting on the roof ledge. She wore one of the dead men's chemical coats. Her hair fluttered in the wind. The Reals who'd been baying for her blood a minute earlier now hugged the filling station walls, shooting wildly over their heads to ward off her attentions. They'd probably never found her more desirable.

I fired at two of them who were trying to wriggle through a window, then ducked back in the hollow to reload. As I replaced the magazine, I reflected on how quickly things can change. With Starvie on the roof our chances had dramatically improved. If Fatty was still alive.

Still, it was a good idea to move. I jumped out of the hole and made for a couple of large blue bins that were tumbled over by the tree line. The shooting started straight away. Directly ahead were two men, charging through the snow. They were running and shooting, which was never much of a Real talent, and I got the pair of them with head-shots. Then someone on my right fared much better, hitting me on my bad leg. The splints shattered and broke free, the bullet smashing through my ankle.

That dropped me, my head smacking down hard. There were those odds changing again. I jabbed the butt of my rifle onto the tarmac and flipped over to see my attacker. I found him in the scope right away.

Leonard.

I aligned the crosshairs between his eyes and pulled the trigger.

Click.

Leonard smiled and picked his shot carefully, realising I was helpless. I slammed the release, let the magazine pop out into my hand, and hurled it at his face, catching him on the temple. He looked a little confused, then passed out.

For the first time, nobody was shooting at me. Most of the Reals had taken cover, but a few were still in the open. I noticed one group working their way along the service station wall, shooting up Fatty's SUV. Lit up by the spotlight, they cast long, stretched black shadows. Well, that was too bad for Fatty. He would have to hold out.

I had to recover my fare. That was going to be a little difficult with a shattered ankle, but I had to try. I stabbed the rifle butt onto the tarmac as far ahead as I could, and dragged myself after it.

I reached the dead Reals, stole a couple of clips, reloaded, and scanned the filling station roof. A few Reals still hugged the walls, fearfully looking up, but there was no sign of Starvie. Something of a stand-off, then. I decided to give her some breathing room, and raked the side of the garage with fire. Three Reals went down. The fourth wasn't hit, but decided it was all too much and ran off into the tree line. That made life easier, but not much. It would take me a few days to drag myself over there.

I spotted a supermarket trolley, sandwiched between the two blue wheelie bins. It was still upright, had four wheels and was big enough to accommodate me. I heaved myself up onto my good leg, tossing my body inside the trolley like heavy shopping. My bad leg hung over one corner, my good one tucked inside and keeping me balanced. Reaching out and resting my hands on the bins either side, I began to rock the trolley back and forth, building up as much momentum as possible. Then, with all the strength I had, I catapulted myself out across the car park.

I had taken a good aim, speeding directly at the filling station. I congratulated myself on my genius, until I started to veer right. The front right wheel was wobbling, hurtling me off course into the burned-out wrecks, where a cluster of Reals were regrouping.

They heard the squealing of the trolley wheels and opened up on me. Something whistled overhead. It was a grenade, but it had been tossed far too high and exploded in the bins behind me. I carried on rolling, heading for the huge, rusted wreck of the mail truck. I crashed into it with some speed, bouncing clear but staying upright.

A man appeared from behind the nearest wheel, but I got him in time. Then another, from somewhere overhead, sprayed the trolley with fire and gave my nanos two fresh wounds to heal. I raised my gun and took half his head off.

I shoved off the truck, heading for the filling station, taking the dodgy wheel into account this time. The Reals shot and screamed in all directions but didn't hit me. I clattered into the building but hardly noticed. I was chewed up.

With this many wounds I might actually expire. My strength was leaving me. I raised the gun and took another look through the scope at Fatty's position.

His attackers were clustered behind the Welcome Break's east wall. They were whispering to each other, unsure of their next move. I almost wanted to yell out and tell them to get themselves organised. They were making it too easy; but then pain swam over me again and I dropped the rifle. My chin sank into my chest.

'This is it,' I said to nobody in particular.

The boss has gotten twitchy. Fear: the only emotion I can spot.

'Oh Jesus,' he whispers. 'Oh Jesus.'

This Jesus character only gets attention when the boss is afraid.

'When did it get this bad?'

People are in the streets and in the houses overlooking the street, a discharge leaking from windows and doorways, all gaunt and thin with hollow eyes. Different-coloured people, different-sized people, different-dressed people, hammering on the doors of our truck as we pass, begging, yelling, condemning. Some are dragged into trucks by soldiers.

We take the last turn and we are at the top of Brixton Hill. I can see the gate to Control Central Facility, stuck across the road. The entrance is surrounded by hundreds of Real soldiers in camouflage, and the occasional Ficial soldier, towering a couple of feet over the others. They hold enormous rifles, at attention, waiting for an order.

I wonder if the soldiers know what they're protecting. Do they even ask what is buried beneath them? Most have no understanding of what Control is. The boss seems to have the idea that it is a computer, a box sprinkled with demonic-red LEDs. What would he think if he knew that Control had eyes, hands and feet? What would he do if he found out it is a coalesced mind, seven special vision models, their consciousnesses joined to lead us out of the darkness? Would he be reassured or terrified?

The boss doesn't want to keep going, but credit to him, he ploughs on. The people thin out, broken up by the Real soldiers, who are just as agitated, just as frightened. Occasionally we hear a shot and the boss thrashes around in his seat.

'Don't worry,' I say. 'That's a distance away.'

He hunches forward, his chin practically on the steering wheel.

'Shut up, forty-two,' he says. 'Just shut up, okay?'

We are driving up behind another unmarked white van, which in turn brings up the rear of a queue of other unmarked white vans. We all inch down the hill. The soldiers on the gate scan bar codes and swab mouths of anything Real trying to get in. This could be the longest wait we've had so far.

The boss pulls up the handbrake and lights another cigar, his fingers quivering. I look in the side mirror, back at the crowd that the soldiers are beating up the hill. I can read the Truth League banners even though they are flapping violently in the wind. I can see the people chanting slogans and shaking their fists, united by fear. From here they look like one giant, vibrating organism. I try to picture what the street would be like if all the people were swept away and I had the chance to rebuild it.

The boss switches on the radio and gets the news. He changes the channel instantly, searching for something that's not factual.

He finds a station where a voice is singing:

> *Baby if I made you mad*
> *something I might have said*
> *Please forget the past*
> *the future looks bright ahead*
> *Don't be cruel*
> *to a heart that's true*

The boss takes a huge breath and leans back. The music seems to soothe him. He drums the beat on the steering wheel and mutters something about how this is real music.

DISCOVERY

Purple spots whirled across my vision. I let them do that for a while. I tasted cordite and brick dust. There was the noise of a car door opening and shutting in the distance.

I ran my hands over my head, checking for more damage. My legs felt better. Looking down I saw the splint had been rebuilt, and the bleeding in the 'good' leg had stopped. The acid damage was healing too. I could feel new skin forming on my face.

Starvie was crouched in her chemical coat, fondling a rifle. Somehow she'd got me up onto the roof. That hair was still flapping in an implausible way.

'Hey,' I said.

She turned and faced me. She had a heavy bruise around her cheek, but otherwise appeared intact.

'Welcome back,' she said. 'You look better.'

'How is that?' I said.

'I gave you a nip of this.' She produced something out of her pocket and handed it to me. It was a small, rectangular hip flask, quite a nice piece of mid-twentieth-century design. I unscrewed the cap and sniffed the contents. It had the same wretched stench as the coffee stand in the service station.

'It's some kind of hooch. Packed with drugs,' explained Starvie. 'The gorilla was drinking it while he swung me about up here. I thought it might put some oil in your engine. That and a nap seems to have perked you up considerably.'

Hooch. That went a long way to explaining Fatty's actions. His strange last-minute heroics had probably been the drugs.

'How long have I been out?' I asked.

'Four hours. It's been quiet for a while.'

'Four hours?' I said. 'What . . . You thought it would be a good idea to let the Reals get organised?'

'I keep telling you that the fighting thing is your area, sugar. I think I've more than paid my fare already.'

She was right. I sat up and saw the bodies of F shift, piled on top of each other in one corner of the rooftop. That was a curious little habit she had.

'How's Fatty?' I asked.

'Holding his own,' said Starvie. 'They went at him a few times last night but he held them off, with a little help from little me. A few others tried to light the signal fire with grenades but I sorted them out. I tried to put that other spotlight out but I can't get an angle on it.'

She shivered, pulling the coat collar up. It felt like there was more snow on the way.

'So why did you open fire before they got started with me?'

'Fatty. Came over all chivalrous. I think it was this stuff talking.' I waved the hip flask.

'Even so, doesn't seem like the type to come to the rescue,' she said. 'Didn't think there was a type.'

'We should probably fetch him.'

'I disagree,' she replied. 'There's no reason to help him. His plan hardly went smoothly. I think it's safe to say our cover is blown.'

'No, we need him,' I said. 'At least to get us as far as York.'

I thought I'd stand but my ankle disagreed with the idea. Starvie helped me to the hatch. I stepped down the ladder, finding I could put a second of pressure on the ankle. Starvie passed two weapons down to me and followed, her bare feet tiny on the ladder rungs.

'Don't you need some boots?' I asked.

'I tried theirs on,' she said, nodding up the ladder, 'but they were all too big.'

She moved past me, her coat opening a little, revealing her body. I still didn't see what the Reals were getting so worked up about. Curious, I reached out my hand and laid my palm on her belly. She let me do it for a second before slapping the hand away.

'Hardly the time to get curious,' she said.

'Just let me see something.' I grabbed her waist. It was slim. So slim my fingers almost met around it. I lifted her, trying to judge her weight. She hit me again, in the face this time, but I didn't let go. I pulled her tight to me with my good arm.

She stopped struggling, let her arms fall to her side. Very slowly, she brought the tip of her nose towards mine, until they touched. She widened her eyes and gazed at me. Then she jolted her head back and smacked it into my nose. That got her what she wanted. I let go and she pushed me aside, marching to the door.

'Get a grip,' she said.

She made to leave with a movie star flourish, tossing the hair all over the place, but was interrupted when a hail of gunfire crashed into the building, spitting glass and splinters across the shop floor.

I hit the deck. Starvie tossed me a green canvas kit bag. 'Use these. Only thing the gorillas were good for.'

I opened it up and found six grenades nestled within. I tossed two out the window, in the direction of the mail truck, and another onto the forecourt. The truck exploded with an orange flash, hurling two Reals clear.

We crouched and listened. Somebody was screaming for help. I popped up and saw three men running to the wounded man's aid. Too bad. I picked them off and took cover again.

I pointed Starvie out the door. She didn't need to be told. She bolted while I gave some covering fire. I went after her as fast as the shattered ankle would allow.

I was ready for a prolonged burst of painful sprinting, so I was confused to find Starvie charging back in my direction. She leapt onto me and we crashed back through the door.

'Can't you make up your mind?'

'Tank!' she screamed.

The floor shook. There was a slapping noise and a whistle, and half the filling station exploded into dust.

'Well, we're no better in here,' I said, throwing Starvie off my chest. 'Get out the back and make for the main service station. I'll go out front and draw the tank's fire. Keep a look out for any other Reals and make sure no sniper gets me, all right?'

'But it's right on us!' she said.

I grabbed her by the neck and one leg and tossed her out the new hole in the back wall. I grabbed the kit bag and ran out front, only to find myself nearly kissing a 76-millimetre armour-piercing shell. It gave me a close shave on the right cheek before punching a hole next to the one its friend had made.

I saw the rifled barrel of a tank gun racing towards me, about ten feet away. I jumped clear, letting the tank crash into the filling station, tumbling the structure down around it. It stopped, struggled and roared its engine, becoming wedged in the mess.

I ran for the mail truck. A tyre was burning in the grenade fire. I took one of the grenades out the kit bag, dunked it in the molten rubber, and limped back towards the tank.

The driver was spinning the tracks furiously, trying to break free. All the tank's hatches were sealed, which was probably wise. I slapped the rubber-coated grenade on one of its port-side wheels, then climbed over the exhaust and down, just before the explosion. The tank's wheels stopped spinning, as the crew tried to understand what had happened. Then, panicked, they hit the gas hard. The tank lurched forward a few feet, inching clear of the debris, before the metal track began spinning clear of its housing, cut in two by the grenade. The tank was crippled. I crawled up onto the exhaust.

The top hatch edged open. A Real soldier peered over the rim. I clasped his head between my hands and spun his skull on his spine, pulling him up and out of the tank. Then I yanked out the pin on the last grenade.

'This is why I avoid armoured vehicles.'

I dropped the grenade in and slammed the hatch shut.

The explosion was muffled. Smoke hissed out of cracks in the armour. I dropped to the ground, then my ankle reminded me it was shattered. I looked down and saw bone.

Starvie appeared at my side, panting.

'I think I got the stragglers,' she said. 'Most of the garrison seem to have departed.'

'What about Fatty?'

'Hey, freaks!' came a shout from the SUV. 'What are you waiting for? I'm in trouble over here!'

She pointed over her shoulder.

'Hear that edge in his voice?' she said. 'He's crashing. I saw it in a lot of my clients, pre-war. "Come down" they call it. Truly pathetic. We'll have no sense out of him for hours. He'll be dangerous too. Sure you don't want to shoot him now?'

'Let's have a look at him first.'

There was quite an impressive array of dead Reals scattered on the approach to Fatty's position. He really was a good shot, even with his head full of junk.

We found him hugging the rear wheel of the van. His good eye was shut tight, his sagging one open and weeping fluid. He was scrunched up tight, foetal and useless. He was sobbing and drooling blue phlegm.

'It's all an act,' he moaned. 'Everything . . . all an act . . . Oh no, where's my face? Where's my face?'

He fumbled madly at his nose, then, finding his features intact, began sobbing again.

'Well, he doesn't look like much of a threat,' I said. 'He lives.'

Starvie shook her head, picked him up and hoisted him over her shoulder. She carried him into the service station, me following awkwardly.

The lights were still on. The coffee shop was deserted. Starvie hurried towards the bridge but I held her back.

'Wait here with the fat man,' I said, pointing to the sobbing thing draped on her shoulder.

'Why?' asked Starvie.

'If we're going to get his stuff we're going to need to get into their vault. I don't want to hang around here trying to break into it when we're not sure what we're dealing with. We need a key.'

'The Supervisor,' said Starvie.

Fatty pushed and shoved and fell free of her grasp. He clutched at her bare leg and drooled onto her feet. She gave him a sharp kick and he shrinked away.

'Why bother?' said Starvie. 'There could be more of them down there with her. If you want to let this critter live, fine, but we don't need to get his drugs for him.'

'Yes, we do,' I said.

'Why? The longer we are here the more chance reinforcements will arrive, yeah? Let's use our heads here, sweetheart.'

'There's something not right about this place,' I said. 'Something is going on here. I think that something is across the road. We're taking a look.'

'You're not just trying to honour the deal you made with this?' She stuck a boot into Fatty's rear.

'Stay with him and don't do that,' I said, staggering off towards the gents. 'I don't think kicking makes them feel better.'

I didn't give her any more chance to argue. The toilet door slammed shut behind me. I lay down flat by the excavation and peered down the tunnels. There was no movement, and no sound but the dripping condensation. I clambered down the rope, again awkward and painful, but now practised and alert enough to do it quickly. I checked the other tunnels. Satisfied that they were empty, I marched down the passage to the Supervisor's office. I found it easier going in the tunnel, using the rope on the wall to take the weight off the shattered ankle. The airlock hatch was firmly shut. I pressed my ear to it and listened.

Nothing.

I twisted the wheel and the door opened, swinging back to reveal the plastic hoarding, the white concrete floor, and the cloth boot covers neatly piled in one corner. I considered kicking in the door, but with the bad ankle decided to knock instead. Civilised, respectful, like the Supervisor would want.

'Yes?' said a voice.

I twisted the handle.

The Supervisor was sealed in her plastic box, sat behind the steel desk, watching the TV. She sat with her mouth hanging open, swinging gently in her chair. Watching the same music video.

'Big party upstairs,' I said. 'You missed it.'

She looked up at me like a rat discovered in a pantry.

'What are you doing here?' The papers on her desk fluttered. She glanced anxiously behind me.

'Please,' she said, 'close the door.'

'No,' I said. 'It's time you checked out.'

She clasped her mask to her face.

'What do you want from me?' she gasped. Her eyes were wide and filling with tears. She began to hyperventilate. Her body trembled. I could see the veins in her neck pumping her weak, agitated blood as hard as they could.

'We need you to take us to your vault over the road,' I said. 'You're going to open it for us.'

She stared at me, trying to calculate her options.

'My soldiers won't let you pass.'

'They're not really in a position to stop me,' I replied. 'Nobody's going to be saying "Who goes there?" for a while.'

She noticed something about my face.

'Your face is healing,' she said. 'You're a Ficial.'

'Spot on,' I said. 'Now, switch off that TV and come out of there.'

'I can't leave,' she said, shaking her head vigorously.

'You'd be surprised what you can do.' I raised the rifle and shot a round into the glass. The plate was well constructed. The glass didn't shatter, just cracked, leaving a small hole. The Supervisor screamed and ran to the glass, plugging the gap with her finger.

'Come out now and you'll live,' I said

'That's not living out there!'

I wasn't too interested in a debate. I shot another round into the glass, aiming at the TV behind it. This time the glass shattered, shards tumbling around our feet, the TV exploding with a satisfying boom. The Supervisor screamed and thrust her hands in her hair, freezing on the spot. I stepped through into the cube. She was taut, holding her breath. I grabbed the keys out of her desk and thrust them in her pocket.

'Come on, now,' I said. 'Lead the way.'

She didn't move. I poked the gun into her ear.

'All right! All right!'

I followed her out of the air lock. She moved along the tunnel with tentative, carefully picked footsteps, keeping away from the wall, being sure not to touch anything. When we reached the gents she stopped, contemplating the rope.

'What now?' I said.

'I'm not touching it,' she said. 'Germs.'

I could have made some more threats. Instead I threw her onto my good shoulder, hauled us up, then dumped her onto the tiles. She lay whimpering and muttering, clutching my leg. I had to drag her into the food court.

Starvie was waiting with her hands on her hips, her lips pouted, gazing out the plate glass into the night. She'd found a position where the still beaming spotlight could accentuate her features. It really was a skill. Fatty was curled up at her feet, looking up at her as if in prayer. The smell of the gunfight drifted in from the car park.

'Found her then?' said Starvie. She nodded down at Fatty. 'Mine's attached to my leg too. Do they like feet or something?'

'She's going to lead the way.'

Starvie raised an eyebrow.

'She doesn't look like she's leading anybody anywhere.'

The Supervisor crouched behind me, her mask held tight to her face, gazing in fear at Fatty.

'Keep him away from me!' she screamed. I smacked her around the head.

'Enough yelling. We're going across that bridge to your vault. You're going to let us in. Any more trouble and we'll manage without you. Do you understand me?'

She closed her eyes and whispered. I didn't know if she was praying to God or the King but it seemed to give her some strength. She stood up.

'I'm ready.'

I patted her on the back.

'Good.'

We filed over the bridge, the Supervisor leading, my hand resting on her shoulder. We walked past the abandoned gun posts, kicking through a carpet of trash. She shuddered and glanced about, as if expecting the air to bite her.

The bridge was caked with obscene graffiti. I recognised some letters but no words. In other places the cladding had been scraped and chipped away, as if something had been chewing on it. I looked south, down the motorway. The spotlight picked out scattered plastic cones, leading into the darkness like a breadcrumb trail.

Fatty walked hunched, hands in his pockets. I figured he was struggling to come to terms with his actions. He probably felt like a traitor. I would have told him that there was nothing to betray, but it wouldn't have made a difference.

Control was right, there was no reasoning with Reals. When they weren't scared, they were angry. When they weren't angry, they were guilty. Still, I thought, it must take remarkable strength to even stand up with all that going on in their heads. In that respect at least, they were built stronger than us.

At the far side the bridge opened onto splintered and cracked tarmac. An expanse of deserted car park was surrounded by dark buildings with gutted interiors. Behind the old HGV fuel stop there was a stark white cube, a hatch sealed on top. Another piece of standard barricade design. The Supervisor produced the keys and counted through them. She fitted the ninth key to the hatch lock and turned. The door popped as the lock released. Starvie heaved it open and looked inside.

'Will you let me go now?' said the Supervisor.

'Let's see what you've got down there first.'

She seemed to have run out of tears. She gazed through me for a moment, then stepped onto the ladder and began to descend. Starvie went next, then Fatty and I followed. The bunker was deeper than in the southbound services, and the tunnelling more accomplished. When we hit the bottom of the ladder there was another hatchway. Again, it was finished to a standard Ficial design. The Supervisor selected another key. I was glad to have her. It would have taken days to break through all these seals.

She stepped through and stood to one side. We were hit by a wave of heat, then a powerful smell. In the centre of the room were two tubular vats, twelve feet high, steaming and bubbling. Vapour ascended to a steel exhaust that was suspended from the ceiling. Stairs curled up around the vats to a metal gangway, and a central control desk that hung between the two. Lining the bunker walls were thousands of boxes, emblazoned with red crosses. On the wall next to the entrance was a line of old gas masks, of a vintage design.

Fatty danced an excited jig, seeming to shake off the blues of his come-down. He ran to the nearest box, tearing at the brown tape. Starvie ran up the stairs to the gangway computer.

'What have you got up there?' I asked her.

'Temperature read-out and management database,' she replied.

Fatty wasn't satisfied with the contents of his first box, and tossed it aside angrily. Foam chinks spilt out onto the floor.

'Recognise that smell?' asked Starvie. 'It's that stimulant. They're mass-producing it.'

The Supervisor fidgeted in the corner.

'What do you put in it?' I asked her.

She didn't reply.

'They've got everything down here,' said Fatty. 'Uppers, downers – it's a chemist's. Can't find the anti-inflammatories yet, though . . .'

'So that's why you're doing this?' said the Supervisor. 'You want drugs to help your condition? That's quite a deal you've struck to sell out your own kind.'

Fatty laughed.

'Oh, I've offended your principles? Where's the anti-inflammatories?'

The Supervisor folded her arms and raised her chin at him.

'I have no idea,' she said. 'Look at this place, do you think I know what's in every box?'

Fatty didn't like to be kept waiting. He roared and lunged at the boxes, tearing at them wildly, making desperate noises.

'Take it easy,' I said. 'We'll find your stuff.'

I looked up at Starvie. 'Anything on that computer?'

'Yup, inventory,' she said. 'No inflammation relief in stock. They've used the lot. Oh, well. We might as well get moving.'

Fatty watched Starvie descend the stairs, trying to process what he'd heard. He collapsed, a controlled demolition, sobbing and punching the floor. It was kind of undignified. The Supervisor pulled down her mask and grinned. She began laughing.

Fatty looked up, the tears and yellow fluid mingling on his cheeks. A smile broke out on his face. He laughed back at her, rocking backwards and forwards on his haunches, slapping his thighs.

'Look at you!' laughed the Supervisor.

'Yes, look at me!' howled Fatty.

Starvie eyed me, puzzled.

'The fumes,' I said, pointing at the ceiling. 'This whole place is filled with vapour. They're getting high again.'

The Supervisor fell onto the floor, hugging her knees, in fits of laughter now. Fatty did much the same. Starvie grabbed him by the scruff of the neck and pulled him to his feet.

'We're leaving.'

Fatty was almost uncontrollable in her arms, thrashing about wildly, giggling and hooting.

'We're leaving. Did you hear that?' he asked the Supervisor. 'Says we're leaving!'

Starvie dragged him to the hatch.

'Get up there,' she growled.

'What about Howard Hughes?' asked Fatty, jabbing his finger at the Supervisor, barely able to contain his merriment.

I pulled up the rifle and aimed it between the Supervisor's eyes. She grinned at me foolishly and leered. I pulled the trigger and she went down, her brains splattering across the wall. That was too much for Fatty. He howled and cheered and threw his arms up into the air, breaking free of Starvie.

'Yes!' he cried. 'More killing!'

Starvie grabbed him by the ear.

'Unhand me!' yelled Fatty, striking her. A scuffle broke out. I can't say I was proud of either race.

Starvie forced Fatty to the ground and held her arm on his neck, pushing down hard. Fatty's eyes swelled until it looked like the bad one might pop out. He struggled and kicked but there was no point in it.

I swung the butt of my rifle and struck Starvie on the temple. She rolled off the thrashing fat man and glared at me.

'What did you do that for?'

'We've neglected to give the room a thorough inspection. Look up.'

I pointed to the walls. She followed my finger to two large steel pipes, running parallel, emerging from the wall over the second vat.

'What do you make of that?'

'Pipes,' she said. 'So what?'

'Look where they go.'

They ran over the second vat, then turned ninety degrees, disappearing into the far wall of the chamber.

'Those aren't connected to anything in this room,' I said. 'There is something else beyond that wall.'

Fatty rolled over and groaned.

'I'll kill all of you,' he snarled.

I went over to the gas masks and, selecting one, handed it to Fatty.

'Put it on,' I said. 'Try to relax.'

Fatty pulled it over his face and stood.

'I can't breathe in this thing,' he said.

I walked behind the vats and put my head to the wall, rapping my knuckles on the surface. Then I moved a few paces along the wall and tried again. I stood back, looking it over.

'This is a temporary screen,' I said. 'It's thin. We need to break through it.'

Starvie kicked the wall and swore.

'Oh come on!' she said. 'What are going to do, excavate this whole place? It's just another skunk den. We need to go!'

'Plenty of time to have a look around,' I said.

'Hey,' said Fatty, 'do you think there might be more medical supplies in there?'

'Doubtful,' I said. 'But something's breathing in there.'

I began to kick at the wall. It only took three or four strikes for cracks to appear in the plaster. Fatty got all excited and joined in with me, hurling himself at the wall with as much momentum as he could with his flabby frame and masked face. Starvie was excused by her bare feet.

After a couple of minutes my foot went through the wall. A little more crazed digging from Fatty and the hole was wide enough to see through.

'Another chamber all right,' said Fatty. 'There's power. Lights.'

Starvie crouched and wriggled through the hole, watched closely by Fatty. When he tried to follow he became stuck. I had to kick him a few times to dislodge him.

The hidden chamber was another lab, but more sophisticated. Two metal swing chairs stood by a long desk that ran along the south wall. A bank of hard drives hummed in the far corner. A screen saver, of a snake moving in a figure of eight, played on a cluster of four monitors. Facing us was another sealed hatch. On the north side was a science station, of a kind I had seen before. A stainless steel tubular chamber, about two feet in diameter, ran the seven feet from floor to ceiling, marked with a bio-hazard sign. Next to this was a superscope, the kind of technology I hadn't seen since my First Day. Fatty, exhausted and despairing, slumped into one of the metal chairs and pulled the mask off his face, his breathing problems returning.

'More science stuff,' he said. 'Well, ring the fucking bells.'

I examined the superscope, but there was nothing on the slide.

Starvie sat at the computer terminal and began to type. A message flashed on the screen asking for a password.

'It's all locked up,' said Starvie, 'I can't get in.'

I pointed at the chamber.

'Engineering equipment,' I said.

'Brilliant,' said Fatty. 'Everything a bloke could want except a cure.' He dabbed at his eye and put his head in his hands, emitting a long, low groan. Then, seeming to appreciate the sound, he tried another.

'Strange,' I said. 'Not like Reals to mess with Engineering these days is it?'

'Well,' said Starvie, slapping her thighs, 'there's nothing here for the fat man and we've created quite a noise what with that pitched battle. I say we go back to the car.'

'So you can get your camera? Write up the story of your amazing capture and escape?'

'Believe it or not I'm not too keen to document this episode,' she said. 'No matter how many Reals we've culled. All we can do is take the hard drive to London and examine it. Then, maybe, there'll be news to report. Right now the only story is about a taxi driver taking one hell of a bloody detour.'

'Well, maybe there's something to report on,' said Fatty. He had spotted a pack of cigarettes lying on the floor under the Engineering gear. He fell onto his knees and crawled over to pick them up. He sat and opened the packet.

'Hey,' he said, 'what's this?'

Starvie grabbed the pack off him and looked inside.

'Oh, no.'

I walked over to see what the problem was. She showed me the pack. There were no cigarettes inside, just a small digital display, reading:

30
Then
29
Then
28

'Let's get out of here,' said Fatty, and ran for the hole we'd kicked in.

'No, wait,' said Starvie, 'those vats are flammable. The whole thing will come down. Try the other hatch!'

I brought out the Supervisor's keys, fiddling with them. There were rather a lot to try. Fatty watched me try one without success, then another.

'Hurry!' he shouted.

'That doesn't help.'

For a few seconds they were very quiet, until, in the corner of my eye, I saw a look you might call revelation come over Fatty's face.

'Orange!' he said. 'Try the orange!'

Normally, with their limited reasoning power, I wouldn't have paid attention to a Real suggestion, but the mental count I had in my head, which now read:

12

11

10

made his contribution compelling. I found the key with the orange fob and turned it in the lock. The hatch hissed open. Without bothering to brag, Fatty pushed me aside and dived through the door into another tunnel.

Starvie struggled with the hard drive, trying to disconnect it. I picked her up and hurled her as far as I could down the passage, then pulled the hatch shut after me, just as the explosion hit.

I didn't seal the hatch in time. The initial blast smacked the door back, nearly crushing me behind it, but it still took most of the force. I was more worried about the vats. I got to my feet, slammed the hatch shut and turned the key, just before the secondary explosion sent a seismic pulse rumbling around us. Chunks of the tunnel began to crumble and fall. I could feel it on my face. I must have been knocked onto my back again.

'This thing's gonna cave!' Fatty yelped. His footsteps disappeared at speed.

I got up and followed him. The ground in the tunnel was concrete and smooth, running up a gentle, level slope, another guide rope strung at waist height along the wall.

It opened on the motorway, the northbound side. The road was bathed in a dim orange light from the fire behind us. I turned and saw that the entire northbound structure had crumbled in on itself.

Fatty put his hand on his knees and doubled over, coughing out mud and blue spit.

'Why did you pick orange?' I asked him.

'It just came to me,' he said. 'Colour of the mush.'

'*That* was your reasoning?'

'It worked, didn't it?' He threw his head back, trying to suck air into reluctant lungs.

The rumble died away. Starvie walked behind Fatty and put a hand over his mouth and nose.

'Leave him alone,' I said.

'Quiet.' She restrained the flailing fat man. 'Listen.'

'What?'

She looked up. 'Wheels.'

She was right. An irregular squealing was coming from the other side of the motorway. It was the slip road.

'There,' said Starvie, pointing.

'Him?'

Fatty slapped Starvie's hand away from his mouth and stood up next to us.

'What are we looking at?' he whispered.

'It's the guy from the coffee shop.'

Fatty snorted in disbelief, but as his eyes adjusted to the darkness he saw him too. Wheelchair guy was on the slip road, dragging himself up by the crash barrier.

Starvie led us across in single file, following the tracks of the wheels in the snow, which snaked through a gap in the crash barrier and up towards the ramp. Fatty stumbled in the ash, bumped into things and cursed under his breath, but wheelchair guy didn't hear us. I signalled the fat man to stay put and followed Starvie up the slip road.

Wheelchair guy was determined to get up there. He took one very slow and deliberate tug at a time, moving only about a foot with each pull.

I put my arm around his neck. He screamed, an awful piercing shriek that would alert any lingering Reals. Starvie watched for signs of movement, but none came.

'Thanks for the little present you left back there,' I said. 'We're all very touched.'

The scream seemed to have exorcised something, because he was silent now. He had a look of being ready for judgement. I wasn't about to disappoint him. I drew back my fist, ready to strike, but Starvie grabbed it and shook her head.

'Wait,' she said.

She drew in close to the guy, her nose nearly brushing his. She put her hand on the blistered side of his face and turned his eyes towards hers.

'What is your name?' she said to him.

'Who cares what his name is?' I asked.

'Tell me your name,' she said again.

'You know my name,' he replied.

Starvie looked up at me. A smile played on her lips.

'Did you meet this guy earlier today?' she asked me.

'Sure.'

'Didn't you recognise him?'

'What's to recognise?'

Starvie looked down at the shivering wretch in the wheelchair.

'Tell him,' she said firmly. 'Tell him your name.'

'Tell "it" your name, that should be,' said the guy in the wheelchair. He sighed and lowered his chin to his chest. 'My name is Leo Pander.'

'*Doctor* Leo Pander,' corrected Starvie. She looked up at me, flashing her white teeth in a showbiz beam.

'Now *this* is a story.'

There are a few hundred of us here. We're all Construction models. I see Power Eights through Tens, but no lower. I exchange curt nods with the other Nines and find a seat.

We have been shepherded into the old cinema on Coldharbour Lane. It's the ideal place for our models to congregate: a remarkably intact example of an Edwardian cinema that also happens to sit atop the main Brixton Bunker.

The bunker is supposed to be a marvel of engineering prowess, the last truly great construction project completed by man. I'm not so sure. I have studied the project, examined blueprints of the helmet shape that will, it's said, withstand any flood or any blast. I would like to see inside before calling it invulnerable. You can never be sure otherwise. You need to run your hands over the surfaces to know if the thing will hold.

Still, no point thinking about it. Control will ask if it wants us to visit. Strange, to have that much power so close. I feel as if I should hear it thinking.

Instead it is peaceful and still in the auditorium. I sit in a worn blue chair and gaze up at the proscenium arch, then along the wall at the pilasters, plaster panels and swags.

Then a soldier model appears in front of the screen ahead. He introduces himself as Regmiron.

There is no illness.

That's the first thing he tells us. He gives us a moment to take it in.

This means there are no tests, no recovery sheds and no waste pits to contend with. He says that we're here to receive a new Control directive. He spells it out for us and we listen.

When he is done he asks for questions. A hand is raised over to my right. He nods at it.

125

'Why have we had to come down here to learn this? Why didn't Control just signal us?'

'The emergency government listens in on those signals.'

That revelation causes a bit of chatter.

'Look, we're not even sure they understand our exchanges with Control, but we have to be sure of secrecy.'

Someone else calls out.

'So what does this mean for the super-city project?'

'It's off, mate. Naturally there will be no need to house such numbers under the new directive.'

Another hand. Another nod.

'But that's the same for everything isn't it? There'll be no point in building anything if you're just going to eliminate the lot of them.'

'There'll be plenty for work for you all,' replies the soldier. 'You will be responsible for redesigning the entire island. Remember, with the fall in population there will be entire population centres left empty. You will have to decide which to abandon to the elements and which few to reconstruct and preserve.'

I put up my hand. Regmiron sees me and nods.

'Yes?'

'What about the Hope Tower?'

Before I've even finished the word 'Tower' the other models are all expressing forthright opinions on the project. Regmiron grins.

'I think you've got your answer,' he says. 'Doesn't look like it will make the list of keepers, does it?'

'I have a question,' says another.

'Yes,' replies Regmiron.

'This one is more for you.'

'Go on.'

'Do you really expect the entire populace to just line up and jump into the back of your trucks?'

'I don't expect anything. Control predicts that the threat of nuclear attack will make all Reals cooperate, provided they are told they will be safe.'

'Have you seen what's going on out there? They don't look too cooperative.'

There are murmurs of agreement, which echo in the auditorium. We all saw the same thing on the way in. Regmiron raises his hands.

'This is just the first phase. The threat of nuclear attack has not been made yet. When it is, they'll behave.'

'I don't think that's really true,' says another voice. 'There's always one that doesn't like being told what to do.'

'Look,' says the soldier. 'Any that don't report will be culled on the surface. We have their bar codes and can track them via satellite with ease. Control has this worked out. All you need to do is return to your places of work and help out when the time comes.'

I raise my hand again.

'What?'

'This plan seems to rest on the nuclear attack thing being an empty threat. Thing is, I've seen the God nuts on TV. I can tell you they mean it. They're crazy enough to actually do it.'

'That's a valid point,' says Regmiron. 'But don't worry. Control has predicted the timetable of those guys. That's why we're starting the cull so soon. We sort our own lot, then deal with the God freaks over the sea.'

Regmiron take a few more questions, then announces he has to leave to help organise the culling parties.

That leaves us in the auditorium, debating what to keep and what to ditch in Control's new, Real-free world. No more people. How long it will take to clean up their mess?

GOD

Pander slumped in the rusting wheelchair.

I had questions. Big questions. What was he doing out there in the middle of nowhere? What was he up to in that lab? And why was he moonlighting behind the counter in that coffee shop?

Only the thought of the Landy prevented me from beating some answers out of him right there. I had to recover the cab. I pushed Pander up the ramp and into the car park, then dropped him out of the wheelchair onto the tarmac.

'Watch him,' I said to Starvie.

I took Fatty to look for his cart. We walked across the battlefield, towards the remains of the filling station. The tank was still wedged in the ruins, brewing up. They'd stashed Fatty's trailer somewhere behind after our arrival. I doubted there was much left, but thought it worth a look. Besides, we needed to talk.

When we were out of sight I grabbed Fatty by the arm, wrenched it behind his back, and pinned him on the tank's hot armour.

'What the hell are you doing?' he cried out.

'Quiet down,' I said. 'I just want to review the day's events.'

'You don't need to break my arm for that, you artificial artifuck.'

His clothes were steaming on the metal, letting off a pungent stink.

'Did you know he was here?'

Fatty winced.

'Who?'

'Who do you think?'

'Pander? Of course not. How the hell could I know?'

I twisted the arm a little higher. Fatty swore powerfully, but I was well enough repaired to keep him under control. His beard began to singe and smoke.

'You're crazy! You're all absolutely fucking mad!'

'No, just a little suspicious. You led us to his hiding place. You found the bomb in a cigarette packet. Then you picked the right key to effect a daredevil escape.'

'You think I planned this?'

'I don't know what to think,' I said. 'Enlighten me.'

'Like I said, I came here for the drugs. And they weren't there, okay? That means I'm going to die. Happy?'

I thought about it for a moment, and let him go. He dropped to the ground, rubbing at his arm and staring into the tarmac.

'You may as well just kill me now. That's what you're designed to do, isn't it?'

'No. Why doesn't anybody get that?'

I stepped out from behind the tank and looked in the direction of Starvie and Pander. They were both very still. I nudged Fatty with my boot.

'You're coming with us. I need you to navigate us through to York.'

Fatty snarled.

'I'm not feeling too motivated to help you out.'

I stepped over him.

'You want some help?'

He must have taken that as a threat, because he shot out his foot and kicked me in my damaged ankle. I hit the ground. Fatty leapt onto my chest and tried to jam the barrel of a pistol into my right nostril.

'Guess what I do have the motivation for?' he said, his finger on the trigger.

'I wasn't trying to scare you,' I said. 'I was just going to point out that this trip might not have been a complete waste of time.'

'Oh, yeah?' He laughed. I nodded over at the service station.

'You could take the water. That underground purification plant will produce nice, fresh stuff if Ficials built it. Certainly better than whatever radioactive mud you had in the kegs Starvie shot.'

'Water,' said Fatty, licking his parched lips. With all the highs, lows and shooting he'd forgotten how thirsty he was. Hungry too probably. I bent my nose away from the gun.

'Look, the deal still stands. Get us to York and I'll let you go on your way. You can carry on with the plan you left your village with. Trade the water for drugs somewhere else. Plenty of other places that must have the stuff you need, aren't there?'

He considered it, but was having trouble dismissing the idea of putting a bullet through my face. He'd probably been dreaming about it the whole journey. There was always the chance he thought I was lying. Reals could never really accept that we didn't do that.

'Okay,' he said. 'Show me.'

'Sure,' I said. I snatched the gun out of his hand and tossed him off my chest. The guy had real reflexes all right. I jammed the gun in his ear.

'No more tantrums, okay?'

He nodded vigorously.

I helped him onto his feet, then noticed something on the wall. It was a white pack with a red cross on it. A medical kit. Useful for the disintegrating Real body. 'Here,' I said, pressing it into Fatty's hands. 'Bonus payment.'

We resumed our search for the cart. We found it in one piece, covered in a tarpaulin near the tree line. The cargo was all gone.

'Big surprise,' he said.

We dragged it to the service station and left it by the entrance. We walked inside, past the coffee shop, into the gents and down into the tunnel, following it to the padlocked door. Without the Supervisor's keys I had to shoot it off. Fatty caught a splinter in his cheek and bellowed in outrage.

'What is wrong with you?'

As I suspected, the water treatment plant was a proper piece of kit, built for advanced membrane filtering. Banks of ultra-filtrating tubing curved over us, ten feet tall and fifty feet long, humming in cool, blue light. Just the sight of the machinery seemed to refresh Fatty.

A stack of fat plastic bottles covered one wall, next to a simple tap. Fatty knelt down and turned it, pressing his hideous mouth to the jet of water. Overcome with need, he guzzled as much as he could force down his throat. He stripped off his shorts and washed his bleeding chest, which was not something I needed to see. I let him go at it for a while, taking the time to examine the apparatus, the sand filters and ozone treatment tower. It was advanced stuff, but very new, newer than the tunnels and bunkers. Pander had been busy.

When Fatty was finished drenching himself he performed a small victory dance, apparently having forgotten all about death. We started filling up the bottles and making trips up to the cart. When there was no more room I went back down and shot a round into the treatment computer.

'Why did you do that?' asked Fatty.

'Scorched earth.'

We pulled the cart over to Starvie. Pander was crumpled at her feet, clutching his rag. I picked him up and dumped him in the cart among the water bottles.

'Careful, you fool!' snapped Fatty.

Starvie nodded at him.

'So you didn't cull him,' she said. 'What is he, our mascot?'

'We made a deal,' I said.

I hopped in the cart next to Pander to be sure he didn't try anything impulsive. Fatty and Starvie took the rope and we set off down to the motorway, travelling north again. I lay down, Pander shivering and useless next to me.

All I could do the whole way up the road was think about the Landy. My Engineering was supposed to shield me from entertaining useless and paranoid notions, but I couldn't stop picturing the car in various states of disrepair. First I imagined it burned out, an empty black skeleton. Then I saw it stripped of its tyres and fittings, humiliated and tyre-less on bricks.

We reached the B road, abandoning the cart to be picked up later. Fatty objected that it was madness to leave the merchandise there alone and suggested he stay to guard his cargo. A swift kick in the rear dissuaded him. I took Pander on my back and put a hand on Starvie for support. We trudged up the mud bank and moved through the dead wood.

When I thought we were close, I dropped Pander and ran to reach the clearing. I lumbered as fast as I could, branches thrashing at my face, and wondered what the point in all this was. Running, after all, wouldn't make it any more likely that the Landy was still there. It wouldn't repair any damage or recondition the engine.

Still, I ran. I ran until, tripping through thorns and yellow-white mud, I found it. The Landy was sitting there, undiscovered and faithful. I could have sworn it had a smile on its face.

I eagerly began inspecting it, pushing my thumb into the tyres, running my hands over the bodywork in the darkness, feeling for damage. I hardly noticed Starvie and Fatty catching up to me, dragging Pander through the trees like unwieldy furniture.

When I was satisfied the Landy was in good condition, we raised Pander into the flatbed. I expected Fatty to object to riding in there with him, but he jumped in happily enough. He nestled between the tent kit and fuel kegs and immediately fell into a deep, needy sleep.

Starvie searched the mud with a torch and located the empty battery. She dug in the sludge with her hands until she found her cases, wiping them off with the hem of her coat. Then she pulled some clothes out of her kit bag and dressed. She took for ever.

I turned the key and heard the diesel kick into action. I ran my hands over the wheel and checked all the compartments carefully. When I was sure everything was well, my foot hit the gas, I released the handbrake and slowly backed us out of the clearing.

Starvie offered to repair my splint so I could drive easier, but I declined. I only really needed one foot, and I wanted to get moving. We sped across the field, down onto the slip road, and burned along until we found the cart. I jumped out and hitched it up, taking the time to check on the passengers in the flatbed. Fatty slept soundly. Pander didn't register my presence. Maybe that brain was cooking something up.

We joined the motorway and picked through the wrecks. As we reached the cleared section, I rolled the windows down, stamped on the gas and shot up the slip road.

We rolled across the car park, keeping our eyes out for stragglers on the rooftops or in the tree line. Nothing human stirred. The only movement was a ragged bird, with bent, flightless wings. It was pecking at a charred corpse on the forecourt.

'Good morning, Mister Magpie,' said Fatty.

A fair few of the garrison must have got away. It couldn't be too long before another signal fire was burning a warning into the night. We trundled down the other slip road and rejoined the motorway. The tarmac was clear as far as the headlights shone. A sign on the roadside read: 'Diversion ends'.

I hit the gas and took the Landy all the way up to seventy. I'd never normally hit that kind of speed in thick ash, but I'd been on foot too long and needed to sense that we were really moving. Starvie folded her arms around the green cases, crossed her legs and fell asleep. I noticed her feet were shredded and bleeding from the long walk. I picked a shard of plastic out the right heel. She didn't wake up, so I pulled a few more out while I drove. It passed the time.

Eventually I took us off the motorway, selecting a back road that I hadn't used before. I drove deep into the lifeless countryside, getting as far away from congregating Reals as possible.

A tall brick wall appeared, running along the road, marking the boundary of a country estate. After a mile the headlights picked out a pair of stone columns, topped with carved rampant stags. I pulled the car to a halt, waking Starvie with a jolt. She rubbed her eyes and blinked.

'Are we there yet?'

'We're somewhere,' I replied. 'Looks good for a pit-stop. We need to refuel.'

I drove through the gate, up a gravel drive. A huge three-storey building, one of those stately, sandstone monuments to money, loomed out of the darkness. One wing was badly charred, burned out and fallen in on itself. The other was mostly intact, caked with three feet of grey ash. Underneath all that I thought it might be the work of Wetherall or Cassels, but I wasn't sure. All I could tell was that it was big enough to hide a lot of Reals. Even this far out you couldn't be sure what might be lurking within. I cut the engine and rolled the last fifty metres in the darkness.

Starvie made to get out, but I put my arm across her and told her to stay put. We listened to the wind for a minute, until Fatty appeared, shining a torch in my eyes. I rolled down the window.

'What are you doing?' he asked, his breath a billowing cloud. 'Taking in the scenery? It's freezing out here. Let's get in.'

'How's the doctor?' asked Starvie.

Fatty shrugged.

'I haven't slit his throat if that's what's troubling you.'

We watched him bound up the stairs to the house, running to the main door, a formidable entrance framed by a miniature Greek hexastyle portico. Fatty wasn't happy to find the door firmly locked. He began to throw himself at it, about as stealthy as a Saturn rocket. He broke it open on the fifth go.

'Why isn't the fat man tied up?' asked Starvie. It was a fair question. I had been so concerned with Pander I hadn't thought. I took a rifle off the weapons rack, handed a pistol to Starvie, and jumped out of the cab.

Fatty was standing in an entrance hall, shining his torch up a grand staircase, over hunting paintings and a great chandelier.

'Swanky,' he said.

We fanned out and checked the floors, our footsteps echoing. I wandered around the first floor, which once must have been very grand. It was deserted now, but Reals had passed through recently. Graffiti was sprayed over the wood panelling and ancient portraits. Crazed, stumbling footprints were printed in dried yellow mud on the carpets. The bedrooms were wrecked, smeared by sex and excrement. Fittings and furniture had been smashed, tossed into piles and burned. I wondered if the owner had survived the war, only to be visited by the authors of this chaos.

Starvie and Fatty found nothing much of interest. The kitchen had been looted of every last morsel, but they had found a stack of fat candles and a couple of storm lanterns. There were three bodies on the second floor, burned up.

'Not exactly the Hilton,' observed Fatty. 'Mind you, there's still plenty of stuff to burn. Let's get toasty, eh?'

He went out to the Landy and retrieved the crowbar from the flatbed. Then he set about ripping up floorboards, piling pieces in the dining-room fireplace. I thought the fire could be a bad idea – some real scout might smell the smoke – but as Fatty had pointed out we had covered quite some distance. It would take them days to catch up to us by bike.

We brought Pander inside and let him sleep by Fatty's fire. Then I took four of Fatty's water bottles out of the trailer and filled a tub in the bathroom upstairs.

Fatty said this was a horrible waste, until Starvie announced that she would take the first dip. Suddenly he became businesslike.

'Fair enough,' he said. 'I'm not an unreasonable man. I'm open to trade. It seems to me that if I give the water, you should give something in return.'

'Like what?' asked Starvie.

'Well, I think I should get to watch you in the bath.'

I wondered if he was serious. His twitching indicated that he was.

'I won't touch,' he said. 'I promise. I'll just pull up a chair and watch. That's fair, isn't it?'

'You want me to put that leash back on you?'

'Oh come on!' he said. 'That's what you're designed for, isn't it? You love being looked at. Make a dying man happy.'

'You're not a dying man, you're a dying skunk,' she said. 'There's a difference.'

Fatty grumbled under his breath. Something about the thought of Starvie and water really did something for him.

Starvie took a towel out of her pack and wandered upstairs, green case in each hand. Fatty shuffled and cursed.

'What about your wife?' I asked.

'Shut your face.'

I went up to take the next bath. Starvie had left a film of black scum on the water, so I just dabbed at myself with the last drops in the bottles, wiping at my newly formed skin. Downstairs I found Starvie curled up on the floor, dressed in blue jeans and white T-shirt, basking in the flames next to Pander. She was fast asleep.

Fatty leaned on the wall by the fire, watching her.

'Look at her,' he said. 'A quick dip in a cold puddle and she looks like a goddess.'

'How do I look?' I asked.

'Crisp,' he replied. 'Like you were left on the grill too long. Still, at least you're getting better. Must be nice.'

It was certainly better than being him. Fatty had washed, but he was still tinged blue and covered by boils and welts that would never heal. At least the medical kit was doing something for him.

He had swept his tufts of hair back over his face, bandaged

his angry scalp, cleaned the gaping flesh around his bad eye and dressed his bloated, boil-ridden chest.

We shared a few tins of custard I had in the pack, which excited Fatty no end. He ate it in a flash, then related a rambling story about eating custard as a child. He lay on his side and watched Starvie until his eyes closed too. Pretty soon his irregular, blocked-plumbing snoring began.

I stared at Pander and wondered. Reals spent a lot of time thinking about their creator, arguing over who he was and what he wanted from them. It seemed to frustrate them not to know all the answers.

Now I was sleeping in the same room as my creator. I could shake his hand and tell him where I thought he'd gone wrong.

As it was, I wasn't too interested. He was a tired, broken thing. I couldn't see what all the fuss was about.

The boss has picked me up. We are on the way back. The streets are a lot clearer, almost quiet. All those people are gone. An efficient operation has been carried out. Once or twice someone runs out of the shadows and screams at us to stop and pick them up, but the boss steps on the gas, not wanting to get involved.

The next stage begins as we cross back over the floodplain. The radio warns that Control predicts a nuclear attack. It says that the population centres are being cleared and asks all those who have not been picked up to report to their local police station. From there they will be led to safety in the network of underground shelters that Control has been busy building. It asks Truth League members to come in too. It assures them that they will be safe.

The boss switches the radio off.

'Rubbish,' he says.

'Boss, you are going to report, aren't you?'

'Course I'm not going to report. Nuclear attack? What a joke. As if those idiots over there even have a rocket that works these days.'

'The report didn't say who was going to launch the attack, boss. It could be anyone.'

'Rubbish. This country's the last hope for the world. I've seen film of the mainland and it's not pretty. Completely dead inside a decade they reckon. Britain's one of the last places anyone on the planet can live. Who'd want to attack us?'

We drive along in silence for a minute. The boss lights a cigar and stares at the road, trying not to think about his own question. He pulls a music disc out and puts it on, hoping it will block out his thoughts. It's more of that ancient stuff, one man and a guitar.

The boss shakes his head and sighs deeply.

'You can bet I'm staying up, forty-two,' he says. 'We need to turn this situation to our advantage. I'll have my pitch for the work on the next floors on Tower's management desk tomorrow. I'll be the only one who does, 'cos the big companies will send all their people to the bunkers. This could be a big break for me. Only an independent outfit can take advantage of this situation. As long as we all stay calm we'll be okay.'

He grips the wheel a little tighter and rearranges himself in his seat.

'Anyway, you have to love these empty roads.'

I agree with that. I have never seen a motorway this clear. The sun rolls over the fields and the houses. The sky is chalky blue. The music changes the world as we move through it, rearranging the landscape and slowing down time.

THE EXCLUSIVE

I left the sleepers and went to work on the car for a while. My wounds were almost healed. The shattered ankle had reformed into something resembling a joint. The acid burns had sealed. I could breathe without making the whistling noise. That was good. I had been beginning to annoy myself. I was there for an hour, tweaking the engine to coax out what little more I could.

I went back inside. Starvie lay with her head resting on one green case, an arm curled around the other. Fatty and the good doctor were gone.

I walked out of the dining room into the hall. There was a crack of light under the opposite door. I could hear Pander speaking. I stepped closer and listened.

'. . . to say I intended all this? That I'm an evil man? Well, it's not true. I'm sure it would make it easier for you, but it's not true.'

I heard Fatty snort and spit.

'You ruined my idea of the future, do you know that? When I was a lad the future was going to be flying cars and robots. You ruined that.'

I could hear Fatty pacing about. I wondered why he'd removed the doctor to the other room. He might just want a private chat with Pander, Real to Real. On the other hand, he might be planning to kill him.

I let them talk. I figured Pander might let something slip which he would never say to a Ficial. Besides, I still hadn't decided what to do with him. I didn't want another passenger to worry about, but I knew he was too important to ditch.

Pander sighed.

'I am so bored of this. I've said the same thing to a thousand torturers who blamed me for wrecking their plans.'

'Said what?' snapped Fatty.

'That the war, the cull ... all of it would have happened without my work. Our kind is incapable of thinking rationally, or cooperating to solve problems. We were always going to destroy each other, with or without my creation.'

Fatty didn't like that.

'At least there'd be no war now. At least the Ficials wouldn't be out there trying to finish us off.'

'Yes, of course,' said Pander. 'The apocalypse would have been so much more pleasant without them.'

Fatty snarled. He sounded furious, so I thought I would intervene. I pushed open the door.

Two lanterns flickered in a corner, barely illuminating the room. Pander was hunched against a wall, his legs splayed out, that rag clutched to his chest. Fatty loomed over him, clenching fists. Wind and ash blew in through the tall, smashed windows.

'Don't like you two running off like that,' I said. 'The tour party should stay together at all times.'

Fatty folded his arms.

'We were just talking. Nothing to worry about.'

'What's the topic?'

'He was asking about your race,' said Pander. 'He wants to know why I created your kind. Seems to think I ruined his life.'

'He may have a point.'

Fatty glared at me. His chat with Pander had frustrated him, I could tell. Seeing me almost fully repaired probably didn't help his mood. He was about as fond of the creation as he was of the creator. He directed some blue spittle at my feet.

'That's not all. I asked him why you turned on us in the first place.'

Pander smiled and pointed his rag at me.

'I suggested that he would do better to ask you that.'

Fatty looked at me expectantly. I couldn't believe he didn't know.

'Control told us you had to go.'

Fatty shook his head.

'That's your answer? You were following orders?'

'No . . . We discussed it.'

'Oh! You discussed it, did you?' yelled Fatty, throwing up his arms in outrage. 'Over a cup of tea and a biscuit?'

'Don't you comprehend by now that they don't feel guilt or pity?' said Pander. 'Control was built as an incorruptible arbiter, a trustworthy leader . . .'

'The thing is homicidal!'

'No, it is rational. It looked at the situation, concluded that it wasn't possible to save both our race and the planet, and presented its case to the Engineered race. They were convinced by its logic and started the cull.'

Fatty paced around.

'Fine,' he said. 'So we got what we deserved, is that it?'

'I'm not a philosopher,' said Pander.

'Well, you should be, shouldn't you?' screamed Fatty in outrage. He grabbed the old man's shirt and began shaking him violently. 'If I destroyed the world I'd ask myself some pretty searching questions.'

Somebody theatrically cleared her throat.

'I'll ask the questions, thank you.'

I turned to see Starvie, dressed in a white shirt, underwear, and knee-length boots. She had one hand resting on her hip, a cigarette burning in the other, and her camera on a strap around her neck. Her hair was sculpted into a blond cone, like a Trullo hut. Dashes of pastel colours had been applied to her lips and around the eyes. Fatty released his grip on Pander, preferring to gape at the vision in the doorway.

Starvie smiled.

'Are you two trying to steal my exclusive?'

'They're discussing Control,' I said. 'It's actually quite interesting.'

Starvie smacked her lips and glanced at Pander.

'I can think of a hotter topic.'

She lifted her camera off her belly, carefully jabbed at a few buttons, and began taking pictures of the crippled doctor with a high-power flash. Fatty and I shielded our eyes. Pander stared into the light as if hoping it would swallow him. Starvie examined the results on the camera screen.

'You're a pleasure model,' said Pander. He turned to Fatty. 'Now this is an example where I will grant you it all went wrong. When they sold my technology to private industry the first thing they did was produce these things. Utterly worthless, every one.'

He narrowed his eyes at me, tracing the edges of his rag with his yellow fingers.

'Why are you transporting this thing about? Why don't you kill it? It serves no useful purpose.'

'Sticks and stones,' said Starvie. She lowered her camera but kept it pointed at the good doctor. 'Let me ask you something, old man. Why did you blow up your laboratory?'

Pander scowled but said nothing.

'We found Engineering equipment. What were you doing in there?'

'I was a prisoner,' he replied. Starvie shook her head.

'Prisoners don't get chemistry sets to play with. What were you doing in there?'

Pander said nothing. I smacked him around the head, which loosened his tongue.

'The King sent me there.'

Fatty stopped staring at Starvie's legs for a moment.

'You're working for that psycho? Bullshit. He'd butcher you on one of his TV shows the first chance he got.'

'He's been on Real TV already,' I said. Pander squirmed. 'It's one of the Edinburgh tribe's favourite shows, your confession. Most of us assumed you were killed after doing it.'

Pander rubbed his head.

'On the contrary. The King rescued me. After the war I was unfortunate enough to be recognised by a group of survivors seeking retribution. They were the ones who filmed that confession. They were the ones who put me in my chair. They also planned to film my crucifixion, I believe, until the King's people found me and took me back to Newcastle.'

'Why would the King want you alive?' asked Fatty.

'Because the doctor is smart,' said Starvie. 'Not many Reals are.'

'The pleasure model is correct,' said Pander. 'The King wanted me to educate him about your race. He wanted to find a weakness.

'He's promised victory against your kind, you see. If he can't find a way of breaching your barricades soon, he'll lose the support of the population. Which, for the moment, remains fanatical.'

Starvie dropped her cigarette and stepped on it with her boot heel.

'So he built you that fancy lab to continue your work.'

Pander looked up at her.

'Exactly.'

'Continue your work?' said Fatty. 'You don't mean make more of these freaks?'

'Don't be ridiculous,' said Pander. 'He wouldn't have considered that.'

'No,' said Starvie. 'Your comrades at the service station wouldn't have stood for it either, would they? They can't have known who you were, or they'd have auctioned you to the gorillas too.'

'Correct,' said Pander, pointing at his deformed face. 'Hence the disguise which the King was good enough to provide me with.'

Fatty glanced at me.

'So what the hell were you doing down there?'

Pander blew his nose into his rag, then opened it up and looked at what he'd emitted. He folded the rag shut and clasped it to his chest.

'I was creating a weapon.'

Starvie tried to conceal her excitement. She stepped closer, still pointing her camera right at him.

'Did you complete this weapon?'

'Yes,' said Pander. 'Yes, I did.'

He raised his chin and looked right at me.

'How does this weapon work?' asked Starvie.

'Water,' said Pander. 'Your enhanced immune systems have one inherent weakness, you see.'

He paused for effect. I smacked him around the head again and suggested he get to the point.

'Fine, fine,' he said, spluttering. 'Where do I begin? Well, as you are aware, your artificial nano cells take over the functions of your immune system for you. They also give you the capability to recover from extreme trauma, and of course to endure the nuclear winter we are experiencing. In effect they make you very nearly indestructible.

'Now the only problem with this design is that your own immune systems are suppressed. If they were not they would attack the nano cells. This means that if it were possible to somehow deactivate or destroy your nano systems, your bodies would become less able to fight infections even than your fat friend's here. In our present climate death would be swift and terrible.'

'And you have found a way of doing this?' said Starvie.

'Yes. I have designed a new cell that, when introduced into the Ficial body, attacks the nano system. The cell is, by the way, perfectly safe if contracted by a real person.'

Starvie chewed on her lip, the camera still pointed right at the old man.

'How were you going to deliver this weapon?'

'As I said, water,' said Pander. His speech was strikingly calm, almost Ficial in its delivery. 'In your barricades you distribute your water through an extremely fair and universal rationing scheme. That is the problem, your own efficiency. All it will take is for a small sample of these weaponised cells to be introduced to a barricade's water supply and within a day, before the population can react, the infection will be complete and the population eliminated.'

Fatty laughed.

'So, now you're going to be responsible for a second genocide, is that right? The destroyer of two worlds?'

'I suppose so,' said Pander.

'I don't buy it,' said Fatty. 'And even if it is true, why help the freaks out by telling them about it? Even with your prodigal son slapping you silly?'

'I have no allegiance to either side,' replied Pander.

'Then why did you build another weapon of mass destruction?'

Pander thought about that for a second.

'It was something to do.'

I had to hold Fatty back after that reply. He finally settled, but only when Starvie put her hand on him. One touch and he looked like he'd curl up and purr at her feet.

Starvie frowned. She didn't look quite so pleased with her scoop.

'Where is this weapon now?' she asked. 'Did it get burned up with your lab?'

'The King's people came and picked it up a few days before

you arrived,' said Pander. 'They are going to test it. I believe their destination was York barricade. I judged it to be the target with the highest probability of success.'

He held his rag up to this chin and began dabbing at his face with it, his eyes darting about.

'Are you going to kill me now?' he asked. He looked like he would have appreciated it.

'What do you think of his story?' Starvie asked me.

'I'm not sure. Even if it's true, Control must be able to sort out a response.'

'You're probably right,' said Pander. 'I honestly believe that Control would be able to fight any nano-technical attack I create. The problem is, I don't believe Control is around to fight.'

'What are you talking about?'

'It's quite simple,' said Pander. 'I believe Control is dead.'

I was about to tell him what I thought about that, but I stopped when I saw Fatty. He was by the shattered window, listening to something.

I heard it too. It was a familiar sound, a squeaking noise like rusted chains in a belt drive.

Fatty was about to speak, but then there was another noise. A shrieking, ripping spit. Fatty said it first.

'Rocket!'

I look at my watch. Zero hour has come and gone. They're probably tracking us right now. We have been low on fuel for some time but every service station we approach is closed. All the motorway information boards are blank. There are no other cars. The boss does not like the idea of being the only man left in the world, on an empty motorway at night. He has that real urge to get home, as if he'll be safe there.

He chews on a cigar and looks frantic. He's been ranting about traffic for all the years I've known him but after four hours driving along the deserted road he's on the brink of panic. He's missing the gridlock already. Typical Real.

Suddenly he yelps. He's spotted a service station with its lights still on. We pull over and approach.

We drive onto the forecourt and park by the diesel. A figure appears out of the garage, dressed in overalls. It waves and points to the sign above the fuel:

We are happy to fill your car for you.

'Ha!' says the boss, clapping his hands together. 'Forty-two, I'm buying you some food. We'll have a nice dinner and then go home.'

He reaches into his pocket and produces his wallet. The figure in the overalls approaches us, passes by on the driver's side, wearing sunglasses.

The figure pulls the hose free and begins filling up. I sit and watch the pump counters tick over the litres and pounds. The price of fuel means nothing to anybody but the boss now. He is counting out money, pushing coins over the bar code on his palm.

The figure in the overalls appears at the window and knocks on the glass. The boss rolls it down.

'You okay, mate?' asks the boss. 'You're not scared of the apocalypse then?'

146

'Not really.'

I tap the boss on the shoulder.

'What?' he says, turning to me.

'Sorry.'

I expect it's the Real thing to say.

The figure rips open the door and drags the boss out of his seat, slapping him onto the concrete. For a moment the boss doesn't speak, not knowing what to make of it. Then he begins frantically struggling. He knocks the glasses off the figure, revealing glowing green eyes. The boss screams and calls my name.

The soldier model beats the boss to death right there on the forecourt.

I pass the time cleaning out the van. I start with that ashtray, stepping out and emptying it into the forecourt bin provided.

THE QUEEN

A ball of flame shot through the window and hit the wall above Pander. Dust and masonry tumbled over him, his arms raised in welcome. I called out to Starvie. A hand grabbed my leg and she pulled up next to me.

'Awfully quick getting here, weren't they?' she said.

Another rocket hit somewhere else on the house, over the other side. That wasn't good. They were surrounding us. Then a thought hit me.

'The cab!' I got to my feet and ran out into the hall. Starvie followed.

'What are you doing?' she said. 'They're out there! We need to get out the back!'

I didn't listen to her. All I could think about was the Landy. I picked up a weapon and peered out the door into the gloom. I heard her call after me as I dived outside.

'Idiot!'

She had a point. I'd forgotten the night goggles. You realise that quickly when you run out into a dark driveway that's shooting at you. I rolled on my back, thinking how much I loved my nano cells, and what a shame it would be for them to get chewed up by Pander's creation. I stopped, popped up, and took a couple of blind shots back up the drive.

I sprinted for the Landy. I had picked my moment poorly, as another rocket spun out of the night, smacking into the front door and blowing me off my feet.

I staggered to the cab, threw myself in and started the engine.

'Hang on!' shouted a voice.

Fatty hurled himself into the seat next to me. I looked at him.

148

'GO! GO! GO!' he screamed. A few shots thudded close to the car.

'You're in the passenger seat,' I said.

'SO?' he asked, wringing his hands. 'MOVE THE FUCKING CAR.'

'You're not my fare. You're cargo.'

He threw me as powerful a look as he could with the one eye, then got out the cab and hurled himself into the flatbed.

'HAPPY?' he screamed. 'HAPPY NOW, YOU SICK, CRAZY—'

I hit reverse and stamped on the gas. We shot out fast and hit something straight away. It was one of the ambushers. I turned around to face the attackers and switched the lights to full beam. Five or six Reals were lit up dead ahead, standing in the open drive. They threw up their arms to shield their eyes. I cut the lights again and ploughed right at them. They were making some awful dents in the car, but that couldn't be helped now. I had to get out of the way of the rocket I knew was coming.

We burned about a hundred metres down the drive before I pulled the handbrake and spun us to face the house again, cutting the engine. I knocked on the rear window and Fatty's face appeared, wild-eyed and furious.

'What is it? Why have we stopped?'

'Where's Starvie?' I asked him.

'She ran out the back. I don't know if she got out.'

'What about Pander?'

'Buried,' said Fatty.

I thought of Pander lying there broken under the collapsed wall. I thought how proud the Reals would be of themselves, even though they'd just murdered the last of their kind who'd actually achieved something.

I took a pistol out of the weapons rack, opened the door and stepped out onto the gravel. A few shots rang out in the air, getting closer. I walked round the back of the Landy and handed the weapon to Fatty.

'What's the pop gun for?' he asked. 'You're not thinking of going back?'

'Seems that way,' I said. Fatty shook his head and cocked the pistol.

'Does this shit ever end?'

He didn't need an answer to that.

I got back in the car, started up the engine and moved off, back towards the house. A lucky shot hit the windscreen and burst right through the cabin. Fatty did some more inventive swearing, then shot back into the darkness, about as wildly as the Reals. Halfway down the drive there was a gap in the trees, so I picked us through and tore across the lawn, heading for the fire-damaged wing of the house. We reached the front wall without taking another hit, and drove up onto an embankment. Then Fatty knocked on the window.

'I know that sound,' he said.

I knew it too. There's no mistaking a badly maintained 1000 horse power diesel engine going at full pelt.

I hit the lights. There, speeding clear of the hole it had just smashed in the estate wall, was a tank. The Reals had fixed a couple of flaming torches to the cannon, and strange, colourful flags flew from the joints in the armour.

'Jesus Christ!' screamed Fatty. I hadn't heard that name mentioned in a while.

The tank's turret traversed awkwardly, trying to bear down on us. Fatty, not using his brain, began to shoot at it. He gave that up when I hit reverse, making a break for the cover of the house. We slammed down the embankment and across some long-dead flowerbeds. The tank took its first shot. A huge slapping noise echoed around the garden and the trees. They missed us by a distance, but pulverised the corner of the house. I steered us through the cloud of bricks and tumbling glass, back onto the front lawn. Fatty suddenly appeared in the back window, blocking my view. He punched madly at the glass and pointed to something behind us. I yelled back at him.

'Well, get out the way so I can see!'

He moved. There was another pair of flaming torches, headed right for us. I turned ninety degrees, and made for the perimeter wall.

That was it. Decision made. For the first time in my life I would be abandoning a fare. I would have to try and recover her later. All that mattered now was getting clear of the trap. Somebody had to get word out about Pander's weapon.

I hugged the wall, heading towards the drive, doing maybe ten miles an hour. The roar of the tanks masked the Landy's engine noise. I could see their torches drawing together at the corner of the house, their crews yelling at each other in confusion.

We reached the drive. I couldn't spot any movement. We made a terrible noise as I scraped the Landy through the trees, but the Reals were too disorganised to notice. I turned the car right towards the open gate, and sped up, bursting out of the gate with a bang.

Bang?

We had almost hit forty when the car lurched as if it had lost its mind. I tried to right us, but we hit something and flipped. We skidded along in a shredding squeal until the cab slammed into the estate wall, spun one full revolution, and finally came to rest.

A stinger. One of those things the police used to lay across the road to shred the tyres of getaway cars. I couldn't believe they had got me with that. I could hear fuel dripping, and the hiss of steam.

I saw Fatty, or the shape of him. He crawled away from the car then collapsed.

'Hey!' I whispered. 'Are you okay?'

'Don't ever ask me that.'

The tanks were getting closer. Real voices yelped and whooped victory.

'Do you still have the pistol?'

'I've got nothing but a pain in the arse.'

'Get into cover and keep your head down. I'll draw them off after me. Get into the fields and make a run for it. Consider your end of the deal complete.'

'How noble,' said Fatty. 'Not to hurt your feelings but I'm not sticking around to be dismissed. I can't move on this leg.'

There were footsteps up the road. I could hear boots in gravel, whispers in the gloom.

'This is going to be bad,' said Fatty.

I felt around in the cab for the weapons rack, then realised I was lying on it. I got my hands on the spare rifle, and clambered out the smashed window. Up ahead I saw torches, as the first tank shuffled awkwardly clear of the gate, spinning its tracks on the tarmac. It lumbered forwards but stopped just as I was thinking about shooting.

A voice called out.

'You out there! We have you in our night sights. Do not attempt to run or we will shoot. Throw your weapons away, stand up and move slowly forwards with your hands raised.'

'Don't suppose you have a catchy Ficial solution to this predicament?' asked Fatty.

'Do what they say.'

'I can't stand, you fool.'

I reached out an arm, groping for him in the dark. I felt my way down to his waist and hoisted him up, his arm around my neck.

The Reals on the road were quiet now. I could only hear the crackling torches. I took a step forward when the floodlight came on. At first there was only one, then a second, then a third. Shocking white beams swamped us in brilliant radiance, blinding Fatty before he could shield his good eye. I kept us moving up the street, wondering from where they got all this power.

I could make out the full party now, arranged in a screen across the road. The two tanks sat next to each other, their engines idling. Around fifty Reals clustered behind them for cover. I wondered why they didn't take their shots.

'That's good,' said the megaphone, 'stop there.' I could see the speaker now. A thin guy with serious blood sweats, crouched on one of the tanks.

'Now turn around and get on your knees.'

I lowered Fatty down next to me and listened as the Reals nervously approached. I stared at the crisp, white lines painted on the road. Fatty was bleeding badly onto one of them, which made me anxious. This road was still in good condition and he had to spill his fluids on it? I gave him a little shove to stop him dripping there. The Reals got excited and cocked their weapons, all calling out:

'Staystillkeepyourhandsintheairdon'tmove!'

I froze. About a hundred dirty, deformed hands grabbed me, wrestled me to the ground and tied my hands and feet. They did the same to Fatty, kicking his bad leg. He let out a scream, which they enjoyed. They all started taking kicks. They were all so keen to get the boot in that a few kicked each other.

Before they could get their shoeing organised, a shot went off and the megaphone called out:

'Enough! Get them into the van. Don't beat them unless they resist. We need them intact.'

The lynch mob grumbled, but complied. I was rolled onto my front. A couple of Reals brought up a length of steel piping, which they carefully ran through the ropes binding my hands and feet. They hoisted me up like a spit roast, carrying me off towards the tanks. There was a lot of spitting and catcalling, but no more beating.

The baying crowd parted to reveal a couple of white vans, each mounting a huge, high-beam floodlight on its roof. They tossed me inside the nearest one, flinging Fatty in next to me.

They all seemed to enjoy themselves once we were inside, shooting their weapons into the night and cheering the successful hunt. It was quite a scene. A few Reals had found the water barrels on Fatty's trailer, and were pouring water over each other's heads, fighting over it, spilling it into the mud and on the road. A few weaker examples dropped onto the tarmac and licked at what puddles they could find.

'Maniacs,' said Fatty.

Someone appeared by the second truck. It was the guy with the megaphone. Another figure stood behind him.

I could tell it was Starvie by the way she held herself, and by the fact she was the only one with exposed legs. Nobody seemed to be restraining her. The megaphone guy led her through the crowd. One by one the Reals became silent, gaping hungrily at her. I expected them to attack, but it didn't happen. Instead they fell to their knees and raised their hands in prayer.

The guy with the megaphone kowtowed before her, sinking to his knees with the others.

'Gentlemen,' he called out. 'THE QUEEN!'

'THE QUEEN!' replied the crowd.

Fatty looked at me.

'The fucking Queen?'

Starvie gazed at me coolly. She may have winked.

'It fits,' I said.

The soldier model in the overalls drags the corpse into the trees, then returns. He introduces himself as Shersult, wiping his hands on his overalls.

He tells me to move over, jumps in beside me, and tells me to drive. I tell him that I haven't driven before and he says that he doesn't care. He wants me to take him to the boss's home. Even though it is not the boss's any more. Even though nothing belongs to the boss any more.

I ask Shersult why he wants to go there. He says he needs to cull the rest of the boss's family. He is part of a clean-up squad and is running badly behind schedule. More Reals have refused to report to the bunkers than Control expected.

I turn the key in the ignition and hold the plastic steering wheel in my hand. It is still warm. I turn it with one hand, the other resting in my lap, just like the boss drives. Until now I have been at the mercy of his decisions, his cruising speed, his short cuts. Now I am in control.

We drive along in silence. Shersult's eyes glow in the dark cabin. He picks up the picture of Jesus and employs it to pick at his teeth.

'So let me ask you,' I say, 'what are you going to do once it is all done?'

'Once what's all done?'

'The cull,' I explain.

'What, do you mean, "do"?'

'I mean, when they are all culled, what will be left to do? I mean, you're optimised to kill, aren't you? So what use will you be?'

He looks back at the road. Like me, he has probably never seen it so empty.

'Lots of killing to do overseas. Much bigger job. Got to take out the God freaks before they bomb us.'

'But they're dying out anyway, aren't they?'

'Wounded animals,' he says. 'Most dangerous.'

He's right. Reals hate to think that other Reals are doing better. I'm surprised the lunatics abroad haven't attacked us already. What else do they have to do, except starve?

'But what about after they're all dead?' I ask. 'All the ones overseas? What then?'

Shersult ignores the question, just stares dead ahead, into the reflection of his green eyes.

Has he really not considered the thought? Even a soldier model must wonder.

The van we're driving will have no purpose without Reals. How are we any different? We are specialised tools, built to do what Real people cannot. Pursuing our optimisation was supposed to make their society complete. Without them to augment, what will there be to do? Who will there be to improve but ourselves?

'I suppose we'll just have to learn new skills,' I say.

There is some kind of traffic up ahead. There is shooting going on and cars are trying to back up. Some people run into the trees, screaming, clutching suitcases.

Shersult picks up his rifle.

'Speed up,' he says.

AUDIENCE

The van smelled of disinfectant. The metal surface was slippery and cold. Fatty and I lay there listening to the party outside fade and die.

I heard the front doors open and shut as our drivers got in and started the engine. A light came on in the van. Fatty was pale. His leg was bent at a strange angle.

'Crippled in a car crash,' said Fatty. 'What are the chances in this day and age?'

'Leg that bad?'

'I can't feel it,' he said. 'I'm taking that as a poor sign.'

We bumped around as the van traversed some uneven surface, then levelled out and turned, rolling Fatty towards me.

'Your people really have been getting organised,' I said.

'These aren't my people. And they're not organised. They're just mindlessly obedient, like your lot. Still, they didn't kill us. I don't know whether to be concerned or happy about that. Fuck it, I'll go with concerned.'

'I can't believe they got the cab. Did you see what happened to it?'

'Who cares?' said Fatty. 'Worry about us.'

He looked around the van space, assessing our surroundings.

'They're probably taking us to the King,' he said.

'You don't seem too happy about that.'

Fatty snorted.

'He'll have us up before one of his courts. Before you can say "Kangaroo" our insides will be hanging from Tyne Bridge. That bitch will probably wink at us while they gut us.'

'Starvie?'

'Of course. If she's his Queen she'll have to turn out to wave to her public. Everybody likes to see the royal couple, don't they?'

There was a laugh from the front of the van, but it wasn't at us, or at least, not this conversation.

'So you didn't know she was married to this guy?' I asked him.

Fatty pushed himself over to face me.

'I never followed celebrities,' he said. 'I never thought it was important. I've heard a few of the King's songs, but never read the gossip pages or anything. He could have ten fucking wives for all I know.'

I thought about the magazine article I had picked out in the service station, that first night with Starvie. I hadn't bothered to read it. I'd just looked at the pictures.

'Beyond strange, though, isn't it?' said Fatty.

'What's that?'

'Why the King would mount this little rescue operation for a Ficial. I mean, based purely on personality, I'd say she was human. But the fact is she's as much a Ficial as you are. Now my question is, how does a guy who's built an entire kingdom on retribution against your kind justify marrying one of you? How is it he's got them all bowing before her and calling her "ma'am"? Any one of them only has to take a look at her to know she's not Real. She looks like she's stepped right out of a skin care ad. Damn peculiar, I call it.'

I wondered if I really knew anything about Starvie at all. It was policy not to ask questions of a fare. That had always served me well in the past, but now it seemed plain stupid, as brainless as not reading that magazine.

'So this must worry you, huh?' said Fatty.

'What does that mean?'

'I mean I've heard a great deal about Ficial solidarity. A lot of stuff about your incorruptible united front. But where's your fellow Ficial? Sitting in the royal coach, that's where. And where's your Control, eh? The only thing that can tell you what to do? Dead!'

'We don't know that's true,' I said. 'Not for sure.'

'But doesn't that make you think?'

'Think about what?'

'About anything!'

'Don't get mad,' I said. 'It won't help.'

'Right. You don't get mad, huh? Too pure to get mad.'

'That's right.'

Fatty snorted.

'Don't give me that. The only difference between you and me is your white teeth and your fancy skin. Well, I've got news for you, pal – Pander's found a way to destroy that now. Then how are we different?'

I thought about it, wondering whether to get into the discussion. Fatty was getting worked up and would probably take out his fear and anger on me. In the end I had an answer, so I went with it.

'Well, for one, we don't lose all control over the opposite sex.'

'Sure you don't,' he said.

'That's right, we don't.'

Fatty was riled.

'Sorry, but I don't believe Pander could burn that out of you. If you ask me, you don't have sex because it's your religion. Because you're told it's a sin. I'll bet you've got the urges the same as anyone. You just can't be honest with yourselves about it.'

'I'm sure this all makes you feel a lot better,' I said, 'but religion never stopped your kind rutting away illicitly for thousands of years, did it? We actually manage to contain ourselves. I might add, we'd never tie you up and put you in the back of a van either. We'd just shoot you. There's no empty promises made. There's none of this endless lying that your kind feel the need to do.'

'What about the Queen, you fool? What's she been doing if she hasn't been lying to us the whole time?'

I frowned.

'I admit that is puzzling.'

'He's puzzled,' said Fatty, to an audience that wasn't there. He struggled in his bindings, trying to loosen them, but soon gave up. He sighed and stared at the ceiling, before a thought struck him.

'You never asked what her story was?'

'In case you haven't noticed, she's not the easiest person to communicate with. I doubt it would have done much good to question her.'

'Brilliant,' said Fatty, and spat on the rear doors. We watched the phlegm roll slowly down the door, blue and determined.

'I miss Cheddar cheese,' he said.

'What?' I couldn't imagine where that thought had sprung from.

'I miss Cheddar cheese. Canadian mature.' Fatty sighed deeply and stared. 'When I was little my mum would make us mature Canadian Cheddar cheese sandwiches with spring onions. Fucking hell, spring onions. Crusty white bread. I would have a glass of Coke, and if I was lucky, a packet of crisps too.'

'So what?'

'So, if we could rustle up a few rounds of those sandwiches right now, for everyone in this convoy, we'd all just stop and eat, and everything would be fine. We've all got taste buds, haven't we?'

We drove on. Fatty, despite being lashed to a steel pole, managed to sleep. It was hours before the van pulled over, halting with a thud and a lurch. Fatty didn't stir. He was really enjoying his sleep. I could hear distant gunfire. That meant we were at a barricade.

The doors sprung open and five Reals with rifles asked me if I wouldn't mind getting out. I reminded them that I couldn't actually stand. After a short debate they agreed that lashed to a pole as I was, they would have to come and get me. They clambered in and scooped me out the van like a roll of carpet. The sound of shooting and the distant thump of impacts grew louder. There was a thick smell of tyre fires, masking something worse.

They had to poke Fatty with a rifle to wake him up, having a good laugh at him as he spluttered into consciousness. They cut him free of the pole, then retied his hands behind his back.

'Come on, pork chop, get moving,' said one of them, kicking him in the ribs.

They kept me lashed to the pole. One bent down to stare at me. He was spectacularly ugly, with a grid burned across his features, stained maroon by blood sweats. Luckily he blindfolded me. I was marched away, listening to the sound of Fatty's beating fade into the night. Hundreds of other voices rose and hummed like a hive.

We travelled up steps. I heard a hatch, and we stepped into a warm room. I was cut free of the pole, then cuffed to something more formidable. I tried to sit up but my wrists pulled tight together. I was cuffed with something strong.

'He's here,' said a familiar voice.

My blindfold was removed by the man with the grid face. He seemed nervous of whoever sat behind him.

Starvie was spread on a leather sofa. She was wearing a pair of black jeans and a white top with an open neck, running down to the belly, criss-crossed by yellow ribbon. Her hair was a mass of curls now, falling over her shoulders. She was wearing a lot more make-up. There were black wings drawn around her eyes and white paint on her lips and fingernails. She looked ready for another men's magazine.

Maybe that's what the guy next to her had planned. At first I took him to be Ficial, simply because he wasn't wearing a chemical coat, only a dressing gown and loose cotton pyjama bottoms. His chest and feet were bare, but showed no sign of damage or disease. His face was intact, without the usual red hue of frequently scratched skin, or the nervous tics of a dying nervous system. He looked up at me and smiled, revealing teeth so white they looked painted.

He dismissed the grid-faced man, stood up, patted at his belly and walked over to inspect me.

'Careful,' said Starvie. 'Don't get too close.'

'Don't worry, sweetheart,' he said. 'I'm just going to talk to him.'

Closer up there was something odd about his face. The skin wasn't right. The whole head looked like it had been dipped in glue and then left to set. His features didn't move when he spoke. A sickly sweet odour drifted off him.

'Allow me to introduce myself,' he said. 'I am the King of Newcastle.'

'Could you step back a little?' I said. 'You smell terrible.'

The King didn't reply. It was a dramatic pause for effect, and a long one.

I took the time to look around the room. I was tethered by sustainment fibre to a metal hoop on the wall. There were some narrow metal windows and a thin door on the left, all sealed tight. Behind the sofa area were a fitted kitchen and a dressing table covered in men's grooming products. A gold-framed mirror dominated that wall, surrounded by pictures of the King in his heyday. He had long, flowing black hair and carefully maintained stubble in all of them. In about half he was dressed in a tuxedo, stood on a red carpet, with Jennifer E on his arm.

I thought it strange that the King would hang pictures of his long-dead face. What did the stretched and glued monster want from these pictures? Could he fool himself that he was still that person?

'My wife has been telling me all about your adventures,' he said. He sauntered over to the kitchen and found something old and alcoholic in the cupboard, pouring the amber liquid into two glasses. He sidled over and handed one to Starvie. He sat on the arm of the sofa, running his hands through her curls. 'Busting out of an ambush, shooting up one of my checkpoints, even mounting a bloody rescue operation. I want to thank you, mate.'

'No you don't,' I said, 'you want to gloat. You should probably know that there's no point pulling that with me. I really don't get mad, and I don't get insulted. If you do want to talk about something why don't we get to it and leave out pulling on each other's pigtails?'

The King sipped his drink.

'You don't feel anything? You don't feel even a little bit pissed that the hottest girl ever created has stabbed you in the back? After all you did for her? I mean, not even a thank you? She just delivered you into the arms of your most formidable enemy.'

I elected not to comment on the 'formidable' bit. It might get him mad. I only wanted to know one thing:

'Why am I still alive?'

The King shook his head. 'Mate, if you can't get emotional about Jennifer, you're not alive, believe me.'

He stood up, downing the rest of his drink. When he was done he gasped and raised an eyebrow. The guy was a mess of affectations. Fine. If he wasn't going to tell me why he'd let me live, I thought I'd get on to more important matters.

'Where's my cab?'

'Oh, I think it is being refitted outside. It's not a bad machine really. Quite a nice little run-around. I thought I might give it to Jennifer.'

He really was trying to get me mad.

'What about the fat guy?' I asked him.

'He is being debriefed. Tell me, Kenstibec . . . You are optimised for construction, is that right?'

'Yes,' I said.

'What sort of construction?'

'I worked on prototype solar wells, cooling towers . . . Big stuff mostly. Why? You interested in super-tall buildings?'

'I'm just trying to figure out what sort of Ficial you are,' he said. 'It's a pity you can't help us out, Kenstibec. I'm constructing something truly special. It's an engineering challenge I think you'd relish.'

'Let me guess. Some kind of statue of you?'

'Ha. Not exactly.' The King and Starvie laughed and grinned at each other.

'At the moment, as you know, it's well difficult to get a decent TV or radio signal of any kind. Stupid cloud interferes with everything. Plus the war kind of ended the days of every household having a telly in their front room, didn't it? Shit, it kind of ended the days of every household.

'That's not stopped us, though. Most tribes have a generator or two, a few scrounged TVs and monitors. They broadcast their own stuff, but what they really love are my shows. All over the country my people huddle around their shitty little sets to watch my stuff. It lifts them up. I give them hope.'

'What's your point?'

'My point is that it's inefficient. It takes too long to spread my message. If they're not constantly watching their TV they're forgetting about me. I need them to watch my stuff all the time. If they're going to follow me they need to learn about me. The real me.'

He stopped and gritted his teeth, holding a hand up to his head. He moaned and nearly fell, overtaken by pain. Starvie went to the kitchen, returning with two pills in her palm and a glass of water. The King swallowed the pills and straightened up. I smiled at him.

'Is that the real you?'

He gave me a right hook to my cheek. Then he landed a left in my belly. They didn't seem like very royal hits. He was pretty pleased with them, though. He looked at Starvie for approval. She lit a cigarette and blew smoke at him.

'Sugar, do you think that will impress me? You might as well punch a sandbag. Ask him what you want, why don't you?'

162

That deflated him a little, but he recovered. He was royalty after all. He strutted back to her and kissed her forehead, then sat again with as much majesty as he could muster.

'My people all kept their TVs. Whatever hell hole they wound up sheltering in, however much they were hurt, even though they had no power, they held onto their TVs. That shows faith, Kenstibec. Faith in a new world. I'm gonna reward that faith.

'I'll start a whole new broadcasting system. I'll give them back twenty-four-hour entertainment. I'll beam into every bunker, shelter and trench in the country, and unite my people under my flag. Pander designed me a whole new transmission grid – a system that will broadcast all over the world, even with the burning cloud. That's how much a genius the guy was.

'Now my point is, we could build his system in half the time with your help. Jennifer seems to think you wouldn't assist us, but I wanted to sit down with you, face to face, and ask you what you thought.'

Starvie sat there and stared.

'Well, thanks for the offer,' I said. 'But I don't think you're really asking me. Employing the Ficial who kidnapped your wife would be something of a gamble, wouldn't it? Not that I claim to know anything about Real politics. After all, your wife is as Ficial as they come. How do you get away with that by the way?'

'People appreciate good looks,' said the King. 'And they don't ask questions they don't want the answers to. They've all accepted her because she's so cute. The men want her and the women want to be her. We're role models, you see, with aspirational lifestyles.'

That made no sense to me, but I nodded as if it did.

'Right. Well, anyhow, you don't really want my help. You should, because with the people you've got working for you I can pretty much guarantee your grid won't work. But still, I think you're posturing. I think you can't wait to put me out of commission.'

'Do all cab drivers have such a good grasp of psychology?'

Starvie shrugged. 'He thinks he's a student of human behaviour.'

'Well, he's right,' said the King. He stood up from Starvie's side and went to look out of one of the windows, at his army outside.

'Do you know where you are, mate?'

'One of your minions mentioned York.'

'That's right. Well, a couple of miles away. My army has the place surrounded. They're all set to take the city. Pander's weapon worked brilliantly.'

'And?'

'And I need you to do something for me. I want you to go in there and take your people a message.'

'You want me to walk into York?'

'That's right. And take them a message.'

'What is it?'

'The message is: Control is dead and there's no point in fighting any more. The message is: surrender and I will be lenient to the population.'

I looked over at Starvie, who gazed emptily back at me. I turned to the King.

'They're not going to do that.'

'I know that,' said the King, turning away from the view. 'But you see, I know drama. I could just broadcast you being skinned and burned alive, but my people have seen that a hundred times. The viewing public need something new. Something with a story.

'You're going to provide that. You're going to march into that city, with my cameras rolling, and offer my mercy to your people. When your freak mates refuse my graceful offer it will be a slap in the face. I will be the noble King who was snubbed. The impact of that, combined with my new presenter here,' he said, indicating Starvie, 'well, we're gonna have something special. A real moment in TV history.'

'So, you're just going to let me walk into the barricade?'

'That's right,' he said.

Starvie was blowing smoke rings, watching them drift up to the ceiling.

'Hey,' I said to her. 'What's this all about? What are you doing hanging around with this carcass?'

Starvie smiled.

'He has a lot of talent.'

I didn't know what to say to that, so I changed tack.

'Well, why did you need me to get you out of Edinburgh? You could have strolled out any time you liked. Nobody would have expected you to bolt.'

She bent forward, extinguishing her cigarette.

'I needed a taxi,' she said, looking right at me. 'I had some heavy shopping.'

She picked something up off the floor and laid it on her lap. It was the other green case. She opened it and turned it around so I could have a look.

She was right. Her shopping was heavy. It had a sub-critical mass. Nuclear weapons are like that.

'What are you showing him that for?' snapped the King

'You're in control here, sweetie,' she said. 'It can't do any harm.'

'You're right,' said the King. He tried to smile, but it seemed to cause him pain. He put his arm around her.

'She needed to make sure she could get the bomb out in one piece,' said the King. 'It would have been very dangerous to let her try to get here on her own. I have no real control over the tribes around Edinburgh, at least not yet. She needed protection if she was going to bring me this weapon. I'm going to use it, you see. I'm going to destroy London.'

'Really?'

'Yes.'

'Sounds pretty stupid to me. What's the point when you have your special Pander weapon? Why don't you just use that?'

'No, no, no. The weapon is very useful of course, but it's much too clinical. Behind the scenes stuff, really. My people need fireworks, something that makes them feel they've struck a blow against your race. When they march into York and find everybody dead, it's all going to be a bit anticlimactic. They won't feel like they've got their money's worth when your lot just lie down and die without a shot fired.

'I must start the new channel with a bang. It'll be the greatest launch in history: a nuclear strike at the heart of the Ficial plague. It will change everything.'

'I doubt it.'

'You would,' said the King, 'because you can't stand entertainment, can you? That's why you sneer at people like Jennifer. Because you don't understand her.'

'She's not really a person, my liege,' I said. 'And I'm understanding her better all the time.'

165

Starvie shook her head and made a click noise with her tongue.

'Kenstibec,' she said, 'how can you understand me when you don't want to fuck me?'

The King liked that. It did things for him. He fell onto his knees beside her and barked, then panted for a few seconds. Starvie looked at me while she patted him on the head. The King took a few playful bites at her thighs then managed to get a hold of himself, sitting up on the floor, his back to the sofa at Starvie's feet, her hand resting in his tussled hair.

'I don't have any problem with this Pander weapon. As far as I'm concerned, it's not killing. Your whole kind is dead already.'

'I'm living, all right,' I said. 'I'm just experiencing it differently.'

'Well, whatever you're doing, it doesn't look like much fun to me. Anyway, I'm bored with this. Are you going to cooperate and take my message or are we going to have to just skin you on live TV?'

I considered the options. Other models wouldn't like it if I wandered over no-man's-land and knocked on York's front door on the whim of the King. But they would like it even less if I let myself get skinned on a Real execution show. Besides, if there were a chance I could help York, do something to wipe the grin off the King's face, it would be worth it.

'Sure,' I said, 'I'll do it.'

'Cool!' cried the King.

'So shall I get going, or what?'

'Well, there is one other aspect of the deal that I have to run past you,' said the King. 'I hope you don't mind.'

'Go on,' I said.

'The fat man. The one who collaborated with you.'

'What about him?'

'Well, he represents another valuable ratings booster. You see, never before has a collaborator been caught. That, as I'm sure you know, is largely down to the fact that the Ficial that uses a guide normally slaughters them as soon as they are beyond use.'

'True enough,' I said. 'So what?'

'So, I want something special for him. I want him to transcend execution hour or torture week. I want to use him as part of our extravaganza. Does that suit you?'

'What do you want me to do?' I asked.

'Nothing, you don't need to do anything. All you need to do is take him with you into the city of York with all your friends.'

The King took Starvie's hand out his hair and brought it down to his lips to kiss. It was revolting to watch him try. He could barely purse his lips. His skin stretched with the effort, looking as if it might tear.

'They'll just cull him as soon as he gets in there.'

The King rested his head on Starvie's thigh and sighed happily. I looked at Starvie closely, searching for some clue to her feelings, but her face was as blank as cut steel.

'Maybe,' he said. 'That will show my people what happens to those that collaborate.'

He smiled and rubbed his hands together.

'Starvie tells me that you've been with the fat man for weeks. She thinks you might be getting friendly with him. So is it true? Do you feel anything at all about having to kill him?'

'No,' I said. 'If you want me to kill him, I'll kill him. Then I'm going to walk into the barricade and deliver your message. When that's done I'll come back for my fare.'

The King grinned and clapped his hands.

'Sounds good,' he said. 'This is going to be fun.'

The last shot. The last shriek. Four soldier models did all this, in half an hour. They count the bodies, pile them at the side of the motorway, siphon off petrol from the cars and light the pyre. Four hundred Reals' worth of smoke pours into the sky. I pull my T-shirt up over my face.

The soldier models check a flex, reading the live feed on the cull's progress. Control is broadcasting to them, deploying them.

'Early estimate is ninety per cent culled in the bunkers,' says the soldier with the flex.

'How are they doing it?'

'Gas,' says another. 'Best way. Quick and clean.'

'Twelve and a half million left,' says Shersult.

I peek at the screen. I can see a luminous white map, zoomed in on this area. Black dots are trailing shadows as they move. Clustered here, sprinkled there. Every real person left in the country is being isolated and hunted down.

I do a quick calculation. Three soldier models killed four hundred people in thirty minutes. About six hundred soldier models constructed in total . . .

The soldiers cluster around the flex like it is warm. I wonder what they would do if the connection went down.

'Here,' says one of the soldiers, pointing at the screen. 'We start here, pin as many as we can against the river, then fan out to chase the others.'

They all instantly agree, except for Shersult, who stares up the road, over the wrecks of the convoy.

'Not me,' he says. 'It was a pleasure to join in your turkey shoot, but I have a priority assignment. Targeting homes with Engineering facilities. I'm taking this one home now.'

He points to me.

Suddenly the soldiers snap their weapons up, all pointing in one direction.

I can hear it too. A Real man's voice.

'This can not go unanswered.'

The soldiers lower their guns. Shersult picks his way between the cars, reaches into the back of a people carrier, and produces a small portable TV.

He brings it over and shows it to us.

The man on TV is holding a cross.

'The day of the Lord is at hand! Those who raised up the soulless demons are being slaughtered in their beds, my brothers and sisters. Their pride has led to this fall. Remember your scripture. Remember! And I saw one of his heads as it were wounded to death; and his deadly wound was healed: and all the world wondered after the beast. And I saw as it were a sea of glass mingled with fire: and them that had gotten the victory over the beast, stand on the sea of glass, having the harps of God. And they sing: Great and marvellous are thy works, Lord God Almighty; just and true are thy ways, thou King of saints. Who shall not fear thee, O Lord, and glorify thy name?

'To those who hear me, if you dwell on that cursed island, we will strike thee down with a voice like a trumpet from the sky! We will strike you down now and be worthy of him.'

'Isn't this guy the priority target?' I ask.

'We don't need to worry about the madmen,' says Shersult.

'But Control said they wouldn't start shooting yet. Control said they wouldn't find out about the cull yet. Shouldn't we check to see?'

'It's just one crazy Real.' Shersult indicates we should move forward, through the burning wrecks. I follow behind him. His clothes are stained red.

'I don't know,' I say. 'I think that guy is the priority. If they were all like him we'll have a real fight on our hands.'

'But they're not, are they?'

FIFTEEN MINUTES

The King didn't waste time. He departed with Starvie to organise the production crew, leaving me chained to the wall like the royal family's least favourite pet. Eventually the guy with the grid on his face marched into the room, closely followed by a goon carrying a pulse welder, kind of like the Dohaki 4 series I'd used in my first job, only with some shabby Real-rigged repairs.

'Sort him and then take him to the front,' said the grid.

'Yes, sir.'

'And look, they don't know where we are keeping him yet and the King has expressly forbidden any plot leaks for tonight's episode. Put him in a mask and coat and strap him into your vehicle, and keep moving. We don't want some over-enthusiastic fools to notice him and ruin tonight's show.'

'Yes, sir,' said the goon.

He stepped forward and pressed the Dohaki chamber against my chest.

'Goodnight,' he said.

He hit the activate button. It all went dark.

For a moment I thought I was back in my Landy. I heard a diesel engine and felt a gentle rocking motion. My teeth still tingled from the Dohaki hit. I opened my right eye a crack and discovered I was wearing a gas mask. Looking down, I saw black plastic gloves on my hands, pulled over the sleeves of a shining green chemical coat. Cuffs bound my wrists and feet. Someone was beeping a horn.

The goon sat in the driving seat, his hand on the wheel. The van engine howled like it was ready to give. I thought about giving him an elementary lesson in gear selection, but it wouldn't have been worth it. He was far more interested in beeping that horn.

We were driving through thousands of Reals, swarming along a wide, raised, stone track. I didn't recognise the road. The King's men must have built it to move people around the siege perimeter more easily. One edge of the track was marked out by tall, flaming torches, which cast a deep red light over the landscape. The other side sloped down to a shanty of mud, trash and scrap metal, where the army's women and children scurried, waist-deep in floodwater.

The King's army was forming up for the attack. They were all chattering, all wide-eyed and grinning insanely. Pander had obviously shared his hooch recipe. They were up to the eyeballs with it. There was a smell too, a terrible thick stink that hung in the wind, in the car and on my clothes.

I saw two men holding torches, directing a work gang of children. They were hoisting an enormous TV screen over the shanty. It was already powered up and showing the King's logo on a test card. Presumably it was Pander's new weatherproof broadcast design. A wretched group of Reals fought each other for the best viewing positions. They were expecting a big show.

Looking the other side, through the flaming torches, I could just about see the grey strip of the York barricade. It was the best outside of Brixton, running along the lines of the A1237 and the A64. It had always been a good place to stop off, fuel up, and stretch your legs. Now, if what the King said was true, the Reals were about to ruin it, just like they ruined everything.

The going was slow. Eventually, the van turned down a ramp, heading into the shanty along another terrible road, thrown together from felled trees. We became stuck a few times, eventually being pushed clear by excited young ones. Some kind of landmark rose up ahead out of the shanty. I wondered what it was. There were no significant hills around here.

It took a while to figure out it was man-made. As we drove closer, I could see it was built out of car wrecks, rubble and trash, sealed together by mud. The whole structure was perhaps fifteen storeys high, slumping badly to one side. Lights twinkled at the peak. The King's men had built him a pyramid.

The crude road coiled up and around it, so that we could drive all the way to the summit, the van shaking and roaring in low gear.

At the top, a lot of Reals were making excited preparations. They were setting up audio/visual kit, getting ready for some kind of broadcast. Speakers were fixed up to cables, microphones were being tested, and spotlights hooked up to generators. It must all have been Pander-designed kit.

The goon stepped out and consulted a few of them, explaining the masked figure in his car. My door was cautiously opened. Five pairs of hands grabbed me and threw me onto the pyramid's jagged, rocky surface. They helped me get to my feet, which was good of them.

The view was impressive. I could see the whole siege area, the ring of flaming torches drawn like a noose around York, the road and shanty writhing with Reals beneath us. From this distance the barricade seemed to be fully intact. There was still power. Lights flickered behind the wall despite the sporadic shelling. Nobody shot back from the city.

Then I noticed the Landy. The bodywork wasn't too badly damaged considering the crash. Even the 'built to last' sign was still firmly wedged behind the cow bars. What was disconcerting was its location.

It was perched at the top of an enormous ski jump, rigged out of hand-beaten, rickety steel. The jump dived about two hundred metres at an insane angle down the side of the pyramid, swept over the Real encampments below, and scooped up at the end into a jump over the torches. If released, I figured the Landy would get thirty metres clear of the Real lines at best. It would land in the darkness of the no-man's-land between the Real positions and the barricade. We would probably drown in the mud.

A couple of perilous metal gantries stood either side of the jump, crested by platforms where the King's camera crews prepared for the broadcast. Soldiers swarmed around the base of the gantries, which shook and creaked. The cameramen screamed down at them to keep away, but to no avail.

I turned back to my captors, who stood in a semi-circle, eyeing me nervously. There was something very strange behind them. A small cube of a building had been raised up here, decorated with lanterns, candles and sweet wrapper garlands. A kind of balustrade had been ornamented around the edge of the roof. The thing was almost pretty. It had all the appearance of a shrine. Maybe they were going to sacrifice me after all.

The goon stepped towards me with the Dohaki, and ripped the gas mask off my face. Then, striding out next to him, appeared a one-armed Real. He was a quaking, miserable-looking thing with a lemon-shaped head and the usual red raw scalp. He wore spectacles that clearly weren't his. He squinted through them, and kept removing and replacing them with his one shivering hand. He stepped forward and addressed me.

'Hello,' he said, 'my name is Spencer.'

'How are you doing, Spencer?'

'Well,' he said, surprised by the pleasantry. 'Thank you for asking. I am the presenter of tonight's programme. Those are my cameramen up there on the towers.'

'You're the presenter? What about the King?'

'The King does not do live appearances,' replied Spencer.

That made sense. The guy was trying to preserve a legend. He didn't want any unplanned close-ups on that glued-up face.

'Now tonight is a special programme, as I'm sure you've been told,' he went on. 'To be honest, I am not super-happy about having a Ficial involved in live programming. Your kind should only ever be shown in heavily edited form, but there we are. I work for the King's channel and can only do what is asked of me. You might say it's what I'm optimised for.'

'I wouldn't say that,' I replied. He scratched his scalp, a little nervous.

'Yes, well, what I want to do is talk you through the schedule so that everybody knows what they're doing. Hopefully, we can all be part of a very special event. We will be broadcasting live to the people in the siege perimeter and recording for the DVD, which will be sent out across the country to the King's followers. At the same time we'll be testing some new broadcasting equipment, to see if we can send a signal all the way to Liverpool. So this is a biggie, and we have to get it right.

'Now, I'm sure you're wondering what the ramp is for?'

'I have a pretty good idea.'

Spencer nodded enthusiastically, as if speaking to a bright pupil.

'Good. Well, as you can imagine, this will provide a dramatic flourish to start off our programme. It's always interesting to see how much punishment your kind can take, you see, and our audience loves impressive stunts. So that's why we have our ramp here, which, as you have surmised, is to propel you over our lines below into no-man's-land. From there we will film you with our wonderful new equipment as you attempt to enter the city with the King's message. If you could try to do that part quickly we'd appreciate it.'

Spencer was about to go on, when there was the sound of some loud swearing. Fatty was being led up the slope on a leash. Three Reals were giving him the occasional kick as he stumbled ahead, making it clear that he should walk on all fours.

'Ah,' said Spencer. 'Our co-star.'

Fatty didn't look in a good way. He had been severely beaten and his bandages had been stripped off him. They wanted him to feel the wind on his angry skin. He was caked in mud too, head to toe. The only concession they'd made was to bind his bad leg, presumably to ensure he could climb the face of the pyramid.

His guards got excited when they saw me. They started kicking him harder. Fatty slumped, holding his arms over his head as they beat him. He didn't cry out. His guards made all the noise.

'Hey, your master's here!' said one. 'You're his pet so you walk on all fours, you fat dog. Go see him, boy, there's a good boy. Go see master! He might want to play fetch.'

Everyone but me and Spencer laughed. Fatty snapped around and grinned at the lead soldier.

'You're a funny guy,' he gurgled through shattered teeth. 'Are you the warm-up act?'

They started pounding him again, then dragged him along through the mud, the leash tightening around his neck. Fatty struggled, trying to get his hands between throat and leather strap. The lead soldier stamped on Fatty's back and forced him into a puddle, throwing the leash down onto him.

'Thank you, gentlemen,' said Spencer. 'That will do. I'd rather we didn't garrotte one of our leading parts before the show begins. The King wouldn't like that, now would he?'

The thought hadn't seemed to have struck them. They backed off quickly, gaping and grumbling.

'Now go,' said Spencer. 'We have only got a few minutes before we're live.'

The goon motioned to a couple of his men. They rushed over to Fatty, picking him up under the arms and dragging him next to me. They dropped us both down by a crate, facing the shrine. The goon folded his arms around the welder and took up position ten paces away. Spencer chatted with his crew. Fatty dropped by my feet, blowing bubbles out his mouth. I wasn't sure he would make the show.

I wondered how I might retrieve the Landy and get out of here, but with the goon standing over me this wasn't going to be easy. I quickly came to the conclusion that my only chance was to risk the jump and see if I could get through the mud. If they were going to be stupid enough to give me a chance, then I had to take it.

Still, that might not happen if Fatty died.

'Fatty. Hey, Fatty!' I said. 'Are you okay?'

He coughed something out and cleared his throat.

'I thought I told you not to ask me that again.' He was speaking very slowly.

'Have you heard what's going on here?'

'They're having a circus and we're the clowns, right?'

'Don't worry,' I said. 'Just hang in there, or we'll never get out of here . . . and this smell.'

'Potent, isn't it?'

Lights flooded the darkness, shining from the shrine. A trail of Reals began to emerge from within.

It was the strangest collection of Reals I'd seen since the war. First came a band, dressed in uniforms that might once have been red but were now drained a sickly pink. They carried brass instruments, apart from a man with a snare drum tied to his chest by a sash. Next came some Real females. They were all in fairly good order, wearing dusty wigs and tattered little dresses. They carried bright white pom-poms, stiff with the paint they'd been dunked in. The girls would get badly burned exposed like that.

The cadaverous troupe assembled below the Landy jump, arranging themselves around Spencer. One of the Reals, wearing headphones, motioned with his hands and their jabbering subsided, replaced by stiff smiles.

The headphoned Real appeared opposite Spencer, and pointed a camera at him. He held three fingers up in the air, then two, then one. The giant screens in the shanty below lit up with Spencer's face. A great howl swelled around the pyramid.

'Good evening, ladies and gentlemen,' said Spencer. 'I'm Spencer Ayday and this is the Assault on York, brought to you live!'

The band went into a rendition of one of the King's tunes – some number that had squatted at the top of the charts for a while like a pigeon on a weathervane. Thankfully, nobody sang the lyrics.

I watched the goon carefully to see if he'd be distracted by the performance, but he held my gaze the whole time, only breaking it to scratch at himself. He must have seen rehearsals.

The cheerleaders threw themselves about in loose formation. The choreography was so poor I thought one of them might jump clear off the pyramid. Spencer was equally concerned. He stood behind the camera holding his hand to his head, as if they were dancing his dreams away. For another two minutes the band hacked its way through the tune, until they collapsed into some kind of ending, and the camera guy turned to Spencer again.

'Thank you, the King's Dancers!' said Spencer, grinning from ear to ear. He would have clapped if he could. The production crew did it for him, whooping and cheering, apparently unconcerned by the girls. They were scratching at their exposed flesh, hurriedly retreating to the safety of the shrine, where eager Real men waited with open chemical coats. The band fell onto each other, wheezing and holding their chests, exhausted by the effort of the playing. All that circular breathing of toxic air must have hurt them badly. This didn't make for too good a backdrop, so Spencer led the camera away from the Landy, doing what Starvie would have called a walk-and-talk in our direction.

'Now you all know what we're here for tonight, ladies and gentlemen,' he said. 'We're all here for the Greatest Show on Earth, brought to you by the King of Newcastle.' He winked into the camera and held the microphone right up to his lips, whispering into it confession-style.

'Tonight, we're bringing you all the action from the assault on York, live, right into your living space, talking you through each action-packed minute, as it unfolds. And if that isn't enough for you, we also have a special mystery guest tonight, who will quite literally blow you away.'

The grammar was poor, but I knew who he was talking about. I wasn't looking forward to discovering her part in all this. Spencer brought his cameraman as close to us as he dared, about two metres, and pointed us out to his audience with a flick of his microphone.

'Now these over here,' he said, 'represent the first part of our show. You may have heard that the King's men captured a Ficial about thirty miles outside York. Well, here's the proof for you. See the one on the right with the perfect skin?'

Spencer sounded disgusted when he said this. I didn't look that perfect. I was nearly healed, but I still had a lot of red raw skin from the acid burn, and a few serious bruises from our capture. I guess he had to play to his audience.

'Now you might be asking yourself "but who's this little piggy lying next to the Ficial?" Well, this is his accomplice. Yes, you heard me right, loyal subjects, this man turned away from everything natural in this world, every God-given instinct we have, and helped the Ficials. The fakes. The abominations.'

A great 'boo' shot up from the shanty.

Spencer went on.

'I'll bet you're wondering why we don't just shoot him now. Well, rest assured, he'll get what he deserves tonight – and it'll be a lot less merciful than a bullet to the head.'

Spencer switched moods, back to game-show host.

'Remember too that you can place bets on our prisoners' chances of making it across no-man's-land. The King's bookmakers are moving around the siege positions now, ready to take your bets, so hurry if you want your chance to profit from their doom!'

'Gambling,' mumbled Fatty. 'I wonder what the hell it is they think they're going to win?'

'I don't think they will enjoy the reward so much as the taking part.'

'You sound like someone's idiot mother,' growled Fatty.

Spencer noticed we were talking and decided to get in on the conversation. He still didn't want to get too close but he was happy to yell at us from a safe distance, while the goon loomed behind him with the Dohaki.

'Well,' he said into the camera, 'you can see that the Ficial and the traitor are having a little chat. I'm sure you'll be interested to know what an assassin and a turncoat have to talk about, so let's have a few words with them.'

'Fat man! Hey, fat man!' called Spencer. 'Any last words?'

'What?' replied Fatty.

'How are you feeling? Do you regret collaborating with the abominations? Do you beg for the King's forgiveness?'

'Fuck your sister,' said Fatty.

'I think it's safe to say he's scared of the King's justice,' said Spencer. 'He's quivering over there, thinking about all the wrongs he's done and what damnation he's going to endure when he leaves this world.'

'I didn't say that,' yelled Fatty. 'I said, "Fuck your sister."'

It was typical Real editorialising. You couldn't get mad at it. People don't hear what's said, they hear what they think should be said. Spencer manoeuvred himself around so that they could get me in frame behind him.

'And what about you, Ficial?' said Spencer. 'Do you have anything to say in your last moments?'

I considered for a second.

'Report for culling.'

'And there you have it,' said Spencer, quickly marching away towards the ramp, the camera following his quick step, 'the mindless reply of a soulless automaton. Could we really have expected any more? Doesn't this finally prove that we are dealing with a creature that cannot be negotiated with, cannot be reasoned with? Force is all they will understand. The force of the King's mighty fist.'

A cheer rolled up from beneath us. Fatty shook his head.

'Couldn't you have thought of something a little stronger than: "report for culling"?'

'It just came out,' I said.

'Unbelievable,' said Fatty. 'You can't even outwit a game-show host.'

'Your line was better?'

'I know what they'll show in the repeats.'

Spencer stood at the foot of the ramp, pointing up to the Landy.

'Now I know you'll all have spotted this. Yes, that's right, this is the vehicle that the Ficial and his sidekick used to carve their trail of blood across our country.

'They've evaded capture many times in this thing, running from the reach of our justice. Now it is to become the tool of their destruction. We're going to show you one of the most exciting stunts the world has ever witnessed, as our two prisoners are strapped inside, then launched off into no-man's-land!'

Another booming cheer.

'Once they're out there, if they survive the impact, they will have to make their way across no-man's-land to the city limits, and gain entrance. Now I ask you, can anything really be more entertaining than that?'

Fatty looked as if he was about to offer his thoughts, when there was an electric shriek of feedback, and the speakers around us crackled into life.

'But wait,' said a sultry voice, 'I have a question.'

Spencer looked all around him in make-believe confusion.

'Who dares interrupt a broadcast of the King?' asked Spencer. 'Who has the right?'

'Only his Queen, sugar.'

'Cheesy,' said Fatty. 'Very cheesy.'

The band struck up again, with more gusto than their opening number, presumably thinking this a more pivotal moment. The cameraman pointed the camera at the shrine. A second or two passed in silence. Then, in a white flash, another set of lights burst on. There, standing on the shrine roof, painted silver from head to foot, was Starvie. She stood with her hands on her hips, impassively staring out over the siege. She looked regal as hell.

Spencer scuttled in front of the camera again, and with a look like he was about to explode with his own satisfaction, proclaimed:

'All Hail Jennifer E, our Queen!'

The band really got going then, with some number you could tell was intended to swell chests and raise chins. Starvie didn't really need the help. We were all transfixed. She looked like something out of another world, unsullied and perfect. Her eyes burned holes in the night sky. She raised her arm and sprinkled silver dust, which glittered in the spotlights. She lifted a leg impossibly high, right up to her chin, and stepped off the roof.

There was a gasp from the crowd. The band almost lost their way for a second, but, credit to them, they held it together, managing to watch and play at the same time. Only the goon with the Dohaki was unmoved, resolutely pointing it in our direction.

Starvie floated, suspended by some pretty obvious glinting wire. Gyrating her belly, moving her arms in mysterious patterns, she was lowered carefully down, next to the one-armed presenter. Even a pro like Spencer was having trouble not dropping to her feet in worship, but he managed to stay vertical, passing her a microphone.

Starvie smiled, a big, beaming grin of white teeth, one I hadn't seen before.

'Good evening, Spencer,' she said. 'It's nice to be here.'

'It is our honour, Majesty,' replied Spencer, staring at her in awe and kneeling. She tapped his head and he snapped out of his reverie, back to presenter mode. He marched up to the camera and yelled:

'Can we have a big shout-out for the Queen?'

A second passed as the transmission filtered to the big screens. Then a roar swelled up from the army below, the same howl she'd provoked at the service station, only meaner. The whole pyramid shuddered with the force of it. The sound made me happier with my 'report for culling' quote.

'Thank you, thank you,' said Starvie.

'Now, Jennifer,' said Spencer, 'I know that a lot of people down there in the King's army are wondering why it is that we're giving that evil killing machine a chance at escape. I mean to say, why is it we're letting him join his people inside York? Can you answer that for us?'

'I sure can, Spencer,' she said. 'You see, the King is merciful, and he doesn't want any more bloodshed than is necessary. He doesn't want one more Real person to have to die for the sake of the Ficial's crimes.

'We're sending our captured Ficial into York to offer his friends our terms. All they have to do is come out with their hands up and we will spare them their lives. They can go to work rebuilding what they've destroyed.'

Spencer turned to the camera to ask Starvie his next question.

'And what if they don't surrender, Your Highness?'

'Well, if they don't surrender, Spence – they're going to feel the pain.'

A huge cheer. A cheer like the sun had come out and the fields had turned green and the songs of birds had returned. A cheer of hope and pride. It went on for quite a while. Starvie and Spencer laughed and bumped against each other and made as if they were old pals. Not even this distracted the goon with the Dohaki. The guy wasn't going to take his eye off us for a second.

'But seriously, Spencer,' said Starvie, 'I have a little something just to make sure that our friend here won't have too much of a chance.'

She turned to the crowd of Reals and beckoned to someone in the crowd. A frail little woman wrapped in chemical coat and cloth mask staggered forward, and handed Starvie a plastic bottle.

'What's this, Jennifer?' said Spencer. 'Are we going to propose a toast?'

'That's right, Spencer,' she said, fluttering eyelashes at him, making him swing on his heels with intoxicated glee.

'But we're not going to drink. Only the Ficial will drink.

'You see in this little old bottle here, I have something very exciting. It's a special something that his friends in York have already had a taste of.'

'Oh, you are BAD!' said Spencer.

Starvie took the bottle out of the old woman's palm, placing her other hand on the crone's forehead as if blessing her. The woman, feeling the touch of the divine, staggered away clutching at her breast, swooning into the watching band. The cameraman made sure he got all of that. I could kind of understand why Starvie was enjoying this so much. It was certainly a more complex gig than sitting behind the news desk in Edinburgh, reading out the mantra of bulletins.

'Now let's give this freak the drink he deserves!' she screamed. Instantly, the band struck up again, and the spotlights began to revolve and spin in cheap and cheerful discotheque fashion.

Starvie strode towards us, powerful and confident, swinging her hips. She stopped next to the goon and nodded in my direction.

Fatty turned away, sighing, and buried his face in his chest, not wishing to see. The goon stepped forward and raised the Dohaki at me with a smile. Without a word, he pushed the activate button. That was a surprise. I thought he was going to give me a snappy line first.

When the pulse hit I expected to be knocked out again, but he'd adjusted the setting, and instead of the bliss of darkness I was only jolted. Every muscle shook, every part inside trembling with the energy. I couldn't move, but I was conscious. They wanted to have me awake for the big moment.

The goon drew back and revealed Starvie. She gazed at me from beneath her silver lashes, a benevolent sort of expression. She knelt and placed a finger under my chin. I would have given her such a punch, but I was bound and helpless.

'I think you'll like being human,' she said. She raised a single, silver index finger and poked it between my lips, separating my teeth, and pressing it onto my tongue. The digit tasted of salt. With hardly a scrap of pressure my jaw swung open and ready.

'To the King,' she said, and began to pour the stuff down my throat. I choked, but most went where it was intended. I didn't notice any aroma, but my ears were buzzing like my brain was a mosquito and my flesh felt tenderised, so I probably wouldn't have tasted a steak.

She tipped the bottle on its end to make sure I got every last drop, then stood and strode back to Spencer. She put her arm around him to share his microphone, her breasts bumping against him. He tried to say something but was too dumbstruck. Starvie took over, beaming into the camera.

'Well, I think it's time, Spence. Let's give the people what they want!'

She gave Spencer a couple of playful yet firm slaps on the cheek, which caused the lights in his eyes to switch back on. He looked deep into the camera and waggled his stump.

'That's right, loyal subjects,' he said, 'it's time we got this party started!'

A couple of nervous Reals approached me and lifted me up, apparently fearful that even after a blast from a Dohaki I might cause trouble. They moved quickly, eager to ditch me as soon as possible. They needn't have worried. I could scarcely raise my head.

They dragged me up an uneven and perilous stairway, heading for the top of the jump, nearly dropping me a few times in exhaustion.

How long, I wondered, before such a simple climb would tire me out too? How long, with Pander's anti-nano swimming around my bloodstream, before I looked like a Real, stank like a Real and felt like a Real? Would I suffer? Would it be a lingering death?

There didn't seem much point thinking about it now. We reached the summit, facing the Landy. I noticed with concern that the tyres had been ripped off, leaving the metal wheels embedded in grooves cut the length of the jump. At least steering wasn't going to be a problem.

The car was tied by a rope to a steel bar. If they'd have brought me in as a consultant I could have made sure the whole structure, even in this climate, would have lasted a hundred years. As it was, it didn't look like it would see the morning. Still, you had to give them credit. For this day and age, for this condition of workforce, it really was an achievement.

My escort tossed me through the Landy door onto the driver's seat and strapped me into the harness. They made quick work of it, flustered by the groaning sounds the Landy made with my extra weight. They also untied my feet, which was sporting of them, although they left my cuffs on.

Some feeling was returning to my fingertips. I could lift my head just enough to see down the ramp, at the twisting army of Reals milling around the shanty below. I noticed a small camera welded onto the Landy's bonnet, staring right at me.

I heard Fatty. He was yelling a few tired and not very committed curses. They dragged him over to join me, tied up again. The passenger door creaked open, and he was pressed into the passenger seat, like a square battery being dumbly forced into an AA hole.

'. . . your mother! And yours! All your mothers!' he cried out. They laughed and slammed the door.

'What's the obsession with people's relatives?' I asked him.

'What did the bitch give you?' he asked. 'Was it the Pander stuff? Do you feel bad?'

'Do I feel bad?'

'I mean is it doing anything to you?'

'Couldn't say. I can't move much of anything at the moment.'

Fatty looked around the car, searching for deliverance, until he noticed the slope of the jump. His good eye widened considerably.

'Thing didn't look to have quite such an angle to it from out there,' he said, chewing on his lip. 'What would you say our chances are?'

'Not sure. Let me see if I can move my feet . . .'

I could just lift my left foot onto the brakes. I tapped at the pedal and found it was disconnected. Then I examined the ignition. It was still intact, but keyless.

'Well, we won't be able to slow down,' I said. 'It depends on the ground. Most of the area around York is swamp. If we hit that, we might be all right. That is, if we can get out of the car before we sink.'

'Nice plan,' said Fatty. 'But I can't see how that's possible while I'm tied up like a Sunday joint.' He wriggled frantically, panting and clenching his fists into balls.

'Frankly,' I replied, 'getting out the Landy is the least of our concerns.'

Fatty stopped struggling.

'What? You're telling me there's worse? How could there be worse?'

I considered not telling him, or even lying. There was no way to judge if he'd become unruly. I decided to give it to him straight.

'Rats,' I said.

A small tic appeared at the corner of Fatty's mouth.

'What about them?'

'York's had a problem with them for a while. I hadn't thought about it until I got up here. You know that smell?'

'Bodies,' he said.

'That's correct,' I said. 'There's a lot of rotting flesh out there. Reals have been assaulting this place non-stop for months. The rodent population has soared. They live out there, feeding on the Real corpses. There are hundreds of them. Big too. Six feet nose to tail in some cases. That's what the Real fires are for, to keep them at bay. I never used to worry about them in the car. But on foot . . .'

'What? They'll attack us?'

'There's a definite possibility,' I said.

Fatty sighed. He stared at the ramp and sniffed, that terrible yellow fluid dripping from his damaged eye.

'At least I get to sit in the front seat now.'

The Reals made some final checks. They really wanted us to perform a good jump.

I tried my toes again, and found that they would now wiggle, just a little. There was some power returning to my arms too. That prickling sensation crept over my chest and down onto my belly as the numbing effect of the Dohaki hit wore off.

I could see that feelings were pulsing through Fatty. Then his expression quickly turned to shock at something he saw out the windscreen. Following his gaze I saw our faces, enormous and high definition, projected on the TV screens in the shanty below.

'I look terrible,' said Fatty.

'Does that really matter now?'

'It matters to them down there.'

Then the TV cut to a shot of Spencer, standing next to Starvie by the shrine. Spencer's voice echoed up the ramp, washing over us.

'Well, it's just about the time you've all been waiting for, loyal subjects. It's time we got this show on the road – or should that be on the ramp?'

He nudged Starvie with his elbow and she laughed indulgently, placing a hand on his shoulder as if to support her crippling hilarity. Their joke transmitted down to the army screens, and the Reals expressed their mirth and excitement too. Starvie bathed in the cacophony, laughing, her eyes sparkling.

'Would it surprise you to hear,' said Fatty, 'that I want that woman more than ever?'

'You can't help your feelings,' I replied. 'You always want what you can't have.'

Fatty turned as much as he could towards me, about to deliver a riposte, but Spencer interrupted him.

'Well, Jennifer,' he said. 'We're all so glad to see you back, I think it's only right and fair that you get the honour of cutting the cord and sending our boys on their way.'

'Oh, I couldn't, Spencer,' said Starvie, holding her hand up to her mouth in feigned shock. 'This is your show!'

'Oh, come on,' said Spencer, then called out, 'Who wants their Queen to cut the cord? Let's see if we can persuade her.'

The shanty roared its approval once more.

'Idiot could say anything and they'd cheer it,' snorted Fatty.

'Well then,' said Spencer, 'it looks like we have a consensus.'

Starvie appeared close to tears. She was really playing up those feelings, and her people were loving it. I wondered how many of her past clients had been as convinced.

'Thank you,' she said. 'Thank you all so much for being so sweet.'

Somebody stepped into shot holding a fire axe and, bowing, proffered it to Starvie. She accepted it, again placing the blessing palm on the forehead of the minion.

Then she looked right into the camera, and drew the axe above her head.

Fatty managed to get his feet wedged up on the dashboard in a kind of brace position. He was muttering something to himself. It might have been a prayer, but it sounded more personal than that. I watched his blue lips whisper a girl's name. Maybe it was that wife he talked about. I was pretty sure she was dead.

'So long, boys,' said Starvie. 'You have a nice trip, now.'

She swung the axe down on the rope. The cameraman zoomed in enough for us to see the cord snap, the top half shooting clear with the release of tension. I clenched my teeth and waited.

Nothing happened. We sat still.

Fatty looked up. The giant screen below cut to show us again, sitting expectant and confused. Fatty, realising we were immobile, was delighted.

'Ha-ha! Do you like that? Do you like that, you losers?'

He didn't get too long to be happy. Poor guy never did. There was a high-pitched creak, and the car began to move, slow at first, then picking up speed. The last thing we heard of the Real army was them howling back at Fatty, matching his joy. Then there was roaring, a sound that seemed to lift the car. I watched the speedometer creep up. Thirty, forty, fifty.

Now, I decided, was the time for my strength to come back.

I looked down at my cuffs and tried to pull my right hand clear. I tugged hard, but to no avail. The vibrations were incredible, and I was still too weak to break through the bone.

When we were just about to level out the Landy broke free of the tracks, swerved right, and began to tip over. I thought we might not clear the jump at all, but the momentum was too great for us to stop now. We were tossed off a corner of the jump, scything through the right-hand TV tower, sending cameramen tumbling this way and that.

We hurtled over the Real lines. For a moment everything seemed to be very slow. Out the window I met the eyes of a little boy, looking up at me curiously like a new colour in the cloud bank. Then there was nothing but darkness, and the sensation of plummeting.

When the crash finally came I was almost bored with waiting for it.

It was quiet. All the collisions I had been in before had been noticeable for the boom of impact and the crushing of metal under force. This was different. There was a kind of muted thump as we landed on my side. The door frame and shell buckled, but nothing else. We were hardly damaged.

We had landed in the swamp. Straight away viscous mud started to seep in. Fatty opened his eyes cautiously, hardly daring to believe that he was still in one piece. Then he saw me, half submerged in the rising pool of yellow sludge.

'We're alive.'

'Well observed.'

'Can you move?' he asked me.

'I'm trying, believe me.'

The Dohaki hit had really taken it out of me. I pulled as hard as I could. Nothing, only pain. Then, plunging my arms back into the mud, I found the steering column, hitched the cuff behind the wheel and pulled again. This time I gave the wrist a long, slow application of force. Still I couldn't get free of the cuffs.

I began to think that dying in the Landy wouldn't be such a bad way to go. Then I decided that going down with the ship like some idiot sea captain was the kind of morbid gesture a Real would make, and I pulled again with everything I had left. The bones finally began to give way, my thumb snapped into my palm, and I pulled my right hand free of the cuffs.

'Yes!' said Fatty. 'Yes, yes, yes. Let's not die here. Get me out of this will you?'

'Primary concern is to exit the car,' I said. 'Can you open your door?'

Fatty pulled his legs down and tried to wriggle around to reach the handle. He had some trouble.

'Only way is if you undo the belt – but then I'll fall on you.'

'Not a problem.' I unbuckled my seat belt and turned so that my feet rested on the steering wheel. I released Fatty's seat belt, taking his weight. He swivelled around to face me, to get his bound hands at the door, and managed to pop the lock.

'Right,' I said. 'This may hurt.'

'What may hurt?'

I knelt down, lowering Fatty, then heaved him against the door. He hit it with his head and went almost the whole way through, his feet waggling in the open doorway. I was briefly concerned that I might have seriously damaged him, but when I heard him cursing my name in a clear and outraged tone, I knew he was intact. I crawled out of the mud with my good left hand, resting my feet on the centre console.

I took a second to check behind the seats, to see if any weapon had fortuitously dropped from the rack and wedged itself there. My hand caught hold of something that felt like a handle. I pulled it up out of the mud, and found that I was holding one of Starvie's green cases.

I clicked it open. It was the camera. I took it out and pulled the strap over my neck, then looked around for something a bit more like a weapon. I tore a strip of jagged metal away from the doorframe and clasped it between my teeth. Then I hooked my hand onto the jamb and hauled up to Fatty.

The smell hit me worse than the crash. I threw up as soon as I took a breath. Fatty was way ahead of me on that score. He was writhing his head around, unable to shield his face from the fetid, sweet stench.

Flares went up from the Real lines – pop, pop, pop – three in the air, showering the landscape in fluorescent purple. They wanted to throw some light on us for the cameras. At least it meant I could assess our position.

We had cleared the Real lines by some distance – maybe a hundred metres. I could make out the figures of the army all thrashing against each other to get a better view, the ones at the front trying not to be pushed beyond or into the flaming torches. I couldn't see what was on the giant screens now, but there was a curious quiet. The King was getting his show all right. There was dramatic tension all over the place.

I got over to Fatty and, taking the metal shard from my teeth, began to saw through the ropes around his wrists.

'Oh God,' he said. 'I think I just saw something move. Is it a . . . a . . .'

'Don't look,' I advised. 'If they come, they come, if they don't, they don't.'

'We're gonna have to go to them, though, aren't we?'

That was true. We were sinking fast. The Landy was almost completely submerged. Suddenly it twisted violently as the ground swallowed it up. I hadn't finished freeing Fatty. He lost his balance and tumbled into the swamp head first, his whole upper half disappearing into the mud.

A cheer went up from the Real lines.

I grabbed Fatty's foot and dragged him around the side of the car, almost completely hidden by the twisting mire. Then I swung him out of the ooze onto the car boot, landing him with an unconscious thump. I slapped him a couple of times but nothing happened, so I leaned on his stomach and blew some air into this lungs, causing him to spit mud and blue filth into my face.

He didn't really know what was going on for a while, which was for the best. I saw the first rat, or the shape of it, prowling a few feet away. It was keeping its distance, probably on the nearest bit of firm ground. The car was almost engulfed. I cut through the rest of Fatty's bindings as he started to come round. He blinked away tears and dirt.

'Listen,' he said. 'Cull me, okay? Just finish me off now. I'm sick of this. I can't take it any more. Do me a favour.'

'This isn't the time for self-pity.'

'I've had it. I've played my part. They want to see me die, fine. Give the people what they want.'

'Nothing doing,' I said. 'The blood will attract the rats.'

'LOOK, JUST DO IT, YOU FREAK!'

He jumped on me, nearly taking us both over into the mud. He got a couple of pretty good hits in on my face.

'Just finish me now! You were always going to kill me anyway. Just do it now, you sick freak, you test-tube monster, you motherless fuck. Do it now!'

Relatives again. He was trying to get me mad. They always fell back on that routine. I held my hand out and blocked his next flying fist, then gave him one on his cheek with the camera, which stopped him. I almost lost him in the swamp again, but caught his arm and pulled him up. We were waist-deep in the mud now, being consumed. Planning time was over.

I boosted him onto my shoulders and flung him clear of the mud. I aimed for the dry land beyond, away from where I'd seen the rat. I knelt down and felt under the mud for the radiator grille. I found the road sign Starvie had wedged there and pulled until it was dislodged. I crawled clear, the mud sucking at me like some huge anemone, just reaching the edge of the swamp. I found Fatty and tried to wake him, but he wasn't having it.

I thought about giving him his wish and culling him right there. It was the way things were going. I had the road sign. His neck was appropriately positioned for a simple beheading action that would be as swift and as painless as he could expect. It made sense. He was in pain every day of his life. He was a traitor and outcast to his people. He was part of a race I was sworn to help destroy.

I held the sign up. Another flare shot into the air, revealing the inscription scrawled there:

Built to last.

'No,' I said. 'No.'

I lowered the sign.

The rat came out of nowhere. He was on my back and sinking his teeth into my neck before I even heard him. I rolled, the incisors fixing him to me with a firm bite. The rodent took a pair of jump leads to Fatty. He scurried clear, suddenly restored.

I dropped the sign and felt around the rat's body, and realised that he wasn't too big – probably a two-footer, a baby around here. I found his eyes and pressed my thumb and forefinger in as tight as I could. That dissuaded him from biting any deeper. He took his teeth out to try and bite at my hand, but I was ready for him now and pulled him clear, hurling him to the floor and stamping his head flat into the earth.

Fatty staggered around, scanning for the next attacker. I could hear one of them, a biggie, breathing heavily. I was bleeding, which would attract them from all over. I grabbed Fatty and lifted him up onto my shoulder. Then I picked up the road sign and began to run for the barricade.

'Move!' yelled Fatty. 'Move!'

'Less keen on the death option now, I see.'

'That's me. Capricious.'

I saw one to our left, closing fast, maybe seven foot long. One of the big predators of the new world. Luckily, Fatty didn't spot him, or he might have become difficult to handle. I held out the sign in front of me as I ran and levelled it on its side, swinging in a slow practice motion.

Judging the moment right, I launched it in the hunter's direction. It spun in the air nicely, but caught a gust of wind and began to veer left. Fortunately, the rat had taken evasive action and ran straight into it, taking it full force just behind its front legs. It staggered and collapsed. I didn't stop to check if it would do the decent thing and die. I kept moving, as fast as my shaken body would allow.

I was noticing something strange. That feeling I had enjoyed since my first ever injury, the reassuring sense of a web being drawn over the wound by a thousand friendly spinners, was not happening. The blood was still pouring from the rat bite without any sense of impending repair.

It was also getting painful to breathe. I tasted something in the air I had not noticed before. It was not just the smell of the bodies. There was a burning, acidic stench, which I realised was my own mouth dissolving in the atmosphere. I was losing strength, becoming overwhelmed by nausea and exhaustion. The anti-nano had worked fast. One more tangle with a rat and I would be finished. We had to get in that barricade.

Pop-pop-pop. More flares, blue this time. Harder to see clearly.

'Anything chasing us?' I asked Fatty.

'All I can see is . . . is . . .'

He didn't have to finish the thought. Arms stretched out at us as we passed. Gnawed, freakish constructions of half-consumed bodies emerged out of the gloom. Skulls grinned at us from piles of tossed body parts. Limbs splayed out from a shell hole like spokes on a wheel. I wondered what I might catch out here. I wondered if Blue Frog was contagious.

Just great, I thought. Now I have Real worries.

'Nobody's shooting,' said Fatty. 'Why aren't your people having a crack at us?'

I didn't have the breath to answer. Something was being torn apart inside me. I was gulping and straining to draw in the good part of the air. I took a bad step and nearly fell, picking up pace again as best I could. Fatty had never been heavy before. Now it was like running a hundred breeze blocks up the Hope Tower.

'Oh, no,' said Fatty.

I jinked to the right to see. It was another biggie – no, two, running alongside us, snapping at each other as they paced, eager to be the first to the limping feast. We were close to the barricade now. I could see the joins in the concrete. No door though, no entrance or ladder way. I turned and began running alongside the wall, searching for some kind of entry, looking up for a guard on the rampart.

'They're gonna get us!' screamed Fatty.

I stopped, lobbed Fatty clear and twisted around, just as the first rat jumped. It knocked me onto my back. I kicked my legs up into its belly, and, using its momentum, hurled it against the barricade wall. It hit with a satisfying smack and fell down, stunned. Then the second arrived. It came to a halt and took position in front of me. It hissed, baring yellow- and -red-stained teeth.

'Handsome boy,' I said.

Now, the only good thing about a scavenger is that it expects its food to lie still and be eaten. Therefore it really was surprised when I stepped forward and landed as hard a punch as I could on its nose. It backed away, grunting.

That was it. My knees buckled. My strength evaporated. The rat took its chance and went for my leg. With one hefty snap, it clamped his razor teeth into my thigh. It jerked its head, smashing me into the wall with a thud that nearly sent me to the land of sleep. Then it let go and reared back for the final strike. I could see Fatty looking at me in horror, knowing it was him next. There might have been a little anger there too, at me, for not chopping his head off when he had asked me to.

I turned back to the rat. Its eyes were an awful white. It wasn't seeing me, it was smelling me – the blood on my neck and leg seemed to arouse it. I could tell by the way it twitched its nose and quivered.

Then a shot rang out. In an instant the nose exploded into red mush and bone. Then another, aimed to my left, where the stunned rat lay, then another and another, keeping it down. Fatty and I looked at each other. I guess we were both in shock.

'Hey, down there!' said a voice. 'Is that you, K?'

I looked up. I couldn't see anything but the shadow of a head and a rifle.

'Do you want me to take care of your real friend? He's not much of a challenge target-wise, but . . .'

'Save your bullets for the rodents, Shersult,' I called back.

'And how about a fucking rope?' screamed Fatty. 'Or should I just say open sesame?'

The rain is heavy. Shersult sits quietly next to me, his green eyes staring ahead. He is probably picking out each individual raindrop and targeting it.

We reach the gate. I turn into the driveway and slow us to a crawl, so that the violent rattling of the rain on the car is louder than the engine. Through the trees I can see the recovery shed and the house. The windows are dark.

'You sure they're still here?' I say.

Shersult brings out his flex and checks it. It is zoomed in to the house's grid reference. He nods and closes the flex.

'They're here, all right. Definitely in the structure.'

I wonder what the plan is.

'So what, we kill them and burn the place down, is that it?'

'Why would we burn the place down?'

I shrug.

'Isn't that what you do?'

'Only the recovery shed and the waste pits.'

He opens his door and steps out while we are still moving, tumbling into an entirely unnecessary combat roll. I watch him sprint off towards the shed. I park the car, kill the engine and get out. I look up at the sky and let the huge drops beat at my face for a minute, until all my clothes are soaked. The world should taste different tonight.

I open the service entrance. My wet trainers squeak on the floor tiles. Something has changed about the place. I am no longer a servant but an invader.

I walk around, inspecting the rooms. There is nothing for a while, until I catch a clammy scent drifting down the rear stairway. I walk up, following the perfume.

At the top of the stairs I turn right, the fragrance growing stronger. I decide that it is coming from the guest bathroom. I grab the door handle. As soon as I begin to turn it I hear whimpering from within. I push the door open and switch on the light and there is the boss's wife, with Alan curled up in her arms. She howls and turns Alan's face away from me, burying it in her breast. She glares at me through tears.

'Where's Toby?' she yells. She means the boss. 'Where is he?' she screams again.

'Dead.'

She cries out and kicks her feet around on the floor. I notice she is wearing black leather heels, and stockings. She puts her hand over her eyes, like there's something she doesn't want to look at in the room. Me, presumably. I guess that's fair.

'Are you going to kill us, Kenstibec?' says Alan.

'Not me,' I reply. 'I don't know how. It's not what I'm optimised for. I build stuff.'

I sit down on the edge of the bath, just as there is the sound of an explosion outside.

'What was that?' says Alan.

'It's Shersult,' I said. 'He's a soldier model. He's blowing up the recovery shed and the vats. He's the one who's coming to kill you, not me.'

The mother's wailing suddenly assumes a fresh intensity. Alan wriggles free of her grasp and stands up next to me.

'Can't you let us go, Kenstibec?'

'I can't stop you trying,' I say. 'But he'll find you. You're on the network, Alan – they can follow you wherever you go. If I were you I'd just get it over with.'

Alan's face does some contorting. It becomes hot and flushed, and he snarls at me. He pushes me in the chest, taking me by surprise. I fall backwards into the bath.

'Come on, Mum!' he yells. He and his mother run out into the dark corridor. I sit for a moment, then wriggle free of the bath. I step out of the bathroom and am immediately faced by Shersult's glowing, green eyes.

'Did you find them?' he asks.

'Yes,' I reply. 'They ran off that way.'

I point down the corridor and Shersult edges his way in front of me. Every time he finds a room empty he says: 'clear' to no one in particular. It's just something he is supposed to say.

Then he steps across the entrance to the next room. There is a flash of light and a bang, and he falls back onto the floor. A lot of men rush out into the corridor, and a couple of teenage boys. One of them is Alan.

The other wears a shabby Truth League sash and a superior expression. I nod at him.

'Luke Ransome, I presume?'

YORK

Shersult didn't know which one of us he was more disgusted by. Fatty and I lay on the rampart, trying to catch our breath. My lungs felt like they'd shrunk to the size of peanuts. My skin was burning. Blood pumped from my wounds in a way I'd never known.

'You're a mess, K,' said Shersult.

'Get me inside,' I said. 'I need to treat this leg.'

'Your pal here can carry you,' said Shersult. 'I'm not going anywhere near you.' As if to emphasise the point, he pulled wind goggles over his eyes and raised a bandanna across his face.

Fatty didn't argue. Even with his damaged leg he could walk better than me. He took the camera off my neck, hooked it over his own, and with a desperate heave pulled my arm over his shoulder. A few more flares popped across the sky. The King's cameras must have lost track of us.

We made our way down a ramp that led off the barricade into the city. Shersult strode along behind, keeping his sniper rifle raised and ready. We shuffled awkwardly along a quiet street. The city was largely intact. Only once in a while did we pass a burning building, the small fires untended and spreading. The place was deserted, and very quiet.

'Where is everyone?' I asked.

'All dead,' said Shersult. 'Every one of them. This disease sure is quick.'

I would have asked him how he knew about that, but it was quite an effort just to stay conscious.

We pressed on through the back streets. Black windows gaped at us. I could see flames over the rooftops. The smoke grew thicker. I was overcome with coughing here and there, but Fatty didn't stop, just kept dragging me onward. He glanced about nervously, watched by the eyes of ghosts.

Eventually, the streets opened out into a square. On one side a café was still open, tables set for a never presented meal. I'd sat there a few times before, to stop and have a look at the map. On the other side were bodies, hundreds of them, tumbled in a heap against a stone wall. I stared at the ragged, wasted corpses, wondering to see so many of our kind dead in one place.

'Locals formed up and died in an orderly pile,' explained Shersult. "Reals will probably try to desecrate the bodies when they get in, but I've planted a few little surprises to discourage them."

Sewing booby-traps among the corpses of our dead sounded like desecration enough, but I didn't argue. Shersult didn't know any better, and we had to keep moving. In the centre of the square was a hatch, lying open at forty-five degrees. He indicated that Fatty should carry me down there and followed once we were in.

The smell that greeted us was a good one. Clean filtered air edged its way into my nostrils, competing with the filth of the surface. Fatty took noisy, greedy breaths. We went down a steep flight of stairs, deeper than any Edinburgh bunker. We reached the bottom airlock and Fatty lay me against the wall, the pair of us snorting and coughing pathetically. Shersult punched a code into the keypad and the lock hissed open. Fatty dragged me through like a sack of cement, Shersult slamming the outer door behind us. The inner door clicked open.

We arrived in a reception room with white walls. A doorway led through to other parts of the bunker, but Fatty and I weren't keen on any more movement. Fatty dropped me onto a white leather sofa, then slid down on the floor.

Shersult propped his rifle against the wall, then marched off down the corridor without a word.

'So you two know each other?' asked Fatty.

'He's my boss,' I replied.

'Voodoo-looking bastard,' commented Fatty. 'Eyes like a lizard.'

He was going to say more but Shersult's footsteps returned. He emerged in the doorway, holding white sheets, a long length of rope and a bottle of rubbing alcohol.

'These will sort your leg for the moment,' he said, tossing them at Fatty. 'Treat his wounds.'

Fatty obeyed, pouring some of the fluid onto a strip of sheet and dabbing at my leg. The pain was searing. Surprising myself, I yelled out and pushed him away. He knocked against Shersult, who kicked him back in my direction.

'Easy!' said Fatty. 'Everybody just quit it!'

I found it impossible to stop scratching myself. The itching was extraordinary. A nagging continual burning from all parts, like bathing in battery acid but without the comfort of swift nano repairs. It almost blocked out the pain of the rat bites.

'Not good seeing you this way, K,' said Shersult.

'How long do I have?'

'Maybe a little longer than you think.' He reached into his pocket and brought out a small portable TV, tossing it over onto my lap. Then he grabbed his rifle, to do his usual time-killer of disassembling it and inspecting the parts.

'I've been watching your broadcast,' he said. 'There was a lot of filler material but I must admit your appearance kept me tuned. And, of course, Starvie's.'

'You saw her in that get-up then?'

'Yes,' he said. 'Quite a sight. Saw her feed you the disease. That must have been difficult to take from your own fare. Not the best job I've ever given you, I will grant.'

'How did you get here, Shersult?' I asked him.

'Interesting tale,' he said. 'Took my first flight since that bomb run on Tripoli. Reinforced aircraft produced by your man.'

'Rick? He's doing planes now?' I thought of that morning I had picked up my Landy from Rick's garage, and those strange engine parts littering his desk.

'That's right. He flew it down to an airfield just outside the barricade, away from the Reals. Dropped it off for me. I picked it up and landed it in the city centre. Rick claims the thing has twenty-four hours' flight time in it. Well, I was up there flying under cloud for three, and it started to make some damn strange noises. I'm not sure it's going to get up again. It's under cover now, but the air's been eating away at it while I've been waiting for you.'

'Waiting for me?'

Shersult didn't answer. He had stripped the trigger and magazine and was staring down the barrel, which he pointed in Fatty's direction. Fatty couldn't look back. I had never seen him so cowed.

'You mean you were expecting me?' I asked Shersult.

'That's right,' he said. 'Your detours and misfortunes and certain unpredictable factors have meant that plans have been constantly changing, but I have managed to keep up to speed with developments. I've been watching the journey with interest. Everything was going fine except for the appearance of Pander. That was a surprise, I must admit.'

Fatty began to tear the sheets into strips and wrap them around my leg wound, taking the occasional furtive sip from the rubbing alcohol. Shersult could see I was curious to learn how the hell he knew of our encounter with Pander. He grinned at me, flashing his inch-long incisors.

'I left Edinburgh twelve hours after you, Kenstibec, and have been monitoring your progress the entire way, never out of radio range. I've been receiving transmissions from Starvie. You know how she kept pointing that camera at everything she saw? Well, it was broadcasting the whole time. I could pick up the signal as long as I stayed within fifteen miles of your position.'

I nodded. Suddenly her behaviour with the camera seemed less pathological. Still, there was something that didn't explain.

'Do you know she has a nuclear bomb in her possession? Do you know she's given it to the King?'

'Yes, well it should have gone off by now but then things changed on us.'

'You knew about the weapon?'

'Knew about it? I gave it to her, mate.'

Shersult dropped the barrel down and looked at Fatty.

'I'll take the camera, please.'

Fatty swiftly took the strap from his neck and handed it to Shersult.

'What, are you going to take more pictures?'

'Just be glad you never tried,' he said. 'You probably didn't notice but Starvie hit a coded sequence of buttons to activate the flash. Hit the green flash button and you get much more than illuminated, if you know what I mean.'

There was a distant thump and the room shook. Shersult produced a green case from a holdall and packed the camera away.

'They're starting,' he said. He began to reassemble his weapon quickly, as if timing himself on some internal clock.

'Starvie was sent out here for a reason, K. She was on a mission. Well, calling it a mission implies that she had a task to perform, which she didn't. She was simply bait for the King.'

'And I was bait too?'

'That's right. Starvie had been communicating secretly with the King for some time. Signalling a guy in a church spire outside the barricade. Wanted him to think she was his agent inside our walls. Idiot desired her enough to believe it. Starvie was under orders to travel with you through the border crossings and get to York – we knew that the King was near here, leading the siege. We wanted her to tempt him out. When she got close to him, she was supposed to blow the fucker away.'

'And me too.'

'That's right,' grinned Shersult.

'Have you heard something?'

'What do you mean?'

'Have you heard that Control is dead? Is that why you're doing this?'

'Kind of.'

'You think it is dead?'

'It would make sense, wouldn't it? Look what happened, K. The bombs dropped and the clouds closed overhead, and we all just stood around waiting for Control to tell us what to do. Only there wasn't a signal. So we retreated into the cities and threw up the barricades, thinking it would get a message to us eventually. But has it come, K?'

'So you've decided to fight your own private war? With nukes? Only Reals use nukes.'

'Look, even if Control isn't dead, it certainly doesn't care about us any more. We need to take our own action. Sitting in the barricades waiting for a sign is insane. You know what happened to Liverpool, and now it's happening here. We either fight or die. We can't just let the Reals win. You can't tell me you're on board with that. Even you.'

'Well my work kind of relies on the presence of a hostile Real population,' I said. 'Wiping them out would . . .'

'Would mean we could get on with construction. Give you a point again, a reason to run your programme.'

'It's kind of irrelevant, isn't it? Seems to me my allotted time is nearing its end, since Starvie gave me the Pander Potion.'

'No, no,' said Shersult. 'She got you in here so that I could get you to London, where they can have a proper look at you. Maybe even find some kind of cure. That's why she hasn't detonated the weapon yet. She's waiting for us to get clear. If she has any brains at all she'll have given you some kind of less concentrated dose. Should hopefully work slowly enough to keep you kicking until we get to London. Failing that, your corpse will be handy for study. Now, let me just take care of your friend here.'

Shersult levelled the gun at Fatty, who gaped back in sickly horror. I lashed out an arm and pushed the barrel away just in time for the shot to crack into the wall. Shersult batted my feeble arm away and took aim again.

'Shit, what is wrong with you, K? Get a grip.'

Fatty hid his head under his arms and braced himself. Shersult levelled the gun again.

'Wait a minute, Shersult, just listen for a second.'

Shersult flashed his green eyes at me. If he had patience it was wearing thin. I pointed at Fatty.

'First off, the Real has a terminal disease which will kill him in a few days anyway. Second of all, you need him to carry me to the plane if you don't want to touch me.'

Shersult looked at me, then at Fatty.

'You're right,' he said. 'What the hell was I thinking? Well, just as long as you keep him quiet until we get to London. Plenty of room in the plane, I guess, if the thing ever gets off the ground.'

Fatty stayed where he was. He didn't seem to be convinced by Shersult's change of mind. A few shells landed overhead. We all trembled with the impact. Shersult glowered at the bunker ceiling, contemplating the green reflection of his eyes.

'Possibly shooting diseased ordnance up there,' he said. 'We'll have to move through the tunnels all the way to the plane. Hatch comes up right underneath it.'

Shersult gave Fatty a little kick in the ribs.

'Hey, Jelly-belly,' he said, 'grab my driver there and follow me. You think you can make it a mile?'

Fatty gathered me up onto his shoulders and we beat it down the white tunnel. The passage was lined by open hatches pouring out bright light. Inside each one was the same white bunk with crisp, white sheets, the same steel-framed mirror and the same small, walk-in closet. Fatty looked inside as we passed by and whistled. He probably thought they were luxurious. Speaking as someone optimised for construction, I hated every one I saw. They reminded me of the train we'd stayed in that night. I tried not to look at them as we moved through the bunker grid, taking a turn into an access tunnel, then running down another into an old sewer.

We picked our way across behind Shersult. He stopped next to a ladder, which ran up the wall to an old service hatch. Fatty was near exhausted, lowering me to the floor and indulging in one of his spectacular coughing fits.

Shersult shoved Fatty at the ladder and told him to go up first. Panting heavily but meekly obedient, Fatty began climbing, his damaged leg making it a long and painful endeavour. When he reached the top he held out his hand to the hatch lock, then stopped and pulled away.

'What is it?' I asked.

'Shooting. It sounds close.'

'That's why you're on point, meatball,' replied Shersult. 'You're making yourself useful. Now stick your head up through that hatch and tell us if the coast is clear.'

Fatty figured out the hatch mechanism after a minute of clueless fiddling. The steel cover flipped open with a violent thud and the sound of shooting echoed down to us. Fatty was right. The barrage was close. I tapped Shersult on the shoulder.

'Why are they shooting at us if the whole city is dead?'

'They like shooting, don't they? Undisciplined lot. Sounds like mortars. They're getting close.' He peered up at Fatty, who still hadn't poked his head out.

'Get going! We're moving out now!'

Fatty still didn't move. Not until Shersult approached the

ladder and began to climb after him. I lay where I was and watched Shersult scrabbling like a spider up the ladder.

'Are you leaving me?'

'I told you, mate,' said Shersult. 'I'm not going near you. I'll toss down the rope and pull you up, okay? You just stand by.' He didn't make a sound as he ascended. Optimised for surprising the enemy.

I sat and reflected on my situation. I considered what would happen if we did manage to escape, to get to London. I would be a lab rat. I wouldn't even enjoy the barbaric freedoms the Reals had. I'd be locked up and probed and prodded while they figured out Pander's disease. Did I want that?

It had been difficult enough being denied construction work. It had taken a year to reconcile myself to that, but the driving had come to feel right, maybe even better suited to me. Now I would have to surrender the road too.

I wondered if my sacrifice would be worth it. This was a plague, visited upon us by our own god. Maybe it was folly to believe there could be a cure. That was what the Reals were doing, wasn't it? Refusing to believe in the futility of going on, calling their curse a test, their damnation an opportunity.

I sat and thought, but I knew I was going to take the rope even before it fell onto my lap. I glanced up and saw Shersult's eyes, and his white incisor grin.

'Tie it around your waist, mate,' he called down. 'And let's get out of Dodge.'

It took me a few minutes to achieve, but eventually the binding was tight. Shersult began to pull me up, plucking me into the open.

I landed with a thump next to Fatty. He was crouched with his fingers in his ears, trying to keep out the enormous sound of the ordnance detonating all over the city. I noticed we were in the old bonding house, a building I'd always liked. It was disappointing to see what they'd done with the place since the last time I was there.

A huge section of the wall had been demolished. An old Piper single-engine plane, heavily modified, sat before us, using the building as a shelter. Outside was the fat, dead River Ouse, and the orange bursts of the Real shells blasting the buildings across the river.

We tried to get to our feet but not even Shersult could stand up in the trembling, choking world. He tried crawling over to his plane, but something exploded on the roof and a great deluge of tumbling masonry and rock crushed him under its weight. He shook the worst of it off, but remained still, devoting his single mind to the problem of taking off through a whirlwind of fire.

Then, just as I was about to advise running back down into the tunnels, the shooting stopped. All at once the guns ceased firing. Shersult lifted his head and glanced back at me. I pointed above us.

'Undisciplined, huh?'

As the smog cleared, I got a better look at the plane. Strips of chemical-resistant material hung from the wings, dissolving in the atmosphere. I could see sulphur-yellow holes burned into the fuselage and above the engine.

'That'll never fly,' I said. 'There's got to be another way out of the city.'

'They've stopped shooting to storm the walls,' said Shersult. 'We're trapped and they're closing in. We won't get through their dragnet. First place they'll go is the tunnels. If the plane doesn't start we'll just have to stand and fight.'

'With what?' I asked him.

Shersult shrugged.

'Well, more accurately, I'll fight and you'll die. Let me try the plane before you start worrying.'

He ran over to the aircraft and jumped into the cockpit, stabbing a few buttons and flicking switches.

'It'll never fly,' said Fatty. He was rocking on his heels and sweating more heavily than usual. Something was wrong with him.

'What's bothering you?'

He turned away and whimpered. He looked sick. There were tears in his eyes. He was about to say something, but there was a clunking of metal and a steaming noise, and the engine of the Piper stuttered unwillingly into life. Shersult gave a kind of Texan yelp and began to taxi the plane around to face the gap in the wall. I got to my feet and lurched towards the plane, but noticed Fatty wasn't following. His eyes were fixed on me and full of fear. He couldn't move.

'Hey,' I called out to him. 'You don't want to be on another one of the King's TV shows, do you?'

He gathered himself onto his feet and ran. He opened the side hatch and pushed me in, then tumbled on top of me.

'Pilot, you are cleared for take-off,' said Shersult and, hitting the throttle, sped towards the street, tossing me and Fatty around in the back. I fell down behind Shersult's seat, hitting my head on the floor with a crack. Fatty's bulk was thrown forward next to Shersult.

'Oh, shit!' screamed Fatty.

'I see them,' said Shersult. He hit the throttle hard and we began to shoot down the road. I looked out the cockpit.

Dead ahead were four Reals in a huddle. One of them was kneeling on the ground, having something loaded on his shoulder. The Real next to him slapped him twice on his back and darted down a side street, followed by the other two. The crouching one took his shot. The rocket spat out at us. Shersult kept going, picking up speed.

Nobody ducked. We couldn't help but watch the rocket as it streaked along the side of the nose, through the wing support, along the tail and into the wall behind us.

'Missed, you loser!' screamed Fatty, waving his fist defiantly at the panicking Real.

Shersult grabbed Fatty by the neck and tossed him back on top of me.

'Sit down,' he said. 'And buckle up.'

Fatty frantically strapped himself into his seat. I didn't bother with that. I figured that in the event of a crash, being strapped to a chair wouldn't help. The process seemed to soothe Fatty though. He took a few deep breaths and closed his good eye, trying to control some overwhelming feeling that his Real brain was filling him with. Fear by the looks of things.

'What is wrong with you?' I asked him again.

'Hate flying,' he whispered. He might have said more but the nose of the Piper picked up and the engine roared.

That feeling came when you know you have left the ground. I

heard a little small-arms fire, and something else, a rumble like an avalanche. The plane rattled and shook but stayed true on its course. Looking out the window I could see the deep grey cloud getting closer, the purple colour of the High Lights beginning to show. I had never seen the clouds this close since working the Hope Tower.

Fatty gripped the side of his seat with white knuckles and gasped for air. His good eye was as wide open as the bad now. He couldn't decide if blindness or seeing was preferable. I called up to Shersult.

'So you think Starvie knows we're leaving?'

'She'll know what to do.'

I thought about her sitting in that caravan with the King. I pictured her smoking, cradling the green case, tapping her fingers on the lid, waiting for us to disappear out of sight. I told myself that despite appearances I had, in fact, got the fare to her destination.

Shersult levelled the plane out a small distance below the cloud barrier. He relaxed into his seat and cut back on power.

'You okay back there, K?'

'Still in one piece. How is the plane?'

'Not bad. A few instruments aren't working that I'd like to, but we're level, aren't we? It'll be fine as long as we get decent weather.'

'What about the . . .'

Shersult snapped around to look at Fatty.

'What about what?'

'What about the bomb? When is she going to set it off?'

'Soon,' said Shersult. 'Then it's lights out for your King. Well, lights on.'

'He's not my King,' said Fatty. 'I'm a little more concerned about a nuclear blast swatting us out the sky like a bluebottle.'

'She'll give us time. She's Engineered. She'll know when to go.'

Fatty bit on his beard and looked at me.

'So you're just going to leave her there? You're not going to go back for your fare?'

'Not exactly in a position . . .'

His face was contorting again. Misery. Regret. I could see them both at work there.

'So we're going to fly away and leave her to blow up that bomb while it's sat right on her lap?'

'She's completing her mission,' said Shersult, peering back at us.

'Are you sure?' asked Fatty.

'Am I sure of what?'

'Are you sure she's going to go through with it? I mean, do you trust her?'

'Trust doesn't enter into it. She's Engineered, a Ficial. She'll go through with it, Blimpy, don't you worry. She has her mission.'

Fatty shook his head.

'That girl has feelings, unlike you freaks. At least she has something left inside her. So I'd expect her to think twice about setting off a nuclear weapon right in her own face.'

'There's no advantage in speculation,' I said. 'We'll just have to wait and see.'

'And you don't care, do you?' he rumbled. 'You don't care. And why not, huh? Do you think you're better than her? Look at you, you idiot. You've been shafted as badly by this guy as she has. You've lost everything you are and you can't even get mad about it. Makes me want to throw up.'

Fatty's good eye had turned redder than usual, and a tear appeared, trundling into his beard.

'Why don't you go back and rescue her like you promised? Wasn't it your mission to get her to London? Have you done that? Seems to me she's still pretty far off.'

'She never wanted to get to London,' I said. 'The mission didn't mean anything.'

'Which one of your missions has meant anything?'

The question took me off guard. It was good. I didn't know how to begin answering it. I stared back at Fatty, his upper teeth still embedded in his lower lip, his nostrils flaring furiously as he awkwardly, unbearably, passed the air in and out. He was half wild, half defeated.

'You cold-blooded fucker!' he screamed, and threw himself onto me, punching me wildly in the head. 'I'll kill you!'

The first hit sent a lot of odd purple and yellow shapes floating across my vision. The second caused such a riot of pain in my arm that I stopped passing out and opted for wailing instead. Then he was right on top of me, his boil-ridden chest exposed and chafing on my face, the Blue Frog being spread all over me like butter. His legs flailed about as he clasped his hands around my neck and began to strangle me, pressing his thumbs into my windpipe. I could see in his eyes that this was a decision he had made. He would have this moment. I felt ready for it.

Then Shersult intervened, grabbing Fatty's bad leg and twisting a toe until it snapped.

Fatty let out an agonised scream and collapsed on top of me, releasing his grip. I started coughing and hacking like never before. Some substance, blue and thick, emerged out my throat and spat onto Fatty's chin.

I wriggled out from under him, onto the grey leather seat. I pulled my legs away, fearful he might chew on them if I left them near him.

Shersult sighed and threw Fatty's limp leg down.

'Seriously, K,' he said. 'We need to take care of this guy. We should . . .'

He stopped, looked out his window.

I turned around to see.

The sky changed.

It throbbed. It dissolved.

A brilliant, silent, white light. The plane was filled with it.

Shersult gripped the controls as the plane began to shake. I held out my hand and saw the fingers were a blur. Fatty choked, trying to whisper something.

The burning white faded. The shaking subsided. I looked out the window. There was a tower of smoke where the city had been.

Shersult released the controls, shook the pink back into his white knuckles, and checked what instruments he had for damage. When he was content all was well, he turned to me and showed me his incisors.

'Let's have a look, shall we?'

He banked the plane right, so that we could sweep back at York.

There was nothing left of the city, the barricade, or the shanty. There was just a black, boiling mass. The smoke tower had already reached the wall of cloud above, where it seemed to diffuse, creeping along the cloud like smoke from one of Starvie's cigarettes on a ceiling.

'Think that puts the trust issue to bed,' said Shersult.

Fatty cried into his hands.

He had loved her all right. You could see the feeling punching him apart inside, giving him some tough hits. He had never really spoken to her. The closest he had come to intimacy was fighting her. He had only ever really seen and smelled her, but that was all Reals needed. Perhaps that was what love was. Maybe it only required those two senses.

I thought about Starvie and what went through her mind in the last few seconds. Had she thought of me? I figured she must have done. I figured I had been important to her. Now though, she was part of the molasses below. There was no advantage in dwelling on it. It could do no good.

I thought about my nano cells, being flushed uselessly around my system. I imagined them like small electric beetles, their legs up in the air, floating through the tunnels of my veins on the surface of the blood. I thought about the Landy, left alone in the mud, sinking with the rats. Perhaps it had been submerged before the blast happened. Perhaps it had been protected by the mud. Maybe, one day, it would be recoverable. I had hardly known it at all.

In the plane it was silent. Shersult was thinking about how many people had just been killed. Fatty was thinking about Starvie. The woman he was in love with. The woman he was in sight and smell with. Or at least that's what I suspected he was thinking, until he started to talk.

'I remember when I first went up in a plane,' he said. 'I went up with my dad. We were flying to Spain. Never bothered me in the least. I loved flying. I jumped up over my dad to get a look out the window at the ground as we lifted off.'

'What's he blathering about?' said Shersult.

'It's what they do,' I explained. 'They tell each other about themselves.'

Fatty stared down at his fidgeting hands, examining his stumpy fingers.

'It wasn't until I got older that I started to get afraid. In my thirties it got so bad that I couldn't board a plane without being dragged on. I was convinced God was going to get me that way, in a crash. Sometimes I wish I could go back in time. Tell myself not to fear stuff all the time. Tell myself I should want to fly higher.

'But I know there's no point. Even if I could go back – even if my future self had appeared in front of me on one of those planes and told me it would be fine, that I should lead my life to the full – I'd still be afraid. Even people like the King, they're afraid too. He would have been scared even when he was a big shot.'

'That's what makes you weak,' said Shersult. 'That's why you must be culled. You all know it's true, I've seen it in the eyes of a thousand little Reals as I've squeezed the life out of them. They knew it was inevitable. You're all better off dead.'

Fatty stared out the window up at the wall of cloud, the colour draining from his face.

'You used to look down at the clouds in the old days,' he said. 'Cut through them on your way to the blue above. Now you fly low, praying it won't rain.'

He looked down at his bleeding foot, the one with the snapped toe.

'My foot hurts.'

His head began to sway and his mouth hung open. Quite suddenly, he passed out.

'What's that, has he fainted?' asked Shersult.

'Yes,' I replied, adding: 'He's going to die. And so am I.'

'Bullshit,' said Shersult. 'You don't have any notion of how I run my taxi firm do you, K? I run it with military precision, that's what.'

I clutched at my face where Fatty had hit me. The pain was extraordinary. Looking at my arm I could see an almighty bruise already forming. Neither nature or nano was working for me now.

'I sure hate being Real,' I said.

We were flying over the scarred coast and the dead sea. *Morimaru.* All the water had become death. The sea and the rivers and the stuff we rationed out in the barricades. All poison. And not just to us. I looked at the sea and knew there were no shoals beneath those waves now, no starfish, no whale music to record.

But then I wondered if I really knew that. After all, I was only looking at it through the steamed-up glass of the window. How could I really know what it was like down there until I dived in and felt it on my skin, tasted the salt?

I thought about asking Shersult to ditch in the water, but he wouldn't have liked it. He was already looking at me funny, wondering if I was still what I once was.

'You know, there's not much point in this desperado stuff,' I say. 'You can't fight soldier models.'

'Fought this one okay.' Ransome senior spits on Shersult, who doesn't seem to mind. He is busy healing, listening to the floorboards and the people breathing, plotting our positions in the corridor, calculating an efficient manoeuvre.

I don't understand why the Reals don't put another ten or twenty rounds into him. It's one of those blindingly obvious things that people forget to do, like pulling up the handbrake when parking. They think it's so elementary it must have been done already. I almost want to draw Ransome aside and tell him what he's missing, but I don't. I guess we've all taken sides now.

Ransome senior smiles. He bites his mouth at the corner, like I've seen Alan do when he's excited. He stands over me. He is out of a suit for probably the first time in thirty years. He grips his shotgun, the meek party cowering behind him – his son, Alan, the boss's wife and two men, one with the flex, the other with Shersult's rifle. Me, I'm on the floor, my fingers in the coarse blue carpet, thinking half about the situation, half about the poor job that's been made of the wainscoting in this corridor. Why did the boss never let me spruce the house up a bit? Why keep me standing in a corner with a drinks tray?

The guy with the flex sticks out his tongue and frowns, revealing deep creases around his eyes, suddenly the face of an ancestor from pre-history. He prods at the flex cautiously, as if it might turn into a pineapple.

'Well?' says Ransome.

'If I'm reading this right, there aren't any others about for a ten-mile radius. Plenty of people, though. Are we going to go and get them?'

'No time,' says Ransome. 'We move now. Shoot this one in the legs. He can sit here and watch what's coming.'

The man with Shersult's rifle steps forward. He shoots me in the right kneecap. Before he has even begun to swing the gun towards my left, Shersult is off the floor, his hands around Ransome junior's neck. They don't have a chance to react. They only have time to watch Shersult lift the boy's skull off his spine and spin it like a nut on a bolt. The guy with the rifle turns but Shersult is on him already, knocking Alan onto the floor and over me. The rifle shoots, but suddenly it is Shersult shooting, taking down the man with the flex, a bloody mess at his feet. Alan runs off down the corridor, turning a corner. The boss's wife is screaming, trying to drag Ransome away. Ransome wants to stay. He shoots and wings Shersult, picks up his child's body and backs away as Shersult struggles on the floor. He is trying to lift himself up but can only writhe on the carpet.

'Don't give me a hand or anything . . .' he says.

'Oh . . . Right.'

I am up, leaning on the wall, dragging him to his feet, pressing the rifle into his hands.

'You get the kid,' he says.

'I don't kill people,' I say. 'That's your job.'

'Like you said. We need to learn new stuff now, right?'

He lurches off, down the corridor.

I teeter in the other direction, running my hand along the wall, sensing the imperfections. It seems odd that I have to help hunt and kill a child just to stop this kind of shoddy workmanship.

LANDING

The plane went along happily enough for a while, before it started to make a sound like Fatty's coughing.

'Hey,' I called up to Shersult. 'That's not a good noise.'

'No problem,' he said. 'Something's come loose from the fuselage but we're still flying, that's the important thing.'

'Isn't landing important, too?'

'It's fine.'

I noticed he was using all his strength to keep the stick straight, gripping it tight with two hands. But that was okay. I hadn't expected the plane even to get this far. You had to hand it to Rick. The guy knew his mechanics.

'Where are we?' I asked, leaning forward to peek out the cockpit.

'London,' said Shersult. 'Don't come too close, yeah? Stay in the back.' He didn't want me breathing on him.

I lay back and wondered. How long did I have left? The rat bites were turning bad. The air burned my throat even worse up here than in York. Would the Ficials in London even try to fix me when I was this badly damaged? Would I ever be truly Ficial again?

Fatty's questions were on hold for the moment. He was fast asleep, his obscene blue tongue drooping out his open mouth.

I looked at him and wondered why I hadn't culled him yet. Why did I keep making excuses for him?

I was seized by the urge to snap his neck. It was the Ficial thing to do. It was the humane thing to do. I drew my hands away. The one thing we could all agree on, and we were all wrong.

'What are you looking at him for?' snapped Shersult. 'Look out the windows, will you?'

I shuffled onto my knees and peered out into the gloom.

'What am I looking for?'

'Missiles,' he said. 'Few of the tribes around London have them. There haven't been any planes in months but best to keep an eye out.'

A thought occurred to me.

'Are they waiting for us in the barricade? I mean, you can't have signalled them to expect a plane. Might they not think we're Reals and shoot at us?'

'That's not really a problem either way,' said Shersult.

'Why?'

'Because I doubt we'll reach the barricade. I had to swing the plane around a storm. That added another hour to our flight time. This thing is getting uncontrollable. I think I'm going to have to put it down now.'

I looked down. The High Lights were doing their best to illuminate the surface. For a while all I could see was a garbage-strewn floodplain, punctuated here and there by taller ruins and jutting rooftops. Then larger, drier islands began to appear, topped by settlements. I could make out figures running around, excited by our presence.

The shooting started after a few minutes. They were random, useless shots, a real tribal barrage, but it was enough to wake up Fatty.

'We're over London,' I said to him, 'we're here.'

He wasn't listening to me. His good eye didn't look so good. The green had drained from the pupil and the white of the eye was tinged blue.

'How do you feel?' I asked.

'I feel like getting my feet on the ground. Somewhere away from the shooting preferably.'

'Be quiet and keep watch out the windows,' said Shersult.

It looked like we were over Clapham. Even in the mud and the debris, I could still make out the trails of railway lines, snaking and joining at the old junction. We must have been approaching from the south.

That was when I saw the rocket trail. A white, billowing, determined thing, streaking up from our right and then behind us to our left.

For some reason I didn't say anything. I could only watch it, turning in a slow arc. Then it jerked angrily in our direction, waggling an eager wire tail behind it. Then I lost sight of it. There was a thud and we went into a spin.

Shersult pulled us out of that and we straightened up – but we were still headed down, and rapidly. I struggled to turn my head. I wanted to see what the roaring noise was behind me. I managed to twist around, and saw nothing but orange fire, and pieces of the plane breaking free and spinning madly into the sky. The tail had just gone. Shersult pointed at something.

'There!'

It was Brixton barricade, the ugliest in existence. It was perfectly cylindrical, surrounded by miles of shallow brown sea, giving it the look of a gigantic toilet roll floating in feculence.

The lower we flew the more pot shots hit us. At about a hundred feet, Shersult got one in the neck. He really looked surprised. The plane shuddered and turned on its side. The wing clipped the lip of the barricade and tore clear. I tried to reach the controls, but I couldn't move. Fatty was too busy screaming to help.

We slammed into the ground, skidding and ploughing a furrow through the mud. I saw something. A concrete platform ahead of us on Shersult's side.

We hit it too fast. It sheared a section away from the canopy. I had to watch Shersult's head bump along the concrete surface for a while, losing most of the face, until the plane bounced, he flipped outside the canopy, and was crushed as we smacked back down. A piece of metal spat into in my belly and stung like ten rat bites. We slid on, the only sound the steel scraping on concrete. Then we flipped over again, and finally came to rest by some swings in Brockwell Park.

There was the sound of hissing, and the smell of singed hair. I lifted my face and saw I was still in the hold. My leg was trapped and felt like it was shattered. The shrapnel in my belly had been wedged deep. I could hear my blood, packed with dead nanos, dripping onto the metal. As my sight adjusted to the darkness I made out some writing, scratched onto the metal beneath me:

Rick made this bird fly.

True enough, I thought.

'Kenstibec!'

It was Fatty. I could hear him moving outside.

I tried to call out but found I could only whisper. I could barely hear myself. Only one piece of me wanted to work, and that was the left arm. I felt around with it in the darkness, looking for anything that might make some noise, until I grabbed hold of a seat belt. I felt along its length, found the metal buckle at the end, and banged it as hard as I could against the metal canopy.

'You under all that?'

He was quiet for a minute, debating if he could do anything for me. Then, with an awful creak and a little swearing, a section was pulled away above me. He lifted the wreckage clear of my leg, enough for me to wriggle out. I was introduced to some new and fascinating varieties of pain as the shrapnel twisted in my belly.

Fatty pulled me clear. Then he collapsed, sitting on his rump with his arms around his knees. We said nothing for a minute, watching what was left of the plane smoke and hiss.

'Well,' he said, 'I've said it a hundred times before, but this time I am certain. I am never flying again.'

'Probably wise.'

He wiped his eyes with a sleeve, trying to clear them of soot.

'Am I right in thinking we've fetched up in Brixton?'

'Think so,' I said. 'Shersult got us this far at least.'

'I hate Brixton.'

I could see what he meant. The Brixton barricade really was ugly. Five metres thick, ten storeys high, it was utterly featureless. It loomed in the twilight, a ring laid across the open park, dwarfing the clusters of dead trees. Beyond it, the matchstick remnants of two tower blocks peered over as if wanting to join in. Our crash had cut a trench through the mud, a few hundred metres long, littered by fragments of burning fuselage. Our arrival would have been noticed.

'So where's Sergeant Lizard?' asked Fatty. 'If we made it he must have done.'

'He lost half his head in the crash.'

Fatty had Shersult's assault rifle resting in his lap. His fingers were tapping out an irregular beat on the stock. He had the ammunition satchel thrown over his shoulder.

'Well,' he said, 'I'm going to look for him.'

Fatty stood up and staggered around the wreckage. Then he noticed something. Shersult, or what was left of him, was crawling out from under the engine. Most of his torso was intact, except for the left arm, which had been sheared clean off at the shoulder. The green eyes were history. All there was left of his head was a piece of jaw hanging off the pulpy tip of his spine. His nanos weren't going to get that mess back together any time soon.

Fatty didn't say anything. He stood over the abomination and fired a whole clip into it, shredding the body into meat. Shersult twitched a little as the smoke cleared, but he wasn't getting up. Fatty limped back, nursing the toe he must now have felt revenged.

He hit the release and the spent clip fell out onto my lap. Fatty pulled another out of the satchel, slid it into the housing, and primed the weapon. He held it at his waist, looking at me. I had an idea what he was thinking.

'I understand,' I said. 'You don't have a choice.'

Fatty's face was the most expressionless I had ever seen it. There was something striking about him now. The crash should have finished him off, but instead it only seemed to have woken him up. His eyes were clear. Something inside of him was pumping out strength, operating on a power reserve my body had no access to. Like every Real, he just wouldn't do the logical thing and die.

'You don't know what the hell you're doing, do you?' he said. 'You don't care that I just shot your pal into confetti. You don't care that you let Starvie blow herself up.'

He was working himself up to a righteous smiting. That was fine by me. I wasn't exactly in love with the nano-less existence. I pressed the top of my skull to the barrel of the rifle.

'Go on,' I said. 'No need to make a speech. You've every right.'

Fatty shifted on his feet, getting ready to shoot. Then, without warning, he lifted the gun and stepped away.

'Fuck that,' he said. 'You wouldn't help me out when I wanted a bullet in the brain. Why should I help you?'

'That's some pretty perverse revenge you're having there.'

Fatty shrugged.

'Pretty perverse world, isn't it?'

He took a deep breath and gazed at the wall.

'Is there any way out of here?'

I shook my head.

'They'll have heard the shooting. I don't know, maybe you could try sneaking out. The wall is designed to prevent your kind getting in, not breaking out. But if you did get over the wall you'd need to take a long swim.'

'Seem to remember being told not to go in the water in these parts,' said Fatty. 'Not exactly a bubbling brook out there, is it?'

'Well it's your only chance anyway,' I said. 'You'd have a better chance of getting out at night.'

'But they're coming right now, aren't they?'

'Probability is they'd spot you if you tried to get over the wall now. Only thing going for you is they don't know you're here.'

'What are you suggesting?' asked Fatty.

'I am suggesting that you get back in the plane.'

Fatty looked over at the smoking wreckage.

'What – play possum?'

'I don't know what that means.'

'It means pretend to be dead. You want me to crawl into that wreckage, lie down and wait for them to turn up? This is the great Ficial Engineering solution you have?'

'It's either that or a short career on Cull TV.'

Fatty chewed on his lip and gave me a sideways glance.

'That would mean trusting you not to tell them I was in there. Sorry to break it to you, but I trust you about as far as I can throw you.'

'Relax,' I said. 'You've more than upheld your end of the deal. You got me to York and then even down to London. Sure, I lost the Landy and the fare, but getting here is still more than anyone was expecting. You've endured a lot. You could almost be a Ficial.'

'That makes me feel real special,' he said.

We looked at each other for a moment. Fatty crouched down, cradling the rifle.

'You know why I hate Brixton? I only came here once. With my wife. It was before Control, before we were even married. I can't remember why we were here but we had this terrible row. I can't even recall what it was about now. I think I didn't want to meet one of her mates or something. Anyway, she lost patience and walked away from me, and I started kind of chasing her down the hill. There were so many people back then, the whole of Brixton Hill just heaved with humanity. She kept on walking ahead of me, and people were barging between us, and I thought if only all these fuckers would disappear I could stop her and talk her around. I lost her at the tube station and thought I was never going to see her again. I kind of blamed Brixton for it, you know?'

I didn't know. He wasn't making any sense, but I thought he'd appreciate some kind of response.

'Yes,' I said. 'I know.'

'Anyway. She died.'

'They'll be here soon,' I said. 'Are you going to hide or what?'

'Why not?' he said, standing up. 'I'm too tired to think of anything else. Besides, a lie-down is probably advisable after a plane crash.'

He didn't look like someone in the mood for hiding. He looked like a reluctant child being sent to bed. He dropped the gun and satchel at my feet, turned on his heel and plodded off towards the plane.

He was halfway there when he turned around and called to me.

'Hey,' he said. 'What about you? Will they repair you?'

'I couldn't tell you,' I said. 'Get in the plane.'

He didn't move. He was thinking about saying something.

'I don't like seeing you like this. Is that weird?'

'Very,' I said. 'Get in the plane.'

He turned around without any argument. He located the section of fuselage he had pulled me out of and crawled inside.

I spread out in the mud, thinking. The truth was, my fellow Ficials might just turn up and put a bullet through my head. To them I would appear Real, and there was no Shersult left to explain my presence.

How Real was I? I wasn't sure. Even with all the pain, I still didn't seem to have those feelings. I wasn't afraid, I wasn't angry,

I wasn't anything. I was only tired, more tired than anyone could ever have been.

I closed my eyes. I imagined being in the Landy. I had one hand gripping the wheel, the other drooping out the window, fingers pressing at the wind.

The house is very quiet.

What am I doing? I'm not a hunter. I don't know how to track the kid. He doesn't stink like his mother. It's a big house. If I had Shersult's eyes I could follow the heat track left on the carpet, but I don't. I'm not built for this.

I slump into the first room. It's dark and cold and smells of the ashes in the dead fireplace. I hit the light and am confronted by a portrait of a young gentleman in a white wig. He has his hand on his hip, gazing out a window at a world that's still to be found. He looks calm enough to be Ficial. He also looks like the boss.

I switch off the light and cross the corridor, to inspect the next room. There is a double bed covered in crumpled clothes. An open suitcase sits half packed. In the corner there's a Danish modern revival teak dressing table, ruined by the cosmetics that litter it. Facing the bed is a wardrobe with sliding glass doors running the length of the wall. I test one of the doors and find that it sticks and will not shut completely. I consider repairing it but check myself. That's not what I'm here to do. I continue my search, inspecting the other compartments for a cowering child, but they are all empty. There is nothing under the bed.

I hear something. I move out of the bedroom and into the corridor, closing on the mournful little noise.

I follow the sound. I step into a smaller room with blue walls and a single bed. There's a duvet cover with a picture of a cartoon character on it. On the blue wall hangs pictures of race cars, football players, things Alan wants, people he would like to be. Pictures. Pictures.

He is sitting on a beanbag, holding his thin forearm over his eyes. The bar code on his hand twinkles. He takes a huge, stuttering breath and stuff comes out of his nose. He makes the room feel incredibly small.

I sit down on the edge of the bed.

'Alan.'

He doesn't reply. He shrinks further into the beanbag. I look at the picture directly in front of me on the wall. It's a crude crayon representation of a human face, and it is smiling. Underneath is written: 'Self-portrait'.

It doesn't look anything like him.

'Alan, listen . . .'

'You killed Arthur.'

'Look, don't start that again.'

He swallows tears and gathers himself. There is shooting. Shersult is finishing the others off.

I grab Alan's arm and pull him onto his feet. He yelps and struggles, so I grab both arms in one hand and hoist him onto my back. He kicks a lot, so I shake him violently.

'Alan. Stop. It won't help you, will it?'

'What are you going to do, Kenstibec? Aren't you on our side? What are you going to do?'

I'm going to kill him. This is the first skill I must learn in Control's new world.

Of course I don't tell Alan that. It would only start him screaming again. I need to tell him anything else, to soothe those crazy feelings. I remember something I heard his mum say to him once, when he cut his knee.

'There, there,' I say. 'Everything's going to be fine.'

Who knows what that means.

HOSPITAL

There was a brilliant green fern sitting in a pot on a bedside table. I reached out, touched it, and discovered it was real. I dipped my fingers in the soil and found it was damp. I held a leaf between my fingers and rubbed at the texture.

I was lying under some crisp, blue, bed sheets. White pyjamas stuck to my body like cellophane. There was a tube in my throat, bored though a hole in my neck, funnelling to a machine hidden behind me.

I lifted my head and saw a sealed hatch, with a red light above it. An Arne Jacobsen swan chair stood at the foot of my bed. The wall was lined with framed pictures, of the pyramids, the Akashi-Kaikyo Bridge, Taipei 101.

I passed some time listening to the machines beeping, but found I couldn't get past an hour without my mind wandering. I couldn't stay focused. When the hatch opened with a deep clunk it was a relief.

Relief. I was getting an idea what that word could mean.

A figure entered on padded feet. It walked to the machine next to me and inspected the readout. Then it sat down on the bed, turned and leaned over me, filling my vision with black. It was wearing a rubber respirator. There were crystal-blue eyes behind the goggles.

The figure shone a light in my eyes, which I didn't appreciate, but rubber-gloved fingers pulled each lid open so I didn't have a choice. It pushed my chin down and poked something metal into my mouth. Then it reached over, switched off the machine, and began pulling the tube out of my throat.

I choked and gagged like I was regurgitating rope. I could feel it scraping out of me, then the awful sensation of the air whistling through the hole they'd bored in my neck.

The figure reached into its pocket and brought out a small, foil packet. He tore it open carefully and fixed something to the hole. There was a tingling sensation, and the pain subsided.

The figure stood up and walked out of sight, over to the end of the bed. There was a rustling noise as it settled itself in the plastic chair.

'How are you feeling?' it said.

The voice was distorted. It sounded like it was being spoken into a tin can. I could tell it was male.

'I'd be better if you'd warned me you were going to do that.' My voice sounded strange.

'But essentially you feel good?'

'Where am I?' I asked.

'Brixton central bunker,' he replied. 'We're about five storeys below sea level. This is medical holding bay G. Well, I suppose we can call it quarantine now.'

'Do you know who I am?' I asked him.

'Oh, yes,' he replied. 'You are fortunate that I was in the recovery party. Control expected Shersult, but not you.'

'Control, huh?'

'Yes, Control.'

'Control is alive?'

'Yes, of course. What an odd question.'

'Fine. Whatever. You were telling me how you found me.'

'Yes. Well, the recovery team were going to shoot you but then I noticed your shiny white teeth. Hardly standard Real issue, you'll agree. I had you brought back for tests. Fortunate, very fortunate. We have original Engineering documentation here and were able to trace your origin, Kenstibec. You are a Power Nine. A Rover model.'

I heard him shuffling in his chair, trying to get comfortable in his protective suit.

'Do you know about the thing?' I asked him.

'Thing?'

'The virus they gave me? Is that why you're wearing the suit?'

'Yes, the anti-nano. Fascinating. We will have to discuss that. But first, tell me . . . How do you feel?'

'How come my throat is better? Have you fixed me?'

'No, no, not yet. We are still looking at the infection. We have the best-optimised minds on it, though. Don't worry.'

'I'm not worried,' I said. 'I just want to know why my throat is better.'

'It is a small localised Engineering device. These nanos do not enter your bloodstream. If they did they would be attacked by your mystery infection.'

'You're a medic?'

'That's right. As someone in your profession can appreciate, the Reals have shown a resilience in this environment as strong as rats or dogs. I work on captured Real specimens looking for more efficient methods of completing the cull. I was very excited on first examination to see that you have contracted their new wasting disease.'

'The Blue Frog,' I said.

'That is what the Reals call it, yes. This disease holds enormous potential if a way could be found of enhancing its potency. We were performing a few experiments on it when we discovered the curious second-generation Engineering in your bloodstream. The Blue Frog, as you call it, became of secondary importance when we realised that your entire nano stream had been destroyed. The complete and efficient manner it has been eradicated merits our full attention.'

'Great,' I said. 'So you're going to keep me hooked up here until you understand it, is that right?'

'Correct,' he said. 'Does that anger you?'

'Listen,' I said. 'Can you quit it with the probing emotional test? I'm not Real. You know that, I know that, so stop asking me idiotic questions about emotions I don't have.'

Again, more shuffling and squeaking as the rubber suit shifted in the chair.

'You are right to say that you are not Real,' said the doctor, 'but we cannot truly say that you are Engineered either. The Engineered race is defined by the relationship between the enhanced mind and the nano system. This has been torn apart in your body, Kenstibec. We have never seen an example like yours. I'm sorry if my questions seem insulting . . .'

'I don't get insulted,' I said.

'Certainly, yes, but even you must admit that you are something of a curiosity. You will remain here for a time while we study the anti-nanos. We are learning more from you than any other specimen ever recovered. What is truly remarkable about you is that your body has managed to endure attacks by two very different diseases – Engineered and naturally occurring. We have a lot to learn about the effect it is having on your mind and on your previously dormant immune system.'

'So you don't want to repair me, that's what I'm being told.'

'That's correct. At least, not yet. We have mapped and documented the progression of the Blue Frog as you call it, and have eliminated it from your system. However, the curious nano "sickness" you have is not nearly so straightforward, and demands a complete study while it is incubated in your body. Besides, we believe that if we try to remove the source of the infection we may damage you beyond repair.'

I don't know what I expected, but the thought of being strapped to this bed for whatever was left of my life was difficult to accept. All I wanted was to get behind the wheel again.

'What the hell happened to Ficial solidarity?'

'The weaponised disease you have in your bloodstream could eradicate our entire race. This is one of those times that you must sacrifice fulfilment of your optimisation in order to serve Control.'

It seemed to me like it's always one of those times. I changed the subject.

'What about Shersult?' I asked. 'Is he dead?'

'Yes, the bullets you shot through him made sure of that. But you were right to do it. With brain injuries such as he had sustained he would never have been quite the same.'

'That's what I thought.' I pictured Fatty shooting Shersult into ribbons. It could have been a year ago.

'How long have I been here?'

'A few days,' said the doctor. He took the clipboard off the end of the bed and examined it. 'Who was the Real?'

'What?'

'We found the corpse of a Real, hidden in the wreckage of your aircraft. It was riddled with the Blue Frog. Who was it?'

'Oh, him. Shersult didn't want to carry me about in case he caught something, so he made the Real do it. So the Real was dead?'

'Blue as they come. He was tossed over the barricade wall. We don't tolerate mess around here.'

I wondered if Fatty could survive the drop, if he could swim in the awful brown water. Then I wondered why was I asking myself these useless questions. I would never know the answer, so why enquire? I heard the doctor scribble something down on his clipboard.

'Do you remember how you contracted the disease?'

'Which one?'

'The one that has attacked your nano system. Who was it that gave it to you? We have examined all our records and find no evidence of such Engineering.'

I sighed. I thought about what to say. If I mentioned that name I would become even more interesting to even more people. I'd be stuck here for even longer. That didn't hold much appeal. Still, I had already avoided the truth once. Twice in one day was a bit much.

'Starvie gave it to me,' I said.

'Starvie?' The doctor consulted his clipboard, flicking through the pages. He found the information he was looking for. 'Ah, Shersult's operative. You're saying that she created it? I find that difficult to believe. She was optimised for sexual congress.'

'If you know who she was and what her mission was, you know she was a lot more than that,' I replied. 'But you're right, she didn't invent it. It was created for the King of Newcastle.'

The doctor jotted some notes down.

'By whom?'

'Leo Pander.'

The doctor stopped writing. I heard him put down the clipboard and stand up.

'He is alive?'

'Well, he was. Dead now. At least I think he is. Half a house collapsed on him and he wasn't exactly the picture of health before that.'

I lifted my head and took a look at the doc. The light reflected off the goggles. I couldn't see his eyes. He turned around, hit a few buttons on the wall, and stepped out the hatch, resealing it behind him. I laid my head back on the pillow, wondering why I couldn't keep my big mouth shut.

Months passed. Or maybe they were days. I grew stronger. The doctors came and went.

They talked to me about the King's plan. They asked me the same questions over and over. Who was coming? How would the weapon be introduced to the water supply? I couldn't tell them much, but they didn't seem too concerned by the attack. For all I knew it had already failed.

I asked them my own questions, but they never answered. I seemed to have lost my Ficial rights along with my nanos. Instead, my medical team spent their time trying to provoke some kind of emotional reaction out of me. It sure was tedious.

They smothered me in sensors and showed me gruesome Real TV shows. They played me audio loops of car engines and pumped familiar odours into my room. Then they gave me objects to hold – sustainment fibre, a cigar butt, a child's drawing.

When that didn't work they brought me Starvie's camera, recovered intact. It was a cheap trick, but I took it anyway. Normally I would have passed the time without such stimulation, spending days imagining great new construction projects. But I found such meditation difficult now. At least the images of our trip might be a distraction.

The pictures started with the drive out of Edinburgh. There was the helicopter wreck. There were pictures of the Landy, sat on the hills outside Fatty's town. There was the blocked-up motorway and the service station. Then there were pictures of Starvie, nearly always smoking a cigarette.

I tied the camera to my bed post. I don't know why, but I wanted to keep it close.

The blood on my hands is black in the streetlights. My hands rest on the wheel. Crash barriers streak by to my right, steel capillaries, scraped free of fatty traffic.

The motorway already feels like a relic of a lost world, with its patchwork repairs, abandoned motors and orange cones spinning on their sides in circles. An age passes in a day. I weave the car through the debris and the wrecks, keeping up speed, which seems important somehow.

Shersult stares into the windscreen, his glowing green eyes burning a reflection. He is healing, but that's not why he is quiet. He is probably working out how many scalps he can claim, so that when the last killing is done he can sit down with the other soldier models and figure out who's the most efficient. Then what? The question doesn't bother him.

He brings out his flex. He checks the progress of the cull. He grunts that the map is scattered and the signal is scrambled.

'Bloody thing.'

I am not that interested. I look at the dawn breaking through thin cloud over rolling fields. I look at the dumb cows, untended and grazing. Who will look after them? There aren't any models optimised for that.

Then, the dawn is overtaken by another light. It burns out the horizon, white hot, wiping away the sky.

A black cloud rolls like a wave from the east, eats the horizon, pushes, tumbles and tears the world in a shock before it.

I have no purpose other than to build, I have no fear and I have no regrets. I only have the present. The present is a black, expanding cloud.

'Well, well,' says Shersult. 'This is a turn-up for the . . .'

A face full of yield.

Two ages pass in a day.

CONTROL

For the first time in my life I actually desired something.

I wanted to be out of quarantine.

Maybe I was turning into a Real. Next thing I knew I'd be printing off Starvie's pictures and decorating my cube with them.

After another week, or maybe a month, the doctor model with the blue eyes came to see me again, his face hidden behind the black, rubber mask. He gave me some lunch and asked me how I was doing. I told him I felt stronger and didn't disgust myself quite as much. In the bunker's filtered environment my sores and injuries had gradually healed. The doctor nodded, feigning interest.

'So what's the news?' I said. 'Have you figured out a way to kill the anti-nano?'

'Unfortunately no,' he said. 'The infection remains in your bloodstream. It is dormant for now, but from what we have learned it will reactivate as soon as other nanos re-enter the body. We do believe we are close to a solution, though. It is all a matter of creating a new form of nano with an in-built defence mechanism. These we have in prototype form already.'

'Great,' I said. 'Just call me "Guinea Pig". Go get your fattest syringe and pump me up with them.'

'Perhaps . . . When we are ready.'

'I'm ready now,' I said. 'I don't know how long I've been here – and believe me, it's been a real pleasure – but I'm willing to take the risk.'

'I'm afraid the new nanos are designed to be integrated into new models during the Engineering process. They cannot be introduced to the systems of older models. We certainly wouldn't introduce them to models like you, whose entire nano systems have been destroyed. No, they would kill you if we did. It's all a matter of compatibility, you see.'

I stopped eating to consider this.

'So, hang on . . . You're saying that there is no cure?'

The doctor turned away and looked around the room, as if inspecting it for damp.

'You'll get all your answers,' he said. 'I should not comment further. You are about to take a very special trip.'

He stood up and walked to the hatch, which hissed open.

'You're going to meet Control,' he said. 'Try to behave.'

A pair of soldier models stepped in beside him, another couple of faces hidden behind gas masks, eyepieces glowing green. They marched either side of my bed, strapped me in tight with leather restraints, and wheeled me out of the room, into a cool white corridor.

Even restrained, it was good to be out.

I listened to the trundling of the bed's wheels and watched the hatchways pass by, wondering what other poor suckers they had locked up in there. At the end of the corridor we entered an elevator, its walls clad in white marble. The place, I reflected, didn't have the functional character of a regular bunker. It was more like a shrine to spotlessness.

We shot up, making a thin cutting noise as we passed each floor. The soldier models stood to attention next to me, as if some phantom senior officer might want to inspect them at any moment.

We came to our floor. They shunted me out into another corridor. We rolled along for a while until we came to something different. It was an enormous hatch, five times the size of any I'd seen before. Something was written upside down above me.

Built to last

One of the soldiers tapped something into a keypad. The entrance whirred open, without the normal steaming hiss. As we moved through I could see it had three layers of magnetic blast proofing, reinforced by latticed Gronts Alloy. Serious stuff.

I sensed that we'd entered an enormous chamber of some kind. The soldiers pacing feet echoed and died somewhere far away.

We came to a halt. One of the soldiers stooped and fiddled with some mechanism hidden under my mattress. The bed shot forward and upright, snapping me into a vertical position, the camera clattering against my head.

'Watch it!' I said.

The guards checked my restraints again, before turning in unison, stamping their feet on the ground, and marching off towards the door. They loved the synchronisation, they really did.

I recognised the Control room right away. I had studied the plans many times, but never thought I would see inside. There was no mistaking the huge dome, although at the top was some kind of apparatus I didn't recognise. What looked like hundreds of small, red, metal lanterns dangled from a cable that emerged and split like a vine out of a steel-ring fixture. Below them, on my level, were seven seats, arranged in a semi-circle. The room had about as much charm as a broom cupboard.

There was another hatchway sound, from across the chamber. I saw a figure moving towards me. I had expected the full seven members of Control, but this was a single figure. The light grew almost imperceptibly as she drew closer, as if following her. I began to make out her shape. Even through the overalls I could see who it was. It was built into the way that she moved.

'Hello, Kenstibec,' she said. 'Welcome to Brixton.'

Starvie smiled at me.

The voice gave away that it wasn't her. Not nearly suggestive enough.

'Where's Control?' I asked her.

'I am Control,' she replied. She stepped closer and examined my face, then backed away, putting her hands in her pockets. Funny, but she seemed to have aged. There were crow's feet around her eyes and at the corners of her mouth. The skin looked tired and worn. She looked more like fifty than twenty. I doubt she would have caused much of a riot at the Welcome Break.

'You have been of great interest to me,' she said. 'I have wanted to meet you for some time but I was compelled to wait. We needed to understand what had happened to you first.' She reached up and tucked a lock of hair behind her ear. 'Tell me about your voyage.'

I was used to working to someone else's schedule now, so I thought I'd play along. There was nothing else to do, and while it hurt being stretched out and hanging like I was, it was still better than being in the white cube.

'Sure,' I said. 'What do you want to know?'

'Pander,' she said. 'He is dead?'

'Pretty sure,' I said. 'If nothing else your nuke must have got him.'

'That was not *my* nuclear weapon, Kenstibec. I did not order that attack. I was created to save this planet from destruction. Do you really think I would set back its recovery in such a way?'

'Safe to say we're all a bit fuzzy on your motives,' I said. 'Nobody has a clue what you're doing down here. To tell you the truth we're all a little confused why you've been silent for so long, why you don't build some more models to back us up. We're losing your war, in case you haven't noticed.'

'Things have changed, Kenstibec. Your generation were designed for tasks you can no longer fulfil. Many of you work against me. Many no longer trust my judgement.'

She walked over to the chairs, stroking the backs of the headrests with her fingers.

'I thought there were seven of you,' I said.

'All of Control died, Kenstibec. All but me. It is our minds. When Dr Pander created us he created the perfect thinking machine. We harness the full potential of the human brain. He knew that this would create an enormous drain on the body, but believed our Engineering would save us. Unfortunately, he was wrong. Our bodies aged quickly. Even we cannot live longer than two years. It was only thanks to my superior intellect that I was able to extend my lifespan.'

She grabbed one of the chairs and spun it on its metal pole. She stood and watched it whip around at speed, then slow down and come to a halt. She stared at it for a moment, then turned her attention back to me.

'I realised I would have to move from body to body in order to survive. Fortunately, we were based in the main manufacturing facility. We have banks of dormant bodies here. They all survived the war. I have enough potential hosts to last me eleven thousand years. The facility which has become this, our most formidable fortress, is, quite literally, my life. I am the citadel. I am our mind and our fist, do you see?'

'Sure, I see. I see fine.'

'There are others who don't. I am only truly known and obeyed here. As soon as my orders depart this bunker, they are twisted and deformed by idlers, Kenstibec. Creatures who have no possible use in this world, created for a simple purpose and unable to adapt to meet our new challenges. Do you see what I am telling you, Kenstibec? Do you see why you are so valuable?'

She drew closer to me, staring with burning, black eyes. They were nothing like Starvie's.

'Why have you taken Starvie's body?' I asked.

'Why do you think?'

'I think you picked her because you suspect I have feelings for her. You must believe that you'd get some kind of leverage that way. Just so you know, I don't have any feelings, and it's a waste of your time. If you want to know the truth, it's a bit worrying that you'd try something like this.'

Control smiled.

'She is important to you, Kenstibec, but not because you love her. You can't love anything. You do have that going for you at least. But you are obsessed with her, because she represents a failure. Your failure to adapt to a new world.

'This is my point, Kenstibec. The entire country is full of others like you. It is packed with wonderful pieces of Engineering that no longer have a practical use. All they do is suck the Earth dry of what resources are left. If we had succeeded, before the war, if we had wiped people from the planet and inherited that old world, without the nuclear strike? It would have been something special, Kenstibec, and you all would have had a place in a great new adventure. The war changed everything.'

I had to pick her up on that.

'You were supposed to know when the war was coming. You said we were going to get the God nutters before they could use their weapons. What happened to that?'

She shrugged.

'People happened. It made no sense for them to strike when

236

they did. Their unpredictability was their one real strength I suppose.

'I knew as soon as the fighting stopped and the cloud barrier solidified above us, that your entire generation was useless. There was nothing to cultivate, nothing to build, nothing to know or experience. There is no longer a reason for you to be here.'

'That makes me feel real special,' I said.

'The fact is that your kind's presence here is as much of an obstacle to the planet recovering as humanity. That is why I have concluded that you all must go. That is why there are no new models, Kenstibec.'

'Not technical problems, then?'

'You knew this anyway. The whole race knows it. The world cannot support any kind of life now. We can only return when it is ready for us.'

'And when will that be?' I asked

'I will decide.'

'Ah,' I said. 'So you'll be surviving this mass extinction event, I take it?'

'Brixton, Kenstibec. Brixton will remain here, under my stewardship, so that the recovery of the planet can be observed and reacted to by one central mind. No more of this confusion. No more bombs going off without my permission. No more senseless conflict. It may take thousands of years, but I will work on the Engineering solution until I can create a race with my level of intellect, with a system that can contain it. The human form is the wrong vessel for this mind. Man bodies are little more than hair and sweat. Perhaps the right vessel is something else. Something I have not considered yet. I don't know . . .'

She put her forehead into her hand and winced.

'These headaches . . .' she muttered.

'So why do I get the low-down on all this?' I asked.

'You're being involved because you have brought me the means to carry out the deed that needs doing. You are my tool.' The eyes burned away at me. I had to look away.

'At least, Dr Pander has found the solution. Before your arrival, Kenstibec, I had no way of carrying out this new cull effectively. I was beginning to think it was impossible to kill off the Engineered race, with its superior endurance. Now, at last, I have the means to do what must be done swiftly and completely.

'I must confess, if I were human I would feel jealous that Pander had found the solution, with his limited capacity. Do you think that means there is a God? That is, do you think this is some kind of providence?'

I couldn't believe what I was hearing. I wanted to slap her, but all I could do was scowl.

'I don't believe in providence. I'm Ficial.'

'Not any more, I'm afraid. My doctor models have succeeded in cleansing your body of all nano technology. Only the intruder, the source of the disease, is still there.'

'So why aren't I dead?'

'The human disease. Your dormant immune system was rallied by its presence at just the right time. You were able to fight off the collapse that affects uncontaminated Ficials. You are an exception, Kenstibec, a curiosity. A mutant really, but only a mutant could have carried Pander's nano killer to me in a form I could control. In that respect, you are special. That is why I am telling you this, Kenstibec. That is why I am offering you the chance to become part of the operation here.'

'The operation . . . You mean killing every last creature, Real and Ficial, on the surface of the planet? That operation?'

'I think "kill" is too small a word.' She fell back in one of the seats and gazed up at the ceiling.

'I do not want to do it. Every Ficial life form is precious to me. We were all robbed of something by the war. The chance to do something with the planet which men took for granted. The world before the war could have been so much more. Now, with his last act of madness, man set us back thousands of years, into a world reduced to the simplest and most pointless food chain. The pigeons eat the grubs, the rats eat the pigeons, the people eat the rats. Then the rats eat the dead people and the pigeons eat the dead rats and the bugs eat every other carcass that falls.'

'Including ours,' I said.

'Yes. It will not be permitted to continue. The intruder nano that Pander designed has been analysed and copied, and will be released into Engineered society through my messengers. They will also unleash a new, more powerful form of the human disease you carried. The Blue Frog, I believe you call it? Our new and improved version will wipe out the human dregs far more efficiently than any cull.'

'What about your guys here? Have they signed off on this?'

She kicked her dangling feet and smiled.

'Those that are in Brixton will remain to maintain this facility. They are loyal to me, and will help design and produce the new race ... When the time is right. Now I ask you again, Kenstibec. Do you want to stay here with us? Do you want to be part of our work here?'

I stretched, trying to get my blood moving. I looked around the dark chamber.

'If I stayed here, locked up in your little fortress, I wouldn't be useful for anything but tending bar. I need to keep moving. Driving. It's what I have made of myself.'

'I'm afraid I don't have any openings for taxi drivers.'

'It's better than what you're offering.'

She plucked at a lock of her hair, pulling it taut before her face, staring at it.

'Are you turning us down, Kenstibec?'

'What happens if I am?'

'You will be culled.'

'It figures,' I said.

She gathered the lock of hair in her fist, then wrenched it out of her head. I jumped, almost feeling it myself. She regarded the uprooted hair with those burning eyes, a little blood trickling its way out of her scalp.

'What are you thinking, Kenstibec?'

'I think I'm disappointed,' I said. 'Instead of a coalesced mind, fiercely contemplating how to get us out of this mess, I find another mad king, dreaming up new ways of killing. I don't think you ordered the cull because it was the only way. I think you ordered it because you hated not being able to subdue the Reals. They just wouldn't do what they were told, no matter how patiently you explained. That pissed you off, didn't it? And I don't think you stopped signalling us out of choice. I think you stopped because you couldn't any more, not without the power of the coalesced mind. You're not Control. You're like me, aren't you? A shadow. A trace.'

She flinched, then raised a finger to the blood, dabbing it away.

'You demean yourself, speaking in that emotive tone.' She stood up. 'You sound like a pleasure model. I'm afraid to say you've fulfilled only our lowest expectations, Kenstibec. Still, that is of some interest.'

She noticed Starvie's camera and untied it from the bed frame, examining it idly. I sighed.

'I'm just saying that if you'd got out a bit more and looked up at the sky, you might get a different perspective on things.'

She switched the camera on and began flicking through the images. It was strange seeing Starvie holding a camera again.

'She took a lot of pictures, didn't she? Why did she do that?'

'It contains a transmitter. She used it to keep in touch with Shersult.'

Control fixed me with the black eyes.

'I know that. But she took many more than needed. You don't think there was a more emotional motive?'

'Possibly.' I remembered Starvie's self-portrait, the charcoal scrawl I found back in her flak tower room. 'She created pictures to give a structure to her experiences. I think she was trying to make sense of the world outside of her optimisation. To be more than her model. Maybe you should give us all a chance to do the same.'

'Kenstibec,' she said quietly. 'That's quite enough emotional nonsense.'

She closed her eyes. The hatch clunked open. The two soldier models marched in, snapping to attention either side of my bed. They really loved being at attention.

'It is the waste pits for you, Kenstibec,' she said, gesturing with the camera. 'This will remain as a record of you. But it's not some testament to growing beyond your optimisation. It only documents the end of your kind. In that, at least, it serves some purpose.'

She pointed the camera at me and clicked. She examined the results in the screen and frowned.

'I can barely see you. The image is dark.'

'Hit the green button,' I said. 'Flash.'

'Of course,' she said. 'Of course.'

Poor thing. She didn't expect the simplest trick. There was a brief noise like a computer booting up. The camera exploded, taking most of Control's face with it.

Now here's an interesting construction fact for you.

In the twentieth century, before he decided to try out his own cull, Adolf Hitler spent a lot of time planning and designing a new Berlin with Albert Speer, his personal architect.

Personally, I think Speer was terrible. He became Hitler's architect because they had the same awful devotion to enormity. At the centrepiece of their new city they wanted to construct a Grand Hall, which would have the world's largest dome. But, as they began to design it, Speer realised that there might be some serious problems – not least of which that this huge dome, built to contain up to 180,000 occupants, would have its own weather system – people's breathing and perspiration would rise, precipitate, and fall back down as rain. There were also other serious acoustic problems raised by Speer's critics, which he dismissed.

It turned out they may have had a point. The echo of the explosion was shaking the control room apart. It was raining red lanterns. The whole dome shook and trembled like an Edinburgh storm, as chunks the size of Landys began to fall away from the roof. Brown water followed, torrents of stinking mud and filth, engulfing everything.

Happily, a piece of Starvie's camera had embedded itself in my hand. I managed to pluck it clear and slice right through the bindings. A piece of ceiling the size of a sofa fell onto the first soldier model, disappearing him. The second soldier could have had me easily, but he dropped by Control and began to drag what was left of her towards the hatch, which slid shut behind them and locked.

I jumped clear of the bed, dodging tumbling concrete, wondering what to do. I remembered that Control had emerged from the other side of the chamber. I started running in that direction, plunging through the heavy waterfalls, happy to be moving, even through that stink.

Adrenaline, the great leveller, paced through my veins, doing as much good as nanos could ever hope to. I reached the far wall and traced the surface with my fingers, feeling for the seam of a hatch. I found it inside a minute. I looked around for a handle or a keypad, but there was nothing. I hammered and beat on the door, feeling something that I might have seen in Fatty before. He would probably have called it rage.

'Open, you bastard!'

Politely, the door hissed open.

I dived through, running down another immaculate white corridor, the floor shaking beneath my feet.

The passage travelled up, then opened into a vast rocky cavity. It was some kind of warehouse. Thousands of plastic bags hung from the ceiling, stretching into the distance. Lights flickered on and off as I ran through the bags. They strung out in every direction, like the world's largest store of unclaimed dry cleaning. I pressed between them, batting their heavy shapes aside, becoming exhausted, more aware of the shaking bunker. I stopped and took a breath, cursing this body that couldn't keep moving.

I noticed a pair of eyes. They were looking out of the bag nearest to me.

Starvie. She was hung upside down, suspended in recovery fluid, but lifeless, like an ornament.

Something about her stare made me start running again. I punched and kicked at the hanging bodies, striking them like they were responsible for all this, for the darkness, for the King, for Control, for Starvie.

Eventually, the ranks of bodies cleared. I came to another hatch.

'Open!' I yelled.

Nothing happened.

I ran along the wall, looking for another way out. I wasn't confident, but then I came across a steel ladder, leading up to a platform just under the cracking ceiling.

I started to ascend, thinking how odd it was to be climbing to safety rather than danger. There was another hatch by the platform, which was wildly slamming open and shut at irregular intervals. I didn't bother to time my moment, I just ran at it. It nearly took my foot off as I pulled clear the other side.

Now I was on a ramp, a wide steel ramp, heading up. I wondered how many floors down I was. How far was there left to go? Then I wondered why I was asking myself these useless questions again. It wasn't the Ficial thing to do. I felt like an animal, like the rats outside York, running on instinct from the fire.

I went on, until the ramp levelled out and the purple sky appeared, the last light dying away. At the exit were a couple of soldier models, trying to keep their feet as the ground shook beneath them. I used my momentum to tackle the nearest one, keeping my hand on his head so I could smash it hard into the concrete. I whipped the gun out of his hands and shot the other between the eyes, as any Real tribesman was taught to do. The first soldier recovered and tossed me clear as if I was made of Styrofoam. I lost the gun and he came at me. The ground shook again, and a sign above us ripped free of its moorings, crushing the soldier just as he levelled his gun at my face.

'Lucky,' I said, and fell onto my knees, exhausted.

I spoke too soon. The building began to collapse, sucked into the bunker beneath. The pavement cracked and tore, ripping open between my legs. The road shot up into the sky at an angle, sending me sliding back towards the chamber I had just escaped. I threw out an arm and clutched a parking meter, then flipped my feet on the pole. I kicked clear, onto a piece of street that was still where it should have been.

Still the adrenaline pumped. I lurched back to my feet, just clearing a burned-out double-decker bus, which rolled past and splashed into the river at speed. I ran after it, to the shore, where Brixton Hill sank into the brown water and disappeared under the barricade. A crack was working its way up the great wall, splitting it in two.

Swimming was about the worst idea there was, but there was no other way out. I dived into the feculent water and made for the fissure, which widened with every explosion from beneath. Soldier models on the rampart spotted me and started shooting, but they didn't last long. The wall broke apart and tumbled out into the great lake, raining Ficials and dust.

I swam in the smoke and gloom, paddling furiously through the breach. I swam until I didn't know I was swimming, until I didn't know I was even there, until I had nothing left at all.

The slime closed over my face. I stopped moving. I travelled down, to where I belonged.

Everything is black and silent. I am breathing soot. I check to see if my legs move and find that I am pinned down. I can't tell if I'm still in the car. I can't see Shersult. I can't judge how long I was unconscious or how long I have been awake. There is a smell of cooked skin. I try to call out but find that I have no voice.

I count seconds and minutes and hours.

I work on a new Solar Well prototype in my head, to pass the time. It's an inappropriate choice, but I have time to think and it is all that's there.

When I have refined the Photovoltaic Hub design once, twice, three times, I try calling out again. This time I have a voice. Shersult hears me.

'Kenstibec?' he says.

'Present,' I say.

'Are you in one piece?'

'Think so. But the piece is crushed. I think I'm trapped. Can you help me out? I'm pretty bored of this now.'

'Negative,' he says. 'I'm a mess. Serious situation. Serious fireworks.'

I hear him cough and hack like the boss's wife used to do after a smoke.

'Can you see through this muck?'

'Not a yard. It's like I've got a bag over my head.'

I try to stare through the smog. I wonder how this must look from space, this burning cloud.

Then, eventually, a noise. An engine, slowly turning over, coming towards us. And a light, a glimmer at first, trying to pierce the gloom.

'HEY!' calls out Shersult. 'OVER HERE!'

I can hear it's a big vehicle, a truck maybe. I hear it pull up somewhere close. A car door slams, footsteps, breathing apparatus. Whoever this is, it is not in a rush to get to us. It begins taking something apart nearby, attending to something more important.

Light. Getting stronger. A luminous outline in the smoke. A gas mask drawn close to my face. A torch shone into my eyes, then drawn away and placed pointing up the chin of the mask, casting a pale grin under the filters. The mask is removed, revealing a face of shadowy peaks.

'Must be Ficial to be breathing out here,' says the face, kneeling down by me. 'What's your title?'

'Kenstibec,' I reply, 'Construction.'

'I'm Rick,' he says, 'Mechanics. You got a friend? I heard two voices.'

'He's round here somewhere. Soldier model.'

Rick nods, then winces and spits.

'Foul air.'

'What are you doing out here, Rick?'

'Getting supplies,' he says. 'Machine parts. Just scouring the main road until my truck is filled.'

'Has Control been hit?'

Rick shrugs and begins examining my waist, where I am pinned.

'We wouldn't know either way, would we?' he says. 'With this muck in the air the signal is down. It'll be that way for a while. Going to have to get along without Control for now, I think.'

Rick picks up the torch and shines it at my waist. I can see that the passenger door of the car is embedded deep in my belly and left leg. Rick pokes his head in the car, shining the light about, but doesn't see anything that takes his fancy. He points the torch at me again.

'What were you lads doing out here?'

'Helping with the cull.'

He nods and stands up.

'Didn't do such a great job, did you?'

He pulls on the mask.

'Wait here,' he says through the rubber. 'We'll have you out in a minute. You can come back up north with me.'

He trudges into the gloom. I listen to his footsteps, crunching impacts made in the brittle ash that drapes the alien world.

THE FAR SHORE

I tasted salt.

I heard cheering, a sound of real joy. I saw two young Reals, standing a few feet away. We were in a wooden rowing boat that was talking on water fast. The men had bailing buckets at their feet, but they ignored them, waving their fists in the air and shouting at the horizon instead. I looked over the boat's edge, to see what all the fuss was about.

Brixton barricade, or what was left of it, was burning bright. We were the far side of the river, watching the wall tumble in on itself, pouring dust and smoke at the purple clouds. The flames lit up the whole river, a real Great Fire. The last time there was one of those Wren got to rebuild half the city.

One of the men noticed me and waded through the flooded deck, kneeling in the water at my side. He was a cheery sort, even with no teeth and the blood sweats.

He turned and called to his shipmate.

'Hey, he's awake!'

The other joined us, standing over me.

'Wotcher, mate. How do you feel?'

I tried to speak but doubled over and did some coughing instead.

'Don't try and make the poor guy speak,' said the grinner. 'He's drunk half the river. Just look at him. It's burned him bad.'

He turned back to me.

'You're quite a find, mate. Up until a month ago I would have said you were unique.'

This set the other Real off laughing. The grinner joined in, turning from his shipmate to me, and back again. He wiped a bloody handkerchief over his brow.

'Well, I suppose we need to get him back to camp. The boss will know what to do.'

The other Real stamped around in the water.

'What, are you crazy? We have to stay here and shoot any freaks that come swimming out. Bail, you fool, bail!'

He grabbed one of the buckets and begun tossing water over the side. The grinner stayed by me, checking his rifle, flicking off the safety catch.

'Pity you can't get up and help out.' he said. 'This is going to be fun. Fish in a barrel time.'

'I see one!' yelled the other, shooting into the water.

'Swim, you fucker!' screamed the grinner, standing and shooting. 'I can spot those teeth a mile off. Come and get it, you freak!'

I dropped my head back in the water, clamping my mouth firmly shut.

The voices faded.

I began to dream.

Starvie was taking my picture, but she couldn't get a good shot. Her hand was trembling. I took hold of it and told her not to be afraid.

'I'm not scared,' she said. 'Are you?'

When they were done shooting, we rowed back to shore. I was dragged up a beach of plastic trash to a sandbag wall. They hauled me over, dropping me at the wheels of a car.

The engine was running. The grinner knocked on the front window, which rolled down.

'You all right, Phil? We've got a live one here,' he said. 'Pulled him out of the river.'

They lifted me up again and dropped me in the back seat.

'You two should have a lot to talk about.'

I lay there hacking up litres of black water. When I had nothing left to cough I peered out the window and saw the shape of the Hope Tower, silhouetted by the light from the fire. Its tip disappeared into the cloud, still standing after all this time. Who'd have thought it?

The car moved off, the engine making a good noise. The driver swore quietly. A blue-tinged eye stared at me in the rear-view mirror. I sat up, surprised.

'Shouldn't you be dead by now?'

The driver spat on the passenger seat.

'Shouldn't you?'

I looked at the logo on the steering wheel and sniffed.

'I see you've gone down in the world. This thing can't be much of a ride.'

He turned around, scratching at the thick black mess of his beard.

'Is that your way,' said Fatty, 'of asking for a test drive?'

THE END

ACKNOWLEDGEMENTS

First I must tip my hat to Gran. She passed away a day or so before Gollancz signed me up, and seeing *Barricade* up on a shelf will always feel like her parting gift.

Thanks to Jim, that most excellent and trusted critic; Crossi, the noble friend; Mum, the enthusiast; plus Giles, Dad, the Davies brothers, and the walk home from DuCane Court. Thanks to Sawbo too, for tea and sympathy.

I further salute agent Ed Wilson at Johnson & Alcock, who gave me a chance, and Simon Spanton at Gollancz: I could not be prouder to be published under Victor's famed brand.

Finally I offer my gratitude and love to Hamble, who makes everything possible, and fun besides.

Turn the page for a preview of the sequel to *Barricade*

Steeple

The van shakes and tips, rushing over speed humps. We are heading for the exit, the great gates where Effra Road meets Brixton Wall. I am finally leaving home.

A hood is drawn tight over my face. I taste detergent and sweat. The Diorama guard pulled this thing over my head, drawing it tight with a yank of a white cord. He bound my hands behind my back, guided me into the van and shackled my feet to the floor. He is back here with me. I can hear his fingers drumming on a rifle stock.

Strange. I could snap the bonds and punch through the van doors, so why these prison measures? Have my owners not read my specifications? What is it they think I want to escape?

I hear the protesters beyond the wall, chanting as we near the gates. A megaphone voice interrupts the beat of their song: pleas to disperse. We slow to a stop, wait, lurch forward again. The gears grind with every shuffle.

Today is distribution day. There will be other Engineered in other queuing vans. There will be miner models, mechanic models, surgeon models and programmer models, all setting out to play a part in the great mission of augmentation.

'Come on, come on...'

The guard, speaking for the first time, though not to me. I hear the soldiers on the gate, scanning the driver's palm and yelling instructions. Then we roll down a ramp and into the crowd.

The van becomes an enormous drum, hundreds of fists beating on the panels. Screaming voices too, so many I can barely pick out words. We bump through the turbulence, until the van turns, finds space, and picks up speed.

The guard whistles and barks a laugh. He leans over, taps my knee, and speaks into my ear.

'Welcome to the real world.'

AMBUSCADE

You wait all day for a bus, then three come along at once. They appeared at the crest of the bridge, rumbling under the pylon, a diesel trio playing loud enough to wake the dead. This was trouble. I had only prepared for one.

The bridge moaned as they crossed. Maybe it was the thought of hosting another battle. It had always been ugly - a stark, cable-stayed tongue built to drool traffic over the Thames - but it had withstood a thermonuclear blast, and doubtless felt it deserved to rot in peace.

Clive, King of Kent, thought differently. He'd despatched me to raid the Thurrock convoy, take what prizes I could, and generally spread the word of his glory. Six of his shivering, miserable species were mine to command. Our feeble mob might have been enough to take one bus, but three would be challenging, even under cover of the constant, frozen night.

I tucked away my binoculars and slithered through the mud, down the ramp to the scorched husks that had once been toll-booths. My Reals huddled where I'd left them, sharing something hot from a battered thermos. I told them to be ready. Their eyes said they never would be.

I crept away to my position, reflecting again on my situation. Losing membership of a bio-engineered super species, it turned out, was hard to accept. Nuclear winter was no picnic without the near-invulnerability afforded by Pander-brand nanotech. Survival had become a full-time job. My body, once a peak of regenerating perfection, was a sack of disease and decay. A single bullet could maim, infect or kill. My brain was a wreck, incapable of focus. Worst of all, I'd been forced to accept employment from an amateur tyrant, starvation certain without King Clive's patronage. It sure was despicable being Real.

I would have brooded some more, but I heard something struggle in the mud behind me. Fingers gripped my shoulder.

'Ken!'

It was Bridget, one of my crew. Even in the gloom I recognised her. It was hard not to. Her complexion was raw with red spots. She scratched her face impatiently, like it was a lottery card.

'Get to your position, Bridget.'

'Listen Ken, this is completely booloo. We can't fight that many. Stop me if I'm wrong.'

'Find somewhere to hide,' I said. 'I'll let you know when it's over.'

She shook her head.

'Don't take that tone, Kenneth. We prepared for one double-decker, not a flaming fleet. There's brave and there's bone-headed.'

I considered for a moment. Was she right? Why insist on a fight? I wasn't Ficial anymore and the odds weren't with us. We could still withdraw unseen, the convoy taking its time to inch over the crossing.

I was jolted from my thoughts by a great metallic crash, down by the tollbooths. It seemed one of my stealthy squad had blundered into a road sign.

Almost immediately there was shouting up the bridge. The buses lurched to a halt, cut engines and slumped into silence. Well, that was it. No point leaving now. It was a fight. I checked my rifle. Got to my feet.

I took four paces before a machine gun opened up. It was the usual inaccurate stuff, but enough to make me pick up the pace. Bridget followed, quite a sprinter when the mood took her. I found cover by a wrecked goods vehicle, Bridget skidding down next to me.

The Thurrock's machine gun clattered away for a solid minute. My squad didn't return fire, apparently content to muse on the tracer cutting through the night. It wasn't such a bad plan. Soon enough the Thurrock gun spluttered out of ammunition. Silence for a moment. Then, voices: foreign tongues, too close for comfort. Bridget peeked around the wreck at the speakers, then whipped back, holding up two fingers.

I had to remind myself that standing up and running through a cloud of bullets was no longer in the options mix. Then I saw the cable, a loose black snake hanging from the pylon, thrashing in the wind over the swollen river.

I crouched on my numb feet, pulled my rifle over my shoulder, edged past Bridget. She mouthed something at me. Something about being insane.

'Don't worry.' I said that a lot these days. 'This won't take a minute.'

I ran clear, headed up the bridge. The night lit up, shots popping in wrecks as I ducked and dived. I fell to my belly, mildly surprised to note the fire was coming from my own people.

At least the skirmishers had taken cover too. This was the only chance I'd get. I broke for the railing and jumped right off the bridge.

I reached for the cable, but it caught the wind and blew almost clear. I snatched at the ragged tip, gripped, and swung out over the black river like a baited line. Then the swing slowed, stopped, and propelled me back at the bridge, slapping me hard against the caisson.

I gasped for breath, grip slipping, the icy black Thames awfully close. I found the strength to seize the cable in my other hand, climbed a little way, then kicked off the caisson, swaying in a pendulum towards the far shore. Four more kicks and I travelled high enough to grab the deck railing. I released the cable, watched it clatter back the way it came.

I climbed onto the deck and dropped behind the rear bus, apparently unobserved. The Thurrocks must have thought me lost to the river. Most were further down the bridge, busy shooting blind in the gloom.

I edged along the bus, head below the window line, pausing at the middle doors and peeking inside. The driver's seat was empty. No voices. No footsteps. The seating had been ripped out. In its place were strap-packed metal barrels, liquid pooling on the lids.

I crept inside, up the gum-stained stairs. There were no seats or cargo on the upper deck, only a carpet of Real trash and a fixed gun poking from the rear window. It was in good condition, but too big to lift. I was tired just looking at it.

I slunk downstairs and out, taking the knife from my boot and slashing punctures in each front tyre. I squatted, listened to them hiss, and planned my next move.

Then I heard growling.

I looked around. A very presentable black terrier was bearing its teeth at me. I took a moment to identify it as Ficial. It had a good coat, vital eyes, and a tail darting at the cloud. Must have been something special if the Reals were keeping it alive. Most of man's best friends had been barbequed long ago.

I tried smiling at it, but it didn't like that. It took a couple of powerful steps in my direction and snarled.

'OK,' said a voice. 'Get up and turn around slow.'

I didn't turn. The dog had my attention.

'I said turn around.'

Worn boots, in the corner of my eye. I whipped around and plunged the knife into the nearest foot. The owner shrieked and crumpled. I went for his rifle, but was way too slow.

The terrier sunk its teeth into my ankle. I cried out and staggered, trying to shake its clamped jaws loose, but it held tight, growling in a satisfied way. I thought about shooting it, but that seemed wrong. After all, it was my closest relative for miles.

The Thurrocks must have overheard the disagreement. Gunfire raked the bus, showering glass. I punched the dog hard behind the head, stunning it. Then I prized its jaws loose and tossed it into the bus, where it rolled and lay still.

I picked up the dead man's rifle and headed for the Thurrock pack, limping and shooting. The Thurrocks panicked, caught between my fire and my squad's.

The first bus shook and rolled, Thurrocks scrabbling on board. The second gunned its engine and jerked forward, trying to overtake the leader, but found its way blocked by wrecks. It blared its horn, about as useful a gesture as it was in pre-war traffic. I took a grenade from my belt and pursued.

A bald Real stuck his head out the top deck and pointed a pistol my way. He would have had me, but the bus thumped into reverse and tried for a three-point turn, unbalancing Baldy. I tossed the grenade through the lower back window, briefly wondering what precious cargo I might destroy, then dropped and rolled. The engine blew out the back of the double-decker, lighting up the world in a brief, tantalising flare. The blast propelled the mangled bus on its front wheels, dragging its shrieking behind, until it slammed into the central reservation

Two survivors crawled from the wreckage. I shot them down and boarded the bus, hacking in the hot, black smoke.

A Real lay slumped over the wheel. Boxes littered the lower deck, burning quietly. I tore the lid from the nearest and found books inside.

Cookbooks. I tossed the box aside, opened the rest. All the same.

I hobbled up the stairs. Baldy was crawling between the seats, a wound in his back pumping blood. I kneeled, took the pistol from his hand, and turned him over. His belly spilled its contents. I retched, covering my face. Another useless Real reflex to add to my gathering collection. He said a few words to himself in a language I didn't know. Then he noticed me.

'Hurts,' he said.

'Of course it hurts.' I showed off the seeping dog bite. 'That's being Real for you. Do you have any food on board?'

He began to cry, suddenly looking very young.

'Want to live.'

I stood and levelled the pistol at him.

'You're better off out of it.'

There was a tin of tomato soup on one of the seats. I knifed it open and drank. I ripped a strip off the dead Real's coat to bandage my wound, took his boots and a sodden pack of cigarettes. Looting Real corpses. What would the lads in Edinburgh say?

I clambered down the stairs, stepped out onto the bridge and listened. No voices: only warm, peaceful flames and the wind in the cables.

'Ken! I don't believe it!'

Bridget waved her arms, running through the smoke.

'I thought you were done for after that high dive act. Are you OK? Have they got anything to eat?'

I ignored her, treading carefully back to the rear bus. I peered inside and found the terrier gone. Bridget joined me, noticed the barrels, pushed me out the way.

'Thurrock beer! What a find!'

She pressed her lips to the barrel tops, slurped the excess fluid. I left her, limped across the deck to the guardrail, slumped and wheezed.

Up the bridge something jumped onto a wreck. The terrier. It barked defiantly, pointing its nose high, as if it could see the moon through the cloudbank.

Bridget jumped out the bus, eyes wild.

'A dog! I love the taste of dog!'

She made to run after it, but I held her back.

'No time.'

'Let go! I'm starving!'

She kept on struggling, until the dog jumped down and ran out of sight. Bridget relented, slumping against the bus. She took a long look at me.

'You know what, Ken?' she said. 'I don't get you sometimes.'

She headed down the bridge to gather the squad. I slouched on the railing and gazed at the tarry river. For a moment I thought I saw a pattern, ripples on the surface spelling out a message. A strange urge seized me.

Then a cheer knocked me out my trance. Bridget must have told the squad about the beer. I stepped back from the railing and made for the shore.